FINAL COPY

FINAL COPY

JAN BROGAN

Jan Brogan

THE LARCOM PRESS, PRIDES CROSSING, MA
2001

The Larcom Press
P.O. Box 161
Prides Crossing, MA 01965
www.larcompress.com

Cover and book design by Leeann Leftwich.

Printed in the United States on permanent paper.

The Larcom Press™ and A Larcom Mystery™ are trademarks.

ISBN 0-9678199-4-6

First Edition

To my mother, Genevieve,
the strongest woman I know.

ACKNOWLEDGMENTS

I'd like to thank the many people who helped me write this book: My writer's group, Barbara Shapiro, Floyd Kemske, Diane Bonavist, Rachel Plummer, and Donna Baier Stein, who supported, guided, and propped me up at critical stages.

For their expertise and assistance in research, Bill Santo on legal and corporate issues, John Yunits and Tom Brogan on legal issues; Tim Fulham on venture capital; Larry Stein and Nancy Stuart on biotechnology; retired police chief Col. Augustine Comella and forensic detective Pat Sperlongano on criminal matters; Jimmy Blue on insurance, Susan Santo-Laidlaw on medical/psychiatric, and Bob Fitzgerald on art.

To my dear friend Beth Kirsch for her methodical and kind editing, as well as her unfailing support, and to Thomasine Berg, who also helped with early editing. To my early readers, Barbara and Bob Brogan, Laurie Mocek Barry and Clare Mocek for their input, and Tom Hunt for his photography.

Also, I'd like to credit as background resources *The Billion-Dollar Molecule* by Barry Werth, *The Mind/Body Effect* by Herbert Benson, *Blueprint for Progress, Al-Anon's Fourth Step Inventory*, and the *Boston Herald* for its coverage of synthetic heroin (fentanyl) overdoses in 1992.

I'd also like to thank Dan Mandel at Sanford J. Green-burger Associates and Ed Breslin at Breslin Literary Agency Ltd. for believing in me early on, The Chesterfield Film Project for renewing my faith in the book, and Susan Oleksiw and Ann Perrott at The Larcom Press for their enthusiasm and commitment.

But most of all, I want to thank my husband, Bill Santo, for his love, his faith, and his great sense of humor.

Book I
The Assignment, June 14, 1991

1

In the politics of the newsroom, the longer the title, the less significant the job. People with long editing titles are often not editors at all—they are reporters who have been demoted. Partly because of the union and partly because newspaper people are proletarian at heart, few are ever fired for basic incompetence. They get shifted to a low-status job with a newly invented title—something like "associate editor for downtown real estate." That's mine. In fact, I'd come dangerously close to being named "deputy executive associate editor for downtown real estate"—a slow and cruel death.

I knew how lucky I was to be invited to the 11:00 A.M. news meeting; to be given an opportunity to come back from the dead was rare, but I also knew that I would be under intense scrutiny. Any hesitation would be analyzed. Every word I said quoted and likely misquoted later in the aisles of the newsroom. Reporters would let their own stories go dim on their screens to debate the ethical errors inherent in mine.

"Did you get the interview?" Mark Schneider, the managing editor, asked me in a low voice.

"I'm meeting him Monday," I whispered.

Mark, who was sitting to my left, offered a drum roll of approval on the table edge. It reverberated under my elbows. "And the profile?" he asked.

"I still have to talk him into it."

Mark's expression tightened. He was highly regarded at the paper for his "creativity," but this also meant he invented stories before we had them. I imagined he had a clear vision of my story on the *News-Tribune*'s front page, down to the layout and headline size. We were to whip all other media with an exclusive profile of this upscale criminal, "Up Close and Personal." Mark did not want to consider failure. "Do your best," he said.

He was diverted by Gerard Hanley, who was sitting on the other side of me, notepad in front of him. Gerard was a wiry, mosquitolike reporter in his midtwenties, whose ambition never slept, never trusted itself to take a minute off from the business of arm biting. Even when seated, his limbs weren't still. Now, his knee was in the midst of a hoe-down, his hand engaged in doodling a map that marked the locations of the synthetic cocaine overdoses. These had been Boston's biggest stories until last week.

Gerard marked in the latest and most sensational of the deaths: Five people had overdosed on less than a single gram of synthetic cocaine at a party in Mission Hill. Gerard, who had covered the story for the Sunday paper, sketched a tall, sticklike apartment building, and drew five black Xs.

The conference room, the only private enclosure in the newsroom, had white, windowless walls and a light switch smudged with newsprint. The wall behind me was pinned with the day's display pages: the front page; the four zoned Metros; Sports; Lifestyle; and Financial. Along the other long wall was a small whiteboard that Mark sometimes used to dissect a run-on sentence or a jumbled paragraph.

We sat at an oblong table, more functional than decorative, with the place at the head reserved for Lev Grabowski, "the editor," who had not yet arrived. Even on days when he wasn't expected, no one else would take that particular seat—no matter how crowded. Mark and Nora Cleveland, who was the City editor, and the few, specially invited reporters, sat on my side of the table. Regional, Suburban, Financial, and Sports editors sat along the other. The new Graphics editor, a woman who was called "the czarina" behind her back, sat at the foot of the table, signifying how much power layout and design had begun to wield in the nineties. Everyone else—the assistants and assistants-to-the-assistants—was crammed together, leaning against the unused whiteboard and the smudged wall.

Reporters were invited to these morning news meetings only when they were involved in a major story. Gerard, the current star of the investigative team, had become accustomed to the privilege. He had an air of impatience about the whole thing, as if he couldn't wait for this bureaucratic stuff to be over so he could get on with the real news. I, who had been excluded for almost a year, felt the thrill, even amid a mixture of anxiety and exhaustion.

I hadn't slept well, and I was more nervous and edgy than usual, thinking constantly about the relief of just one Serax. Still, I'd been able to maintain a semblance of "stomach calm" during the critical phone call this morning.

"Well, let's get going," Mark said. He had a boyish face that from a distance might be mistaken for an intern's. Even up close, he didn't look like he was in his late thirties, but you could see the authority about his mouth, the resolve of his expression. In the last year, he had taken to wearing elegantly tailored suits. This made him appear to be from advertising rather than news.

Everyone began consulting the budget, which is a list of local news stories and photographs for the next day's paper. Most national stories, like the recession, or the Persian Gulf War victory parades, were handled by wire services, and unless we sent our own correspondent, rarely discussed at this meeting.

The term *budget* refers not to financial calculations, but to the need to plan and conserve inches of space. A routine political story out of the City Council may be allowed to run fifteen inches. A reactive front-page drama, twenty-five to thirty. I used to do in-depth investigative pieces that were budgeted over sixty. These were the kinds of stories that brought prestige to the paper and won me the 1989 New England Investigative Reporter of the Year award. But that was before my brother died.

Today's news budget was two pages long with the Francis Marquesson murder listed as the top story under "City." Last week, we'd reported that venture capitalist Francis Marquesson's plunge from the balcony of the Harbor Inn Hotel and Convention Center was "an apparent suicide." By this week, "unnamed sources" in the Boston Police Department began speculating about the possibility of murder, and by yesterday we learned that his business partner, Kit Korbanics, was a suspect.

Now the newsroom buzzed with the information: I had dated Kit in college—a fact responsible for this most recent turnaround of my career.

If Gerard hadn't been hot on the investigation of the synthetic cocaine overdoses, he would have been assigned to Marquesson's plunge: a gruesome, middle-of-the-day drama, attracting a crowd of spectators that tied up traffic on Atlantic Avenue. As it was, the two police reporters had gotten the front page headlines, pushing Gerard's copy to the inside of the paper.

As was the custom, suburban news coverage, which the *Boston News-Tribune* knew to be its best edge over the *Boston Herald*, was addressed first by the Suburban editor. Nora, the City editor, usually presented her budget next, but she waved the Regional editor on to give his rundown on New England stories.

The meeting proceeded tediously to the various departments. Then, at the end, just as the Lifestyle editor was giving her spiel, Lev Grabowski, "the editor," appeared at the door, a newspaper folded under his arm. Lev was a tall, stocky man with a square forehead and brightly suspicious eyes. These eyes, some sort of blue-green combination, were like security system sensors that made an electrically charged notation every time anyone flinched. Lev could be uncomfortably silent or intensely heated about an issue no one realized had his attention—like unnecessary hysterectomies for women over fifty. He came in on this topic, which had everyone else dozing, and suggested three possible sources at the Brigham and Women's Hospital.

The Lifestyle editor was a quiet, fashionably dressed woman. She wrote the information down with a sly smile. The male-dominated news editors tended to snicker at Lifestyle stories. Lev's interest was a political victory. Lifestyle could now be fairly certain about a front-page promo on the story and advance radio advertising.

I stared down at the news budget while Lev walked past my end of the table to take his seat. The newspaper he carried was a tab—most likely the *Herald* folded over. He laid it on the table, one elbow resting on its ink, as he leaned forward to grouse about the medical establishment and how it went through "surgery crazes" to the detriment of innocent patients. Several editors mumbled their agreement.

Not Nora. She did not openly toady to Lev. She nodded an acknowledgment of his presence, but went on to show it did not affect her pulse rate. She spoke in a slightly bored tone that conveyed that the news was just another day's business. Presenting the City budget in an inverse order of its significance, she began with the most nasal, most mundane actions of the Boston School Committee. She worked up the list and arrived at the investigation of campaign spending by the former mayor.

This last was a story that would have been mine had I not been "promoted" out of the investigative team. At one time, I knew the intricacies of state election law and our database of campaign filings better than any other reporter on the staff. Even with the possibility of the Kit Korbanics story before me, I felt a pang of jealousy.

The meeting had progressed to the bigger stories, and Mark took over again. "What is the DEA saying about leads?" he asked Gerard. This was a reference to the U.S. Drug Enforcement Agency, which so far had been baffled by where the synthetic cocaine was coming from.

"Officially nothing. But I got a source that says he thinks it's local."

"Local, meaning Boston?"

"I think the source meant Massachusetts."

"A metropolitan suburb, perhaps?" the Suburban editor asked. This was a joke, so no one answered.

"When will you have something on it?" Lev's tone was gruff and demanding, but he wasn't fooling anyone. A paternal look softened those sharp eyes when he gazed at his golden boy.

Gerard was prepared. He did not flip nervously through a notebook to pause for time, but raised his doodled map to illustrate. "All depends on the DEA. In the meantime, I'm putting together an in-depth piece on the victims, who they were, where they all lived, and what went wrong with their lives that they wound up snorting cocaine."

"But you did a piece like that on the last victims," Nora objected. She had little sympathy for cocaine users, whom she tended to regard as affluent, undisciplined holdovers from the eighties. Besides, her domain was daily news and she tended to resent the developed pieces, the long and unwieldy stories that were taken out of her possession and handed up to Mark.

"But this would be different—this would be a long-range piece, looking at all the victims—what they had in common, how they differed," Gerard said.

What this meant, of course, was that Gerard would be unavailable to cover any daily stories. There was a moment of silence as the editors weighed this consideration, which appeared to vex Gerard considerably.

"You're going to give all this play to one man—who may or may not have murdered his partner—because he's a rich guy and you think the people in the suburbs will relate to him. But a story about a drug that murdered five people this week, twelve altogether—just because they're from a lower echelon— that gets second billing?"

"A businessman ends up splat on a sidewalk on the water-front in the middle of the day and it tends to capture the city's imagination," Nora said dryly.

"It's just a question of how we allocate our resources at the moment," Mark intervened. "If the Grand Jury indicts Korbanics, we're going to need your help to coordinate some of the daily stuff coming from court and the DA."

Gerard didn't reply, but it was obvious he was appeased by the recognition of how badly he was needed.

Lev picked up his newspaper from the table and turned it over. I could see now that it wasn't the *Herald*, but the *New York Post*. From the way he was looking at it, there was some-thing inside he didn't like. Whatever it was, he brushed it aside. "Is there going to be a Grand Jury?" he asked Nora.

Nora lowered her voice, as if maybe there were television spies among the editors relegated to the wall. "I think so. Rumors are that forensics found fibers on Marquesson that match Korbanics's jacket."

This produced a buzz in the room. Mark leaned forward to catch my attention. He wanted to make sure that I realized the story, *my story*, had just gotten better.

Lev, who used to be a police reporter, was known to call the DA himself if something about a murder story intrigued or perplexed him. Those laser eyes of his lit up. "What else are they supposed to have on him?"

"They're not saying anything on the record. But a source at the hotel says one of the chambermaids told a detective that she saw Kit entering Marquesson's hotel room about twenty minutes before the fall," Nora said. "And the insurance motive."

She was referring to a story the *Herald* had run yesterday about Kit and Marquesson's venture capital firm, The BioFund, having a key-man life insurance policy worth five million dollars. This was supposed to pay either partner enough to buy out the heirs of the other in the case of death.

Gerard was being unusually obtuse about the significance of this story. He had decided to minimize it rather than compete for it. Either that or he wanted to hear more about how the paper couldn't handle it without him. "You really think this guy would shove his buddy out a balcony window for the insurance money?" he asked me.

"Wouldn't you?" someone quipped.

Gerard ignored the laughter. "I thought insurance companies didn't pay out on suicides."

"They usually have only a two-year exclusion clause on suicide," Mark explained.

Gerard rolled his eyes. "There's got to be an easier way to bump off a business partner. I mean talk about attracting attention. Midafternoon during a national biotech conference? Wouldn't a smart guy go for poison?"

"Hanging him in the shower would have been a lot quieter," someone else suggested.

Lev became impatient with the banter. "Did he agree to meet with you?" he directed this question at me.

"Yes," I answered swiftly. I expected this to produce a nod of approval, but there was silence, so I continued. "I talked to him this morning."

"What's his alibi?" Lev asked, focusing his eyes sharply on mine.

I realized in that awful moment that I'd spent a half hour on the phone with Kit Korbanics that morning and hadn't asked the single most important question. But I could not explain to Lev that I'd had so many years and awkward memories to bridge, so much to overcome in just *making the connection* that I'd simply allowed Kit to talk. I hadn't challenged or demanded specifics. I'd focused solely on getting him to agree to the personal interview.

"He had to consult his lawyer before making any statements," I said.

There were several groans of sympathy at the reference to the lawyer.

"So is he a *big* guy?" Dave, the Sports editor, asked. The Sports editor enjoys the admiration and envy of all men, even the publisher, and can interrupt whenever he wants to. There had been extensive debate upstairs in Sports about what size a man had to be to pick up another man and throw him off a balcony.

"Six-four, six-five," I answered.

The men in the room nodded at this impressive height. But Lev was not entirely satisfied. "And capable?" he asked.

I hesitated. "Athletically, you mean?"

"I'm not asking you for judgment on his soul *before* the interview," Lev said. "No matter how well you knew him."

There was a rustle of laughter as people, at first, took this as a joke. Halfway through the room it died.

"He used to do a lot of 10K races," I said. "I imagine he's kept himself in shape."

"How long ago did you go out with him?" Nora asked in a quiet voice.

Every pair of editor's eyes turned on me and I felt the white-hot, investigator's light. "Fourteen years ago," I said. "I haven't seen him since then."

I didn't add that maintaining this kind of distance had required effort on my part. Kit had also been my brother Rory's college roommate, and up until Rory's death, the two of them had remained close friends.

"And only for a few months," Mark said. Actually, it had been closer to a year.

"Still, I don't see how you can assign a reporter to write a profile about someone she used to go out with," the Lifestyle editor commented.

Several assistant editors voiced their agreement. The room began to rumble as the debate took off.

"How can we pretend she's objective?" the Suburban editor asked.

I wanted to shut my eyes, hide my face in my hands, but I had to sit there, back straight, eyes level, staring into the center of the room, as if it weren't all so desperate. These people didn't seem to understand that I hadn't gotten Kit Korbanics to agree to anything. And that if his lawyer, Estella Rubin, was as good as she was supposed to be, she'd talk him out of seeing me by Monday.

At that moment the debate was cut off by Lev's secretary, who appeared with a yellow memo slip, which was handed across the table to Lev.

"WRKO's saying the Grand Jury convened this morning," Lev informed the group. Then he raised his wrist to his line of sight—as if there wasn't a clock dead ahead of him on the wall—and announced that the news meeting was over.

"You three stay." He pointed his finger at me, Gerard, and

Mark.

The assistant editors, who were accustomed to hanging around until the bitter end trying to make insightful wisecracks about whatever politician was in trouble, looked at each other, brows arched at the official dismissal. Slowly, they began to gather their scratch pads.

When they all filed out, Lev picked up his newspaper and began flipping through pages. When he found what he wanted, Lev pushed the opened newspaper across the table to Mark.

Mark quietly scanned the news item.

"They picked up the *Herald* story yesterday about the insurance motive," Lev said.

This information sunk in. If enough major urban newspapers across the country began picking up a story like this it could take on a life of its own, gaining momentum. "If the Grand Jury indicts and this thing goes to trial, it could be a *national* story."

"Maybe I *should* get involved," Gerard said. His dedication to those twelve victims from all walks of life evaporated quickly in light of the possibility of a national story. "Addy can press Korbanics to let me come with her this afternoon to meet him."

Mark and Lev were nodding at each other, like yes, this would be a good idea, send a competent reporter along. Gerard nodded back.

I'd worked with Gerard on the investigative team and knew what to expect. First, he'd put on a great act of working cooperatively: offer me his notes, pass along photocopies of the DA's legal documents. But then, when he was close enough to Kit, he'd sabotage me—steal the information I was collecting for the profile and turn it into a front-page daily under his own byline. He'd done that two years ago when I was doing an investigation on a shopping mall developer who'd bribed local officials in seven different states. Gerard had gotten a regional reporting nomination for a story based on information it had taken me months to collect.

No, I would not allow Gerard Hanley to get his fingers on *my* profile. "Korbanics is gun shy of the media right now." I tried to sound concerned about this, worried rather than defensive. "I don't want to blow his trust."

Mark was staring at me hard, trying to interpret my response. I held steady, meeting his gaze. I didn't know if Mark would be putting his faith in my substance abuse meetings and shaky self-discipline if he had Gerard Hanley in place.

"Gerard's involvement would relieve a lot of the pressure on you, Addy," Mark said, in a kind manner that scared me.

"I can handle the pressure," I replied.

Mark smiled weakly, as if he wanted to believe me.

"But that's not the issue," Lev said. "The real issue is how can you report objectively about a man who used to be your—" Apparently, he could not bring himself to say the word *lover*.

Mark said, "Frankly, I think Addy's closeness to the murder suspect is an asset, not a liability."

"Maybe for the profile," Lev said, although his tone was doubtful. "But not daily coverage. We've got to have Gerard involved."

Anger and anxiety bubbled to the surface, but I fought to keep them submerged. I had to think coolly. I knew that the sole reason they were willing to take a risk on me was because I was the only one with access to Kit. If I shared it with anyone, I would lose my only shot at a comeback—a shot at what might become a national story. "I had a hard time convincing him to even meet with *me*," I protested.

Gerard fixed his gaze on me shrewdly, at once suspecting my resistance. Mark and Lev exchanged a glance.

"This is a very big story, Addy," Mark said, after a bit.

"I think I'm aware of that."

Gerard had begun fidgeting with his notebook. "Can you at least give me his home phone number?"

"Part of our agreement is that I not give out his number. It's unlisted." This had never been mentioned but I could not have Gerard calling Kit at home, spooking him.

"Fine." Gerard did not try to mask his annoyance. "I'll stalk his office then."

"No, you won't." This came from Lev, who looked disgusted with both of us. "We have a chance at blowing everyone else out of the water and we're not going to risk losing Korbanics—not this early. You'll cover everything that comes out of the district attorney's office, and we'll have Addy get the responses from the defense team. She'll turn over the notes to you and you'll write the daily stories."

To me, he said, "You focus on getting that profile. An in-depth piece showing you know this guy like no one else. His bad habits. The kind of car he drives. Whether he gets along with his parents. You talk to people who like him. People who hate his guts. We want the definitive piece on whether this is the kind of guy who could do something this gruesome."

I nodded.

"You got two weeks to put it together. Mark will keep close tabs on you every step of the way. He'll need a lead and first draft midway."

It was Friday, which meant I had little more than a week to collect enough information about Francis Marquesson's death as well as try to determine whether a man I hadn't seen for fourteen years was capable of murder. I scribbled Lev's commands in my notebook, underlining bad habits. "I think Kit drives a Porsche," I offered.

Lev was not impressed. "Given the significance of this story, I have no choice but to depend on you. But let me tell you, if you screw up again, you start giving us bad information, or you miss deadlines again—"

"I'm not going to screw up," I said, meeting those investigative eyes head on.

"Good. Then while you're at it, find out what Korbanics's alibi is, will you?"

I nodded.

"We've got the lead on every other newspaper in the country. You blow this story, Addy, and you'll be out of here."

In the eight-year history of my employment at the *News-Tribune*, I'd never before heard of any editor threatening any reporter with termination. But I nodded as if it would be completely expected, completely within reason.

"And, Addy?"

"Yes." I was stone cold.

Lev was smiling now, pleased with whatever vengeance had come to mind. "If I wind up firing you—I'll make sure Gerard's the one to rewrite the profile."

2

I was on a balcony, braced against a cast-iron rail. The slider to the hotel room was sealed tight, the glass smudged and cloudy. I peered into the room and saw Kit lying on the queen-size bed. Beside him was a woman he caressed. He turned and saw me. No expression. The balcony rail gave way. I was flailing, twisting, hurtling down. . . .

I sat up in bed, the cotton blanket kicked to the floor, my heart racing with such a pounding ferocity that my whole body throbbed with a machine-gun beat—at my temples, wrists, ankles.

I put my hand to my heart, trying to quiet the pace of the chambers firing. It was 1:00 A.M. One half hour after I had dozed off.

I've awakened in this state of panic every night since my brother died. Every single night as I am about to slide into some deep delta phase of sleep, I awake with a jolt, reliving the moment of Rory's death. The last flash when he knew his body was shutting down. But tonight, it was worse. Tonight Kit had put in an appearance, raising himself from the lower levels of consciousness where I had so skillfully kept him submerged.

I leaned over and flipped on the light. The flood of halogen electrified the cornflower blue wallpaper and revealed the chaos of my life—newspapers stacked against the wall, my khaki pants on the floor where I had stepped out of them, a half-eaten bowl of cereal on the desk.

In the mirror over the bureau, I could see a rattled woman sitting up in bed. My face looked thin and desperate; my shoulders absent in a T-shirt that was ghostlike in form. I had lost both the figure and the boldness that had once attracted Kit. I looked as if I hung by a thread.

I stood and began pacing around the single bed. The room was small, and except for the wallpaper, undecorated. The only carpeting was the stacks of newspapers I saved because they carried articles I meant to read.

I paced to the window that overlooked a narrow side yard between the closely spaced houses and pulled up the ill-fitting plastic blind. Outside, the Brighton neighborhood was silent. The lesbian couple who lived upstairs were like mice; I knew they were there, but I never saw them. College kids lived on both levels of the two-family next door and often came home late. I yearned for their activity—the sight of someone else's life.

But tonight I was alone, except for Rory, I supposed. He had been dead for over a year now, and I had not let him go. I walked to my bureau and picked up the picture I kept in a Lucite frame.

It was from my cousin's wedding in St. Louis, taken six months before Rory died. My brother, who had been an usher, wore a tux. It was a small wedding, and neither of us brought dates. We spent most of the night dancing together. At the end of the evening, I brought out my camera, snapped the bride and groom at my parent's table, and then found my brother at the bar trying to pick up one of the bridesmaids. Rory, who never smoked, had lit the woman's cigarette and even taken one for himself in the grand strategy to get laid. I zoomed in close and caught him in laughter, his head tipped back, his lips still in the O-shape of an exhale, his dark, intelligent eyes amused. He'd succeeded with Renda, or whatever her name had been. A mystical smoke ring floated near his face.

My only brother, so sharp, so witty, so alive. Having Kit reappear in my life made it seem like Rory, too, could emerge from some shadow. His sudden, inexplicable death and my parents' choice of a closed casket made it hard to believe he was, at only thirty-five years of age, decomposing in the ground.

But at the same time, I felt his death in my bloodstream. He was my sibling. In some ways, he *was* me. The DNA we shared had to respond, had to relive the moment of his panic again and again.

Only the Serax had given me relief. I put the picture down and turned back to the bed, sitting on its edge.

Go on, Addy, just wallow in it. I could hear Rory, frustrated by my grief, my overindulgence of emotion. My inability to let things go.

I reached into my nightstand drawer and foraged through the pencils, papers, and cough lozenges. Did I really think that I was strong enough to take Kit Korbanics on? That I could use our past and not succumb to it?

I'd thrown out the Xanax, which had been my first choice of sleeping pill, but there was still a bottle of Serax. Untouched for almost three months, it was stashed inside a knee sock—as if the acrylic blend would negate its existence. I lifted the plastic bottle from its sheath and stared at the red-and-white capsules inside. Every single day the battle raged and my opponent never weakened.

I shook the bottle. There were a dozen left. Each one a potential confession to my substance abuse group. I pushed away images of all that concern. The mix of disappointment and understanding on all those faces. I wanted to toss down the pills, swallowing without thought or water.

I uncapped the bottle and smelled the wonderful acridity. I

had to face Kit tomorrow. I had to be smart, skillful. I laughed aloud at the thought.

One pill. I would hardly feel the effects. It would just slow my metabolism, so I couldn't keep pace with my racing fears, couldn't answer my own rat-a-tat of painful questions.

A good night's sleep. I told myself I deserved it. I had a trained throat. The capsule went down effortlessly. It was followed by a powdery aftertaste I always associated with peace.

#

On Monday, Kit called to say he wanted to meet at the Eliot Lounge, the sports bar outside Kenmore Square where Rory had bartended during law school.

I tried not to be resentful about his choice of location, but after last night I wasn't in the mood to face more memories of my brother, to see him working behind that bar—his earnest, rapid-fire efficiency as he spun drinks and snapped off the caps of imported beers. And I didn't like being pushed into it by someone who hadn't shown up for the funeral.

The taxi was hot, the windows rolled up tight. The cabby, an aging hippie with long, dry hair in a ponytail, was under the impression the air conditioner worked. When I moved to open the window, he barked at me. I might have barked back, but there was something fierce about his driving, his way of weaving around traffic on Storrow Drive at a speed and angle that went beyond the standard hack instability. I inched toward the middle of the split vinyl seat, tense and silent.

I used to keep my prescription bottle with me in my leather satchel. Thirty milligrams and the cabby's violent right turns wouldn't bother me anymore. Sixty and I wouldn't see my brother so clearly behind that bar. Ninety and I could pretend it wasn't Kit whom I was meeting.

I didn't need to chastise myself for taking the Serax. I would do my penance tonight by confessing to Dennis and the group at my substance abuse meeting. That would be punishment enough.

Now, I had to focus on being the competent reporter. I had to come back to the newsroom with an exclusive profile.

At the Eliot, I'd insist on a table away from the bar. I wouldn't allow myself to engage in any memory lane chitchat with Kit Korbanics. I had to keep in mind that he was a man who might have thrown his business partner from an eighteenth-floor balcony—that he was a man who I knew lied.

I paid the fare and asked for a receipt, which the paper always requires. Despite an undeserved tip, the cabby didn't even bother to grunt or shake his ponytail when he let me out at the corner. He started moving through traffic before I slammed the door behind me.

The Eliot Lounge was housed within the Hotel Eliot on Commonwealth Ave., but the entrance was around the corner in a markedly different world. On Mass. Ave. the sidewalks were dirtier, the horns honked louder, and the more dangerous elements of the city screamed an occasional threat as they whizzed by.

Inside, the bar decor had been redone. It had been dark, with warm woods, burgundy carpeting, and marbleized Formica cocktail tables when Rory worked there during college. Updated in the optimism of the eighties, it was now all bleached oak and fertile green. The artificial lighting glinted off the polished brass.

Kit Korbanics was standing at the rail beside a woman in a business suit. He was turned to the wall examining the framed sports photographs, most of them chronicling some aspect of Boston Marathon history.

Even relaxed, Kit radiated intensity and purpose. He had an electrical field that was like a woman's perfume. Even before I opened the door to the bar, I had sensed his signature charge.

Tall and athletic, he was wearing a nylon warm-up suit, the jacket sleeves pushed up to his elbows. Like a student, he hauled a canvas backpack over his shoulder. He turned, and gave me a wry smile that acknowledged the bizarre conditions under which we now met. I had to take a breath to steady myself, but I managed a return smile that affected a casualness about our meeting. As if I hadn't avoided him for fourteen years . . . as if I weren't here because he was suspected of murder.

He made a move toward me and for a second I was seized with panic from the fear that he would kiss me hello. At the last minute, he must have remembered that I was there not to forgive him or be friends, but because I was a journalist. He allowed this to play on his face so I could see all that he understood. So I could imagine it pained him. Then he reached for my hand, holding it, rather than pumping it. His eyes peered into mine, searching for something I wouldn't let him see.

"I'm so sorry about Rory," he said.

"Yes," I lowered my eyes in acknowledgment, although I discounted his sorrow. My brother had died more than a year ago, and this was the first I'd heard about Kit's grief.

The woman in the business suit took a step closer, letting me know she was a part of this reunion. Kit gestured toward her. "Adelaide, this is Estella Rubin, my attorney."

Normally I tried to avoid shaking hands with lawyers— even though Rory was one and my father still is. I figure that within the news jungle, we are natural enemies. But I reached for Estella's hand, if only to avoid reacting to Kit's use of my full name, a familiarity no one but Rory and my parents ever used.

Estella, in her late forties, was one of the city's most prominent defense attorneys. You would never know this from her appearance. She was under five feet tall and wore long, feathery earrings with an off-beat business suit that looked like it came from a vintage clothing shop.

From the clips in the database, I knew that she had grubbed her way up to the Lloyd and Hodge law firm via the Justice Department's Organized Crime Strike Force, where she had made headlines in the mideighties as the lead prosecutor in the Anguilo brothers' trial. She had a small but firm handshake, and a quiet manner. Absent was the nervous, excessive voltage of most defense attorneys.

Very matter-of-factly, she told me that she didn't approve of this meeting, but that Kit insisted and she was here today to limit the damage. She pulled a tape recorder from her briefcase. "I'll be taping," she said.

I found myself looking into my satchel, an enormous leather bag with no compartments, no attempt at organization. Pretending to search for my own tape recorder, I allowed papers to fall out onto the floor and then swore to myself as I crouched to pick them up. "Oh Christ, I hope I didn't leave it in the cab."

This is an old habit burned into my operating software from long ago investigations; it happened now without me pushing the buttons to issue the commands. It was a ruse—searching for the nonexistent tape recorder. I never used one. It froze a subject up—at least at first—and I could never trust that it was working. But I had long ago discovered an advantage to having people—particularly lawyers—think that I was scatter-brained. They took less caution in forming their answers.

Kit started to bend down to help me, but I jumped up, stuffing the papers back in my satchel. There were only two other customers in the Eliot—two men playing cribbage at the bar—but they stopped their game to watch me scramble. I stepped beside them and ordered a soda water from the bartender, a pickled, square-set type who looked disappointed at my choice of drink.

The Eliot Lounge had three levels: the main floor, where the bar was; a small balcony; and an equally small downstairs, which was an alcove on the way to the cellar. Kit and Estella headed up the stairs. I followed.

When we sat down, I noticed that Kit's beer, an imported label, was one of those nonalcoholic varieties.

In college, when the rest of us were drinking too much beer, Kit had displayed a rare moderation. When Rory and his friends experimented with pot, Kit refused to participate. He would leave. Often with a woman. For a while, it was me.

Apparently, he'd maintained this moderation through the excess of the eighties and it served him well. At thirty-six, Kit didn't look much older than when we'd been in college, except that his hair, an unruly blond, was darker, the curls shorter and better tamed. His jawline, a wide angle, jutted, and there was a coarseness to his beard, maybe an early shadow. But the blue eyes were no less brilliant, no more muddled by life or compromise.

As he settled into his chair, Kit pulled the backpack onto his lap and removed a small, silver tape recorder and handed it to me. "Here, you can borrow this."

It was just like Kit to bring an extra tape recorder to an interview with a journalist. I waved it off, pulling a pen and notebook out of my satchel. "This will be fine."

He laid the machine on the round cocktail table and pushed it toward me. "Go ahead. Really, I don't need it."

"It's all right," I said, leaving the tape recorder on the table. Kit had been known for his generosity. When we were going out, he was always buying me things for my dorm room or lending me his car. I turned over a fresh page of my notebook, frowning at the lines as I fended off memories.

Normally, the goal was to make this kind of interview as informal as possible, as if we all just found ourselves in a room together and were killing time by having a little talk. But suddenly, it was important that Kit Korbanics not think he was charming me. I was not the college freshman all aflutter over her brother's friend.

"The paper wants to do a profile of you," I said. "There are two ways to do it. One where you talk to me, you give me an insight into your life, your relationship with Francis Marquesson. And the other where you refuse to talk and I have to rely on other sources."

Kit fixed his astute blue eyes on me. "You mean people who might want to screw me?"

I met his gaze. "People who have their own agendas."

"How about you?" he asked. "How about your agenda?"

I was prepared for some variation of this question. "Kit. That was fourteen years ago. I stopped thinking about it."

"I haven't," he said softly.

I did not respond. Estella, rather than showing any awkwardness at being a party to this conversation, was peering at me as if she knew all about Kit and my history and was openly gauging my sincerity, my ability to forgive.

"How would it work?" Kit was asking.

Estella pulled out a yellow legal pad—apparently she didn't trust her tape recorder either—and poised herself to take notes.

I explained that it would be a front-page story that would lead the Sunday paper in two weeks, that I'd need to spend the next three or four days with him in various settings, like at his home and at his office. I'd be asking questions about his personal life, as well as investigating his career, his business, and his relationship with Francis Marquesson. I let him know I'd be collecting information from other sources: his friends, his enemies. "The difference is that this way you get a chance to refute what they say."

"Do I get to see the story before it goes in the paper?"

"No," I said. Everyone asked this question.

Estella was shaking her head. "Too much to lose," she said to Kit. "This woman can write a story making you look like a raving lunatic."

"I can do that with or without his participation," I said swiftly.

Estella was taken aback, but Kit appeared amused. "She didn't get on that investigative team without playing hardball," he said.

I was surprised he knew I'd been on the investigative team and grateful he didn't know I'd been thrown off.

"You can do the story without him, but Kit's cooperation gives you an exclusive, doesn't it? An edge over all the other media. What do we get out of it?" asked Estella.

"You get a fair story," I said.

She rolled her eyes, a shake of the feather earrings discounting the value of the exchange.

But Kit looked thoughtful. "I've read your stuff over the years. You seem like you're fair."

"I try to be," I said.

"I want to do the profile," Kit said suddenly, his intensity focused. "Even if there's no indictment, people will think I did it. I *need* good press. Otherwise, I could be ruined financially."

I retracted from his gaze, stiffened against the back of my seat. I thought I had made it clear I wasn't anybody's advocate. Least of all his. "Kit, I'm not promising you good press. I'm a reporter. My only obligation is to tell the story as I see it."

There was a second as he considered this. "That's all I ask."

"That's all you'll get," I said, to reiterate the point.

This was not the way you got people to drop their defenses, not the way you got people to tell things they should keep to themselves. But with the distance established, I felt relief. Kit, too, looked as if he might be satisfied with this businesslike approach—one professional to another.

Estella, on the other hand, wore a troubled expression. "I want the record to reflect that I'm against this," she said.

"Duly noted," Kit replied.

"And you're not going to talk to the *Herald*?" I asked.

"I hate the *Herald*," he replied.

Had the *Herald* sided with the Cambridge neighborhoods that opposed the expansion of the biotech industry in the mid-eighties, I wondered? I picked up my pen and notebook, trying not to show my satisfaction too openly. I adopted a businesslike tone. "Now, I know we talked about some of this over the phone, but do you want to start at the beginning and tell me what happened?"

This roused Estella again. "As long as it's clear that everything said at this meeting is off the record."

"Off the record" meant that you could use the information but couldn't attach the source's name to it in print. From a background source it could be useful, but not from the subject of a profile. The exclusivity of Kit's innermost thoughts and fears was worthless if I couldn't attribute them to him.

"Off the record" wouldn't get me anywhere with Lev Grabowski.

"Estella doesn't want anything in the paper before the Grand Jury decision," Kit said.

"Neither the judges nor the bar in Massachusetts looks fondly on lawyers trying their cases in the press—particularly before the case even starts," Estella explained.

I looked at Kit. He shrugged as if to say it was out of his hands.

"So you're not saying this is off the record, you're saying you want me to embargo it until the Grand Jury decision?"

Estella glanced at Kit; he nodded.

"And you'll still talk to me if the Grand Jury doesn't

indict?" I asked.

A dark look crossed his face. "A Grand Jury will indict its own mother."

"Not when there's no evidence," Estella interrupted. They exchanged a look that said they'd already had this argument.

"Indictment or not," he said. "I'll still need to set the record straight."

After another pause, he began speaking in a factual tone, extricating the emotion, as if I were the prosecutor. "I was in that hotel room and like I told the DA, Francis and I did have an argument—but I left at least half an hour before the time they say he jumped."

I glanced back at my notebook, where I had scribbled the time on the inside cover: 1:22 P.M. I was about to say it aloud, but stopped myself. I didn't need to impress him with my hard-ball anymore. I needed to find out how often he would lie.

Kit was smiling at me, as if he had heard my interior mono-logue and found it amusing. "One twenty-two," he said, affirming my own note. "I went up to his room after the keynote address at the luncheon—which was over at twelve-thirty—and I only stayed fifteen minutes. I caught a cab, and was across town at the Esplanade by the time Francis did it. I admit we had a pretty loud argument. Jesus, you know my tem-per, Addy, I had to get the hell out of there before I *did* throw him out the window."

I bristled at this reminder of our intimacy. I hadn't seen him for fourteen years and did not consider myself an expert on his temperament. "What did you fight about?" I asked, in a clipped manner.

"Business. What the hell else do partners fight about?" he asked. "Although, I suppose I could have been sleeping with his wife."

Estella lurched forward to shut off the tape. "Jesus Christ,

Kit—"

"Oh, come on, the woman is fifty-six years old. Not bad for fifty-six, but I've never been into women twenty years older. Lighten up, Estella, Addy knows me, remember?"

"She's made it pretty clear that's not going to help you," Estella said.

"But it will." His blue eyes locked on mine, and despite my best efforts, I could feel myself responding. He had always had this capability—this way of zeroing in with an intensity that was so sharp and sudden it threw you off. But he could zero out, just as quickly, I reminded myself.

"Addy is not going to deliberately screw me when she knows I'm joking," he said to Estella.

"Are you clear that he's joking?" she asked me.

"On this particular point," I said. "But you should advise him in the future not to joke."

"No joking," she said.

Kit shook his head in mock disappointment.

"So what do you think made Marquesson so upset that he threw himself out of a window?" I asked. "You think someone else might have been stepping out with his fifty-six-year-old wife?"

Kit declined this opening. "Ann-Marie is not the type. I mean, obviously you never know about people, but she hovered over Francis a lot. Calling all the time at the office, meeting him for lunch and dinner."

"Maybe he couldn't stand her anymore," I offered.

"No. Francis liked her. He never complained about her and when she called, he jumped to answer the phone. He was a pretty quiet guy—I got the feeling she was his only friend." There was respect in Kit's voice, as if he had given their relationship thought and admired it a little.

"What exactly were you two fighting about? Payroll? A bad

investment?"

Estella became quite vocal. "I have to advise Kit not to answer that. The BioFund's investments are all in privately held companies, which means none of the financial information is in the public domain. Kit cannot speak openly of BioFund matters. He has a fiduciary responsibility to his companies that cannot be breached."

Her use of the word *fiduciary* had an impact on Kit.

"The capital market is a small community. Rule number one is keep your mouth shut. I start blabbing about our in-house squabbles over investment companies and my career is over. It'll ruin me." He smiled that rueful, wise smile again. "More than an indictment for murder."

Kit stared off, over the rail of the banister toward the bar below, where the bartender was polishing the brass rail with a soiled rag. In my college days, I had often waited on this balcony after closing hours, watching Rory clean the bar, polishing half-heartedly, putting down the rag to pick up his beer, cracking jokes with the waitress. He was always on the make. I closed my eyes, forcing away his image.

"We put ourselves under a lot of pressure," Kit was saying. "We make risky investments—shit, that's our business, to put our money into companies that have every possibility of going under. I mean if they weren't risky, they'd be going to the bank for debt instead of giving away their equity. But when you go into the venture business, you start to expect yourself to perform miracles. And the limited partners expect you've got the prescience to know which companies are going to strike it rich—rich enough to go public within our ten-year time frame. I think we all put too much faith in biotech. It takes a lot longer than anyone thought to produce a viable product. People used to be able to raise money on a good story. But not now with the economy in the tank. I think I understood from the beginning that it's all a big crapshoot. But Francis, he was the scientist, the insider to the industry. He expected that on the basis of his research, he would be able to pick the winners."

"And when he came up with losers, he threw himself off a balcony?" I asked, but I moderated my tone of disbelief.

Kit was still staring at the bartender, but his eyes had a glazed, abstracted quality and I was not sure what he was seeing. "I think we all have a lot of fear and anxiety inside us—and it kills us in different ways."

His eyes shifted and focused now on me. There was a definite message he was trying to transmit. I realized suddenly that he was talking about Rory.

"I've been reading up on this sudden death stuff—you know, the arrhythmia—trying to understand it," Kit said.

"You have?" I spent the first month of mourning seeking my relief in research. I desperately sought information as if understanding how and why Rory died would make it less of a tragedy, less of a deprivation aimed solely at me. I talked to the doctors who treated him at Mass. General and I read all sorts of medical books regarding the heart. I had a hard time imagining Kit doing the same thing.

"Well, yeah. I mean, how many perfectly healthy people do you know who die for no good reason—just some sort of electrical discharge?" Kit didn't wait for an answer. "Christ, it's like being struck by lightning or something, but at least lightning you can see. And you hear all your life about it striking people dead. But this arrhythmia—it's like crib death—only for a thirty-five-year-old man. But you know, have you ever read *The Mind/Body Effect*?"

That book was probably one of the reasons I couldn't sleep nights. The analogy played over and over in my head—that arrhythmia was the developed world's equivalent of voodoo death. Instead of the enemy casting the spell, the victim cast his own spell—his misery or feeling of hopelessness causing his heart to misfire.

"It's a pop medical book," I derided it the way Dennis had at my substance abuse meeting. "Just one theory, meant to sell self-help. Not exactly given fact."

"Yes, but Rory was miserable. I talked to him the week before," he said quietly.

"Lots of people are miserable about their jobs," I shot back. "Their hearts don't stop."

"Maybe not." Kit and Estella exchanged looks. Her expression was full of sympathy. I suddenly wanted to leave.

"But sometimes they do jump out of buildings," Kit continued. "When people see themselves as failures—or when they face financial ruin—they have been known to jump out of buildings."

I should have been writing this all down, but I wasn't. I wasn't thinking about Francis Marquesson at all. "Rory wasn't facing financial ruin," I said. "He might have been unhappy where he was, but he knew he could leave. My father had already offered him a job in Worcester."

"That's right," he said. "I'd forgotten that."

But he hadn't, I could tell by his expression. Kit had seen I was getting upset and decided to shut up. He knew as well as I knew that to Rory, taking a job at my father's one-man practice in Worcester was the very definition of failure.

"Look, I'm sorry if I've brought up something you're not ready to talk about yet." Kit reached across the table and put his hand on mine. "I would have liked to have used my connections to get him a job at another firm."

I didn't know how to respond to his agonizing, his good intentions on behalf of my brother. My hand lay limp under Kit's fingers. The cool of his silver ring, one of those Irish rings with the heart facing out, slid over my knuckle. I withdrew my fingers. This was, after all, an effective way to divert me, to gain sympathy. Set the interview up in the bar where my brother had worked. Make the reporter into mush. If Kit had honestly felt this way about Rory, why hadn't he come to the funeral?

"So let's go on the record for a minute. I realize you don't want me to print all the details on where you were, but I need an official statement on your alibi for tomorrow's paper."

"We're working on it," Kit said.

"That's off the record," Estella leaned forward again.

"Come on. There'll be a story about the Grand Jury convening. I think it would be to your advantage to have a statement about the alibi."

"Off the record, I'm not going to start trying my case in the paper when I don't think there's going to be a case. My position, off the record, is that the state doesn't have enough evidence to even consider Francis Marquesson's tragic death a murder. Off the record, you print one word of this and the deal on the profile is off." All this was said in a measured tone, but she pushed her tape recorder toward my mouth for an answer.

Kit shrugged again.

"No comment from the defense as to Kit Korbanics's alibi," I said into the microphone.

Estella smiled a funny smile, as if gee, these reporters think they are so *clever*. "No, I want you to say Estella Rubin, attorney for Korbanics, was not commenting on the case yesterday."

I was not prepared to take dictation from a lawyer. I looked to Kit, hoping he would override her again. But although there was a twist in his lips, I could not tell if it was bitten-down objection. Whatever it was, he restrained himself. This was his first concession, the first sign he gave that he knew how badly he might need Estella Rubin's renowned abilities in the months ahead.

I made a pretense of writing Estella's quote in my notebook

before turning to him. "Off the record, do you have any witnesses to corroborate where you were when Francis Marquesson went over that balcony?"

Kit looked at Estella for guidance. She glanced at her watch. "We've got a meeting with Linscome and Kelley in fifteen minutes," she said.

Linscome and Kelley was a private detective firm. I imagined they had hired a detective to hang around the corridors of the Grand Jury to see who came to testify.

"Why don't we meet tomorrow at the Esplanade?" Kit suggested.

"Anyone see you at the Esplanade?" I asked.

"I don't want to see the word *Esplanade* in the paper," Estella said coolly. "Not yet."

She then began consulting her daytimer, trying to see what meetings she could rearrange so she could be on hand to chaperone, hamstring the flow of information. We set our date for noon. Then I made note of my deadline and hurried downstairs, out of the stale light of the afternoon bar.

3

"How did it go?" Mark materialized before me as I stepped off the elevator.

We were standing in the newsroom's reception area, where a tall counter stocked with back issues and a bulletin board pinned with tearsheets of stories created a natural loitering spot. The receptionist had already left her desk for the day, but three City reporters, holding cardboard cups of coffee, turned to see who Mark was tailing.

I smiled the kind of half smile the reporters would recognize. I was like a pregnant queen who knew she was about to give the throne an heir.

"What is it? What have you got?" Mark asked.

"He agreed to the profile. I'm meeting him again tomorrow."

Mark held up his thumb in congratulations. One of the reporters, a woman who had once sat diagonally from me when I was on the City staff, raised her coffee cup in a salute.

Mark and I passed into the newsroom, a large, open room divided into departments only by the configuration of desks and half-wall cubicles. The openness is to "expedite the free flow of communication" as well as to share the light of the tall Palladian windows. Rory used to call the noise level "appalling," but I found it invigorating, an electrolyte drink I could always devour.

"City" is the undefined bulk of the room centered around "the Desk," where Nora, Mark, and their assistants sat. At this hour, it was at peak capacity as day and night shifts overlapped. The major news had congealed for the day. The tension rose as the reporters covering Boston's City Hall squabbles and Dorchester drive-by shootings rushed to put the stories into keystrokes. Copyeditors, who sat at a U-shaped configuration of desks called "the Rim," hunched over their video display terminals moving early copy.

"He's not going to talk to the *Herald*, is he?" Mark asked in a loud voice. The phones rang incessantly and two television sets produced the added drone of CNN.

"No," I said, smiling.

Mark was pleased by this, but he allowed only a momentary pleasure. Quickly, he resumed the look of a harried manager. He checked his watch, a paper thin rectangle overly elegant for a newspaper man. We were in front of the conference room, just right of reception. He leaned into the doorway to see how many editors had already assembled for the Five O'clock. A half-dozen people milled around the table.

"Talk to Gerard," Mark said, briskly. "He's on his way back from the DA's office now. He'll need your notes."

Over my left shoulder, I saw Lev and Nora walking together up the central aisle of the newsroom. Like everyone at this hour, they had a hurried gait, as if racing for a bus that was already departing.

"I can't give him my notes," I said. "They talked to me off the record."

"Off the record?" Mark asked, turning away from the door.

"Till the Grand Jury decision," I explained.

"What about Korbanics's alibi?" Mark's eyes were past me, focused on Lev.

"Kit's going to walk me through the whole thing tomorrow."

"Tomorrow?"

His voice had risen another level. Two assistant editors, heads down, walked delicately around us into the conference room. A pack of reporters returning from a dinner break glanced over their shoulders as they hustled by.

As evenly as I could, I explained Estella's position, that she did not want to try the case in the press before there was a case.

Lev and Nora were now upon us, a look of acute interest on both their faces. Mark filled them in on my meeting with Kit. It now sounded something less of a triumph.

Lev offered congratulations for procuring the profile, but it seemed muted in light of the more immediate concern. "So we've got nothing on Korbanics's alibi for tomorrow?" he asked.

"An official 'no comment' from the attorney," Mark clarified.

"Who's his lawyer?" Lev asked, although he knew who Kit's lawyer was.

"Estella Rubin," I said quietly.

Lev glanced at Nora. I imagined a previous conversation in which they assessed my chances against a defense attorney of Estella's stature.

"Can't we go with the 'no comment'?" I asked. We did it all the time.

"Maybe," Lev said. "But try Korbanics one more time. Call him at home. Without the lawyer."

There was no arguing with Lev about the futility of one of his commands. I plunged my hand into my leather satchel as if already foraging for the phone number.

To Nora, Lev added, "It's doubtful Rubin will budge, but see if you can get Gerard to give her a call."

Gerard. I felt a flush rising up my neck and bent my head, looking deeper into the folds of my satchel. Lev and Mark marched into the conference room and Nora set off in the other direction, backtracking through the newsroom to leave a message on Gerard's desk.

There was little else I could do but make my way around the periphery of the newsroom to my desk in Financial. The department was in the back, righthand elbow of the room, set apart by half-wall cubicles. When I'd first been reassigned here I felt like I'd been confined to "solitary."

It was quieter than City, especially at this hour with the stock market closed and most reporters gone home. Judy Owens, the Financial editor, was at the Five O'clock meeting. A lone copyeditor banged away at his tube.

So meaningless was my job covering real estate that last Friday when Mark announced I was being taken "off staff," as it was called, reassigned to the Korbanics profile, Judy Owens had not raised the usual department-head objection. She already had an "economic development" reporter who covered real estate transactions of any significance. As associate editor for downtown real estate, I wrote and laid out puff pieces like "Brownstone of the Week," designed to satisfy the Realtors Association, which so heavily supported our classified ads— despite the economic slump. This Judy could do without.

The department was L-shaped, with my desk in the furthermost nook, pushed against the half-wall cubicle that divided me from the rest of the newsroom. As I turned the corner, I noticed Lorraine Javitz was still there. Her desk was opposite mine, facing the window. Her back was toward me, and she was sifting through a pile of documents with such piercing concentration that I knew she had no idea I had arrived.

Lorraine and I had started at the *News-Tribune* together as suburban reporters in the Waltham bureau. She'd become a business writer for the regular hours, "the normalcy of life," as she put it. In the suburbs, we often had to work nights covering the verbosity of a school committee meeting or waiting for the police details of a Route 128 fatal. Lorraine said she never wanted to ask another grieving mother how she felt about the death of her child.

In short, she refused to make any of the sacrifices usually required to succeed in the news business. And yet she managed to become a star, having developed a network of sources in the business community no one else could match. She had turned the "Tech-Talk" column, which once had been mostly product announcements, into drama—full of personal rivalries, colossal misjudgments, and an occasional fraud.

She was a good friend who had hovered over me after my brother's death, worrying about my uneaten lunches and buying me those god-awful nutrition bars she procured from some home-health vitamin distributor. Later, when I started to show up for work medicated, she steered me into the ladies' room and made me brush my hair. She went out and bought me a toothbrush once, but she never questioned me about the obvious. Never asked what I was on. Even now when I made reference to my "meetings," she never acknowledged that I'd had any unusual problems.

I threw my satchel on the floor and sank into my chair, a tweedy, ergonomic leviathan the union had fought hard for. I rested my spine against its promise of lumbar support and found it wanting. At the Five O'clock, I hoped the discussion would be of my in-depth profile, but I feared it would be of tomorrow's deficit, the absence of Kit Korbanics's alibi.

Deputy associate editor of downtown real estate. The new title flashed in my mind.

I pushed away the thought and began scouring through the papers on my desk for Kit's phone numbers. Lorraine turned around. She wore typical business attire—an Oxford shirt with the sleeves rolled up to the elbow and a navy skirt—but there was something defiantly offbeat about her. Her hair was long and her glasses John Lennonish. She had taken them off to read and now peered in my direction without her normal focus. "Addy? How'd it go?"

Briefly, I filled her in on the day's interview as well as the task ahead. Afterward, she twirled back to her desk so as not to distract me. It was now a quarter past five. I tried Kit's office at The BioFund, but only got his voice mail. Recalling that he and Estella were supposed to meet at the detective agency, I found the number for Linscome and Kelley in the *Yellow Pages*. No one picked up: no secretary, no answering service, no machine.

"You think you're going to get him to change his mind and go against his lawyer's advice?" Lorraine asked over her shoulder.

"No." Still, I ransacked my drawer, looking for Kit's home phone number.

"I mean the man's not even indicted yet. He'd be a fool to start spouting off in the press." Lorraine turned around again and was facing me.

"I know." I had little hope of persuading Kit. I wanted to show Lev that I had at least reached him—made the effort, followed through. My stomach was beginning to feel painfully empty. I had forgotten about lunch again and had to settle for a pineapple-flavored Lifesaver I found in my drawer, dusted with eraser shavings.

Even if Kit were to go straight home from the detective agency, he likely wouldn't be there yet. Still, I hunted for his number, which I found on a torn piece of paper wadded into the corner of my satchel. The answering machine told me he was not available. It must have been programmed not to take messages. No beep. I talked to the blank airwaves anyway, asking Kit to call me as soon as he got home.

"Hey, you *got* him to agree to the profile. If you can't get him on the record for tomorrow, you can't get it, " Lorraine said.

Lorraine always seemed baffled by my anxiety. She was extremely rational and seemingly immune to pressure from editors. She wrote her column, motivated by some sort of responsibility she felt toward technology rather than whether anyone at the paper would pat her on the back. As a consequence she paid little attention to either criticism or praise.

But I couldn't afford her attitude. I glanced at the clock, hoping Kit returned to his town house before the news meeting broke up at six o'clock.

Lorraine picked up a bound publication from a stack of financial documents on her desk and waved it at me. "Look what I got," she said with a sly smile.

"What is it?

"The BioFund prospectus. Details on Korbanics's investment companies."

The BioFund, a limited partnership, owned pieces of small, private biotechnology companies. It did not hand out its prospectus like cocktail napkins. Our chairs were on rollers. I glided across the carpeting, parking the arm of my leviathan beside hers.

Lorraine handed me the prospectus. The print was small and dense.

"Where did you get it?" I asked.

"One of my sources. I've been following that Fenton Biomedical merger. A French pharmaceutical, Lavaliere, is buying them. Turns out The BioFund owns a stake. Anyway, the *Herald* keeps writing that Korbanics needed to bump off Marquesson for the insurance money because The BioFund's investments were deep in the tank. I'm trying to figure out how deep."

"Kit said he and Marquesson were fighting over BioFund business," I told her.

She considered this for a moment, before shaking her head. "Yeah, they had a lot to fight about. But probably not Fenton. From what I can tell, it was their least troubled investment. Fenton has had this agreement with Lavaliere since May. The BioFund stands to *make* money on this merger."

"You writing anything for daily?" I asked.

"No. Just scavenging. It'll take me a while to wade through all of this." She gestured to the stack of documents, which she identified as scientific journal articles.

Lorraine took the prospectus out of my hands and loaded it into her nylon briefcase. She was meeting her latest MIT boyfriend in the North End and wanted to know if I'd join them for dinner. She had an odd preference for brilliant but socially immature men, the kind who might reconstruct a neuron path with the spaghetti. I said no thank you, but I'd like to see the prospectuses after she was done. She nodded her assent.

As I watched her head to the elevator, it occurred to me that Kit Korbanics was probably on his way home from the Linscome and Kelley meeting by now and that, most likely, he had a car phone. Step one in doing a profile: Get all of the subject's relevant phone numbers. I returned to my own desk to check the inside cover of my notebook. It was blank.

I tried Kit's home number again, reached the answering machine, and hung up. I stood and peered over the cubicle half-wall. The Five O'clock meeting had not yet broken up, but Gerard was at his desk. I could see his shoulders bent toward the computer screen as he typed at a manic pace.

I sat, swiveling my chair toward my own tube. Reporters working on stories were cautioned to "save" or enter their copy into the system at least once every five minutes in case the central minicomputer crashed. This way a copy of the work could be retrieved by the "white knights"—the mysterious saviors who worked upstairs in the data center.

This meant that if Gerard had "saved" his present story at any point, I could call up a copy of it on my terminal. All I needed was to figure out the story's "slug," or computer title.

First I typed in *Korbanics*, but got nothing. I tried *KKorbanics*, *KitKorb*, and *Korbanics1* before I realized the proper perspective. Gerard's slug was *Marq*, short for the victim rather than the accused.

I hit the key that pulled forth his working text. The story appeared on my screen in its partially written state.

A Suffolk County Grand Jury, impaneled to investigate the dramatic death of former scientist Francis Marquesson, began hearing evidence yesterday of a possible murder.

Marquesson died two weeks ago after plunging from an eighteenth floor balcony at the Harbor Inn Hotel and Convention Center. The fall, which stopped lunchtime traffic on Atlantic Ave., was originally called a suicide.

W. Christopher Korbanics, Marquesson's partner in the venture capital fund, The BioFund, is believed to be the only suspect in the possible murder.

A source connected to the investigation said yesterday's Grand Jury was to hear physical evidence linking Korbanics to the hotel balcony scene. A spokesman for the district attorney's office would not comment.

There were three or four carriage returns Gerard had made to create space for a response from the Korbanics camp.

The story picked up:

Marquesson, a former professor at MIT, was a
molecular biologist, best known for his work on
the immune system. The BioFund, launched in 1983,
funded startups in biotechnology. With the failure of
several of its companies to produce a product, the
fund appeared headed for insolvency, according to
sources.

The text ended there, where Gerard had last remembered to save the working copy. I stared at the big white space. Gerard was probably on the phone right now trying to reach Estella.

I supposed I would be exonerated when he, too, failed to get anything out of her. Still, the glaring hole in Korbanics's responses wouldn't reflect on Gerard since I had effectively denied him all access to the murder suspect. It would reflect on me, the reporter who had promised the editor to ask the key question and then could not procure an answer.

Had I been dulled by last night's Serax? I'd felt slow in the morning, perhaps it had carried through into the afternoon. I sent Gerard's unfinished copy back into computer blackness and stared, full of self-doubt, at my now-empty screen. The deadline for the final copy on the Grand Jury story wasn't until 9:00 P.M., but Lev would want a report on my progress before he left for the day at seven.

I got up from my desk and headed out of the Financial department to the open newsroom. The meeting had begun to break up. Lev and Mark were standing with Gerard outside the conference room.

I moved between the aisles of desks, where reporters sat staring into computer terminals or frantically glued to the phone. I glanced up at one of the clocks, which hung on the wall like a supervisor with a shotgun, and told myself I still had plenty of time.

Mark stopped midconversation when he saw me approach. "You got anything from Korbanics?"

I stood outside the little male ring and explained that I hadn't been able to reach Kit, but that I remembered he'd been on his way to a private meeting at a detective agency with Estella Rubin when they left. "I'll try him at home again in another half an hour."

Gerard reached forward, a comrade. His hand touched my shoulder, urging me to relax. "Don't worry about it," he said. "I've got a response from the lawyer."

Lev gave him a round look of approval: If he could count on nothing else, he could count on his boy.

"Estella talked to you on the record?" It came out of my mouth sounding like an accusation.

Mark's expression told me my tone was out of line, but Gerard did not seem to notice. He continued in his effort to soothe. "She had no choice, really. I told her I heard there was evidence Korbanics's prints were found on both sides of the glass slider to the balcony. He needs an alibi. She said he left the hotel by cab and took a walk on the Esplanade. I convinced her a front-page piece in the paper was just what she needed—publicity to get witnesses to come forward."

I looked at him dumbly. He took it as praise.

Mark scribbled something on his yellow legal pad and showed it to Lev, who grunted, "Yes, good idea." The three of them would meet first thing in the morning to review how best to deploy Gerard to maximize his raw investigative talent.

Then Lev asked Gerard to send copy of the rough draft to the editor's queue. Lev wanted to read it through before he went home for the evening. Normally, he let Mark or Nora make the call, but tonight, he wanted to be the one to decide where to position Gerard's story on the front page.

4

I followed the scent of overboiled coffee downstairs to the church basement, where the unqualified support of strangers was supposed to deliver me from my demons.

The meeting room, a creation of blueboard partitioning, had a well-worn air about it, as if all the support groups in the world were held within its confines. Yellowing substance abuse posters vied with AA slogans for wall space, diminishing the statue of poor Jesus with his shepherd's staff that hung above the blackboard.

Beneath Jesus, Dennis stood at the desk, his foot resting on an open drawer. He was telling a rapt audience about the rules he had devised for avoiding a bad batch of cocaine.

The group surrounded him in four semicircular rows of folding chairs. There were maybe twenty-five people—a small sampling my age and older, but most in their late teens and early twenties. They listened attentively, engrossed in the finer points of the drug life they were trying to shake.

Normally I took a seat in back, next to the cubbyholes of art supplies and brightly colored toys that led me to believe that during the day, preschool children pondered the poster of pills and capsules caught in a swirl of a flushing toilet. Today I forced myself into a seat in the second row. The look in Dennis's eyes told me he noticed the deviation.

"Welcome, Addy," Dennis said in the compassionate tone they teach them all in rehab. In cadence and gesture, Dennis attempted to underscore the spiritual connection we were supposed to share. Sometimes it was comforting. At the moment, I found it onerous.

"Hello," I answered, and there was nodding around the room.

When I had first met Dennis, about three months ago, I thought he was some sort of Southwestern cowboy. He had longish hair and a mustache, as well as an extensive collection of silver and turquoise jewelry on his fingers and wrists. As it turned out, he was a transplanted New Yorker, but also a folk singer who played at coffee houses and "western nights" at a few Allston bars. He used to subsidize his music by dealing cocaine. Now he drove a cab he'd bought with the illegal proceeds.

His eyes remained on me longer than was necessary before he announced that it was time to turn the meeting over to open discussion.

There was a pile of pamphlets on the empty seat beside me. The first few times I had come, I had taken the pamphlets and turned them over to Mark as proof of my attendance—like the church bulletin for my parents when I used to skip Sunday mass. Now, I picked one up, scanning it to hide my face.

Except for Lil, a grandmother who had been off Valium for so long now I couldn't figure out why she still came to the meeting, and an anesthesiologist who had been caught anesthetizing himself, this was primarily a tough Brighton crowd. Cocaine was the drug of choice, but sometimes crack and heroin. Many were here as a condition of their probation. Open discussion often led people to admit their experiences breaking into people's cars to steal stereos or hocking jewelry that belonged to their mothers.

We all knew it was my turn.

Dennis sat down at the desk, hands clasped behind his head, waiting for someone to speak.

Initially, I was put off by his drug dealer stories. He talked openly of the marijuana distributorship he gained after years of driving carloads of the stuff up from Florida, of his promotion to selling cocaine and the high-life parties he threw in the eighties. At first these parties were peopled by semiglamorous participants: roadies from important bands, a DJ from the hip Boston radio station, and a few well-known restaurateurs. As the decade changed, the partygoers became more desperate: a high school algebra teacher who lost his job, a stripper who couldn't get herself on stage without cocaine up her nose.

I once felt outclassed by the housebreakers and jewelry thieves. I might have missed a few deadlines, embarrassed a state rep by confusing his name with an opponent, but I hadn't done anything criminal. I hadn't smuggled illegal drugs across state lines or corrupted young minds. In college, Kit and I had left parties where cocaine turned up on mirrors. At first, I couldn't relate to these people who voluntarily took drugs to increase their heart rates.

But now I felt differently. Dennis had made me see that my dependency was no nobler, nor did it require any less strength to overcome.

Perhaps because I'd come to respect his opinion, I was finding it hard to confess to my weakness of the night before. Odd, I couldn't admit to a man who used to transport kilos of illegal substances that I had swallowed one doctor-prescribed antianxiety pill.

Christy, an eighteen-year-old with chronic boyfriend problems, filled the silence by telling the group how difficult the weekend had been, how she spent Saturday night watching a video with her mother, and how she had to slam the door when

Elio showed up at her apartment at midnight with a six-pack of beer and a crack pipe.

The group cheered a show of discipline that had eluded me. Dennis was carefully watching my reaction. I lowered my head. There was a lull, the odd moment when people were trying to decide what to say next. I wondered if they would notice my leaving.

"So, Addy, how did it go? Did you get that assignment?" Dennis asked. This was a clear break from the way group discussion was supposed to work, but Dennis was not one to adhere too closely to rules.

"Yeah, I did." Generally the group cheers even the most minor success, but something in my tone must have made them hold back.

"You all right?" Lil asked from behind me.

Honesty, Dennis liked to say, is different from truth. Truth is a fact. Like I only took one thirty-milligram pill. Honesty is the heart's appraisal: The prospect of seeing Kit Korbanics had made me fall apart.

I told them about the bottle in my nightstand, the panic attack, missing my brother, and about needing to block it all out to go back to sleep.

I got no credit for it being a single pill. The hardest junkies in the room looked at me with disappointment.

I told them of my anxiety about seeing Kit for the first time in fourteen years, although I was careful not to use his name. "I was afraid I wouldn't be able to handle him any better now than I had when I was a freshman."

"*Him*, the old boyfriend?" someone asked.

"Yes."

"If this guy flips you out so much, you shouldn't see him," advised Christy, who kept returning to the boyfriend who beat her.

I told her I had to see this man to do my assignment. And that I had to do the assignment to regain my career.

There was a blank look among the people in the group and I realized that many had never held jobs. Lil, the grandmother, said that if it was a choice between recovery and career, I should choose recovery.

"Career *is* my recovery," I said.

"It wasn't last night," someone else commented.

"She doesn't have to choose." This came from Dennis, at the desk.

I gave him a grateful look. He told me once that he could never have gotten straight without his music, without spending long hours playing the same songs, going over the same notes to stay focused on something other than cocaine.

"I think what you need is to put things in the right order in your head," he continued. Everyone else fell silent. "Did you handle this guy any better today than you did when you were eighteen?"

I shrugged. "I thought I did until tonight, when the editors—"

"Forget the editors," Dennis interrupted. "How do *you* think you handled him?"

I hesitated. "All right, I guess. Better than I thought."

"Cool," Christy said.

"But it's not just that," I addressed myself mostly to Dennis. "I mean, it's complicated. This guy was my brother's best friend. When I hear his voice I go back in time. College. When it all was ahead of me. When Rory was alive. When everything was going to go right."

There was a murmur around the room. My brother's death was not an unfamiliar topic.

"But you're not eighteen anymore," Dennis said gently. "Now, you *know* things don't go right."

I was silent.

"When you're taking drugs, you're not dealing with anything." Dennis's tone had shifted, grown darker. I knew he was thinking about his girlfriend who had died of an overdose. He sat absolutely still behind the desk as his audience drew closer. At the end of my row, a young woman who had been rifling through her backpack put it down to listen.

He stared down at his turquoise bracelet as if it were a watch with its timepiece missing. "I was so screwed up after Andrea's death. So guilty. I couldn't face it. I stayed awake snorting coke; at dawn I took Tuinals to sleep. I slept right through her funeral—out cold when they put her in the ground.

"I couldn't face myself so I stayed high for eight months. I didn't get over the grief. You pay now or later. You don't skip the suffering part because you're high. When you get straight, you start from square one—dealing with the real shit. The guilt, you know. Andrea didn't die on *my* coke, but maybe she wouldn't have done coke at all if she hadn't hooked up with me."

A painful silence ensued—an agony everyone seemed to relate to. The turmoil in my own stomach had begun to intensify. My feelings of guilt about Rory's death. The reason I awoke every night in a panic.

Voodoo death, Kit had called it. Rory's arrhythmia was so sudden, so strange. Kit had been suspicious enough to look it up in the Benson book.

I tried to tell myself that Kit had his own motives. He was a murder suspect trying to manipulate me, trying to use his concern about my dead brother to convince me he was not the murdering kind. But I couldn't get the thought out of my mind. *Voodoo death*, a semi-involuntary suicide.

The meeting was breaking for coffee. People stood up and stretched, headed to the coffee table in the back. A hat was passed into my lap. I added a limp dollar from my wallet and sent it on.

Suddenly Dennis was next to me, his silver-laden arm on mine.

"Throw them out," he said.

He meant the Serax. I nodded.

"You can't have that shit around. You never know when you're going to have a bad night."

"I'm over the worst," I said, not too convincingly.

Dennis wore an expression of sadness, not of his own sadness, but of mine. "No, Addy. Not really. You've just begun."

#

The last time I saw Rory, I was under deadline. Nearly the entire time he talked to me, my eyes were on the clock.

It was a Saturday afternoon and I was working in City, sitting at the elections database desk, set apart from the rest of the newsroom, near the window. I'd been following up on a tip that a state senator from Mattapan hadn't filed reports on his fundraising and campaign expenses for the 1988 election. Keying his name into our database, which contains the current filings at the state office of campaign and political finance, I'd found that the senator not only had forgotten the 1988 six-month filing, but for the previous election as well.

I had fifty minutes to double-check all this and to put together a lead that would convince Mark my story deserved front page. Rory appeared over one of the guardlike file cabinets that bank each side of the desk.

Seeing my brother and me together, no one ever failed to identify the sibling relationship. We were the same reedy physical type, although he was more substantial, and had the same coloring—the odd Irish combination of dark hair with a never-exposed-to-the-sun fairness. He looked particularly pale that day,though at the time I attributed it to our fluorescent lighting.

I could tell from his outfit, the sports jacket thrown over an Oxford shirt and jeans, that he'd come from his office at Keenan and Quinn. Unlike most lawyers, Rory did not work eighty-hour weeks trying to make partner. But on the rare occasion when one of his clients was actually innocent, he sacrificed a Saturday.

"What are you doing here?" I asked.

"You have time for lunch, Brenda?"

Rory used to call me Brenda Starr. We both knew I was no voluptuous, eye-twinkling comics heroine, but it was meant as a compliment, a tip of his hat to his sister's inner glamour.

Normally it made me smile, but not this day. "Does it look like I have time for lunch?" I asked, turning back to the PC.

"No, it doesn't." He watched me enter keystrokes in silence, then added, "But do I stop by much?"

To pick me up when we had something planned, yes, but to drop by the newsroom, unannounced? Maybe once or twice, during the entire time I'd worked downtown. The newspaper, overlooking the expressway in the industrial section of the South End, was not on Rory's way home. Somewhere in my cold heart, I knew he needed to talk to me, but I did not turn to examine his expression. I had to connect the dots. Make the story. Make the page.

To emphasize my impatience, I glanced at the clock.

"It's about Keenan," Rory said.

The firm, which always seemed to be representing someone I despised, was not my favorite group of lawyers. Rory had his complaints about his employer, but he liked the opportunity to do criminal defense work at a downtown location that was within walking distance of his racquetball club.

"I don't have time to breathe right now, let alone stop for lunch. How about later? Dinner?" I asked.

"Got a date with Karen."

The lawyer with the great body he lusted after. Let her console him, I thought.

"Call me tomorrow," I said, abruptly. I had misspelled the senator's name and was now looking at a screen of someone else's filings. I stabbed the escape key to start all over.

"Yeah, all right," I heard him say. I did not look over my shoulder to see him leave. I did not take my hand off the keyboard to wave good-bye.

I didn't think about Rory again until after my story was filed and slated for Page One. Even then, I was diverted by a group of reporters who invited me to go out for drinks. It wasn't until I got back to my apartment at almost 1:00 A.M. that my mother finally reached me. She was calling from the hospital to tell me Rory was dead.

#

So now, when I wake in the dark, I don't have to turn on the light to check the clock. I can tell time by my wild, pounding heart—it's one in the morning.

Tonight, as the fear and panic subsided, I was left, not with the blankness I usually took for relief, but with an excruciating hollowness. I let the tears fall on the pillowcase.

I turned on my right side so as not to put pressure on my heart, but found myself facing the nightstand drawer where the Serax was still hidden in the knee sock. *Pay now, or pay later,* Dennis had said.

I did not dispose of the Serax as I'd promised, but I did remove myself from its presence. Grabbing my damp pillow and cotton blanket, I went to the darkened living room. I curled, fetal-like, on the nubby Haitian-cotton couch to wait out the pain, far enough away from the nightstand and the easy reach.

5

On the Esplanade, I sat on a bench by the river making note of the whitecaps on the Charles as I waited for Kit and Estella. Despite the June sun, the air was fresh and clipped, kicking the river into a turmoil of current. The lone white sail on the water was hard-heeled, its rail dipped into the water as the sloop tacked its way back to the Community Boating boathouse.

I was supposed to meet them at the Arthur Fiedler memorial, which was at the base of the footbridge not twenty yards away. We were to spend the afternoon retracing Kit's innocent walk, the one he was supposedly taking while his business partner plunged to his death.

I turned and saw Kit crossing the footbridge onto the path. He was wearing running shorts, a Gore-Tex jacket, and a pair of Ray-Ban sunglasses. He was an impressive figure, seeming taller and larger from my seat on the bench. He appeared to be alone.

He saw me and strode past the Fiedler statue, center lane, making a passing bicyclist veer to the grass. "Adelaide!" he called, using the familiarity again and peering at me in a way that made me feel self-conscious. I didn't normally spend a lot of time in front of the mirror, but that morning I'd applied makeup, trying to offset the dark circles. With Kit staring at me,

I felt suddenly silly about my efforts, exposed somehow.

"You look good," he said, a slight smile on his lips.

I mumbled a thanks and bent my head, flipping over the pages of my notebook in a noisy, businesslike fashion.

"Estella's not coming," he said.

"She changes her mind a lot," I said dryly.

Our eyes met as he searched mine for meaning. He seemed not to understand.

"Yesterday at the Eliot she threatens my life if I mention the Esplanade in print. Two hours later, she gives Gerard Hanley the whole alibi. No sweat."

He seemed surprised by my tone. "She had no choice."

"What happened to her qualms about the Grand Jury? Not trying her case in the press before there was a case?"

"Hey, he cornered her. Besides, he's from *your* paper." His eyes, wide and blue, pleaded no apologies.

I spent a moment considering whether to enlighten him about in-house rivalries, but decided there was no point. The bottom line was that Estella had been serving his interests. How upset could he get?

"Lousy photo," I said.

I was referring to the morning's paper. Alongside Gerard's story, the paper had run its most recent photo of Kit Korbanics, taken outside the police department last week when he'd been called in for questioning. Shot at a distance, the zoom lens had not angled close enough. He'd been caught as he turned sideways to Estella, an unintelligible profile.

"I like being a blur," Kit said, attempting irony, for he was now long past being a blur. There was an edge to his voice, a tension to the acknowledgment. With the news that an investigative Grand Jury had convened, his picture had been everywhere. *Herald* photographers had gotten a clear shot of him, which was run two columns on the front page. The three network affiliates had shown his defiant jawline on both the six and eleven o'clock news. This explained his sunglasses.

Kit was checking his runner's watch, a large timepiece with an extraordinary number of digital windows. "It's almost one o'clock. I'm going to try to keep this in time with the real walk I took. Prove I couldn't have been at the hotel."

Did he think matching up the times would prove anything other than that he could read his watch? I wondered, but nodded. He must have some other strategy.

"Come on, I'll show you where the cab let me out," he said, and began a brisk pace back toward the Hatch Shell.

In New England, few people squander a sunny and clear day, and a lunchtime crowd was just beginning to empty onto the Esplanade. We traveled against the prevailing throng, over the danger-ridden moat of Storrow Drive, maneuvering among businessmen, rollerbladers, dog-walkers. Coming around the last curve, we dodged a scavenger propelling a grocery cart filled with cans and bottles.

We made our way down Embankment Road, a half block to Beacon Street. At the corner, Kit pointed to the curb. "Right here," he said and consulted his watch. "Five to one, that's pretty close."

I dutifully pulled my notebook out of my satchel and jotted it down. After a minute, I asked, "So did Gerard's story start the phone ringing this morning? Any witnesses?"

"Not yet. But if the Grand Jury does indict me, we can subpoena the cab companies. The way bill will show a fare dropped off right here."

"What kind of cab?"

"It could have been any of them," Kit gestured to the taxi-laden traffic whirling around the Public Garden behind him. "I was all pissed off. Not paying attention. But I gave the guy a twenty-dollar tip. That I remember."

"More than the fare?"

"Yeah, probably. I didn't have anything smaller. Hopefully, the cabby remembers."

"You paid cash then. You don't have any kind of company account?"

"I'm a small businessman, a rather unsuccessful small businessman at the moment. And if I had an account, I'd know what cab company it was," he returned.

I took a minute to let him cool off. "There are certain things I have to get on the record, Kit," I explained.

"I'm sorry," he said. "It's just that there's a Grand Jury deciding my fate at the moment and this cab thing has me frustrated. I usually ask for a receipt to keep track of my expenses. Why the hell did I have to forget this time?"

This was a good quote, full of human emotion and versatile enough to be played a number of ways. I jotted it down, aware that Kit was watching me record his apology and yet unable to pretend this was just a personal exchange. Nothing was personal. He'd have to get used to that.

After a minute, he turned and began retracing our steps to the overpass. We walked side by side as we crossed over Storrow Drive again, and it occurred to me that to the passersby, we looked like a couple—a couple with something troubling between us—off for a stroll along the Esplanade.

We crossed the footbridge and landed back in front of Arthur Fiedler. Kit stopped, staring at the statue in an odd manner.

The statue is an enormous head of the late Boston Pops conductor, a computerlike drawing transformed into three dimensions by the horizontal layering of steel. "You know, I think there was a circle of people around here when I passed, some sort of tour group." Kit had a puzzled expression, as if remembering this for the first time.

"Tourists with cameras?" I asked. Just after one o'clock. With some difficulty, this could be checked out. There were only a couple of agencies whose walking tours of Boston included the Esplanade.

"No. Like a field trip, with kids."

I jotted this down in my notebook. Schools would be harder; the kids could come from anywhere. "Did it look like a tour guide leading them?" I asked hopefully. "Or just a teacher?"

"Jesus, I don't know."

"Well, how many adults were there?"

He closed his eyes. "I don't know," he said after a minute. "I didn't even remember there was a group until now."

When you made it up on the spot? I wondered. "How old were the kids?"

"I don't know—nine, ten, maybe twelve. Who can tell kids' ages?"

His lack of specifics could mean he was lying, but it could also mean he didn't know that much about kids. Either way, I'd be forced into at least some attempt to confirm or refute it. To be fair, I'd have to call some of the elementary schools in the Boston area. "Were they wearing uniforms?" I asked, hoping to rule out the parochial schools.

He closed his eyes again. "I don't think they had uniforms. I'm pretty sure I did not see uniforms." He still seemed vague about the recollection.

"Did anybody in the group see you? Any kids turn your way?"

He thought a moment. "Not that I remember, and I was walking by pretty fast." He turned away from Arthur Fiedler and began heading toward the bike path. We walked along the river in silence and over another footbridge, which left us on the back side of the Hatch Shell.

I forced myself to jot down more little landmarks as we

passed. The gold-lettered names of the composers written on the exterior walls of the Hatch Shell; the pathetic looking steel animals in the neglected playground; the crowd of masts bobbing on moorings before the Community Boating boathouse. But I wasn't really seeing any of it. I was thinking about Kit, and thinking that his uncertainty seemed as frustrating to him as it was to me.

Three women, power walkers lined up like a brigade, pumped toward us. I was trying to recall the person at the substance abuse meeting who had talked about exercise as an aid, an alternate addiction, when Kit pulled me by the hand, steering me to the right of the path to avoid the vigor of the women's arms.

I felt an unexpected warmth, a sensation I did not want to acknowledge. I reminded myself that Sir Walter Raleigh here was on a mission. He'd be laying his Gore-Tex jacket over puddles if he thought it would convince me he wasn't at the hotel when Marquesson went flying. I wanted to pull my hand free, but decided it would make too much of his courtesy. Instead, I waited until the women had passed and Kit let me go to consult his watch again.

"One twenty-five, already," he informed me.

Three minutes after Marquesson smashed to his death. Did he think that by telling me today's time, I'd be convinced? I pulled the pen out of the wire binding of the notebook, anxious to re-employ my still-warm hand. My change of subject was more abrupt than it should have been. "How would your fingerprints end up on both sides of the sliding glass door?"

He took off his sunglasses to better meet my eye. He wanted me to know that while my tone had surprised him, the question was fully anticipated. "We had that hotel room as a business suite," he said, after taking a moment to pocket the sunglasses. "I had meetings there with investors and potential clients the night before and that morning. I'd shown at least three or four people the view from the balcony."

"Will any of them testify to it?"

"They'll have to fly back from Japan, but yes, if they have to, they'll testify."

If they have to. I scribbled this quote in my notebook. Yesterday, he'd been certain of an indictment. Today, as the Grand Jury went into its third day of weighing evidence of murder, he entertained the possibility there would be no need of witnesses.

Rory used to say that a Grand Jury would indict anyone on the thinnest of evidence. But of course, that was a criminal defense lawyer's perspective. I had to check myself: Any reporter in my position would *want* to believe Rory, would want to believe this case would go to trial.

It occurred to me that I was making a tactical error, asking the most aggressive questions first. I had an enormous amount of background information to collect. There was no need to constantly remind Kit I was the adversary.

I turned toward the tall rectangles of MIT looming on the horizon and struck a more casual tone. "Some of your biotech startups must have originated at MIT. Isn't that where Marquesson came from?"

"Yeah. He taught molecular biology," Kit said. "You know, he should have stayed in academia. He wouldn't have made the money he did—but he wasn't motivated by money, really. So why put himself under the kind of pressure we were under?"

It was the first note of sympathy I had heard from him. "Why did he?" I asked in a softer tone.

Kit peered back toward MIT. His voice got hard again. "Because Marquesson was under the delusion that he was a businessman."

"Why was it a delusion?" I asked.

"A man who is best in the world at identifying the target proteins of autoimmune diseases can come to think he's brilliant at everything. The international scientist assumes all problems are science problems. But he hasn't a clue how to manage other scientists. Or cash flow.

"He had no temperament for the day-to-day pressures and had to hire a manager for the biotech company he founded. Although he stayed on the scientific advisory board, he had to turn the reins over to a real CEO—a guy named Beane. I think Francis felt a little desperate to prove he wasn't a failure in business. That's when he decided he was more of a deal maker than an entrepreneur."

"The BioFund?" I asked.

"I was working at an investment banking firm in New York when Francis approached me. He had the stature, and I knew the mechanics of raising money. I was young, too young not to swallow the bait."

I asked him what went wrong.

"I mean it didn't take long to figure out that Francis didn't get the venture capital business, either. The point of a fund is to bring a return to the limited partners. It's not about having the best science."

I was writing swiftly, trying to get it all down. Suddenly, Kit's tone changed again. "If Marquesson wanted to win his fucking science awards he should have stayed at MIT."

Kit was staring furiously at the river as if he would throw Marquesson in if he could just get him up from the grave. "And if he wanted to kill himself, he should have shot himself in the fucking head."

I stood completely still, afraid to remind him I was a reporter by making a single notation.

"I'm sorry," he said, after a minute.

I shrugged.

"It's just that the great man of science has been a pain in the ass for the last eight years, and now, he managed the final fuck you. If he had shot himself, at least there would have been powder burns."

He had said too much for me to try to remember it later and yet I wanted to preserve the illusion that I was not recording all this fury. I looked off toward MIT for a few moments, then opened my notebook slowly, as if deciding to resume a lapsed interview. "So what's your theory? What caused Marquesson to jump off the balcony? Your fight?"

"I don't know," Kit said, with irritation. "Like I said, we've fought enough before. I mean, we never agreed on how to handle our client companies."

We had resumed our walk and I was trying to keep pace while getting down his quote about wishing Marquesson had shot himself in the head. I missed most of what he went on to say about Francis's "scientific arrogance."

When I looked up, Kit's eyes were fixed on my notebook. "You getting all this?"

"Yeah." I turned to a fresh page. "Slow down a little."

He hesitated. "The difference this time, I suppose, was the economy. The recession. And we were nearing the end of the life of the fund."

I gave him a look that showed my ignorance.

"A venture capital fund has a set life span—this one was ten years. We were in year eight, which meant we had only two years left to make our investment in companies liquid. Money is tight nowadays. And the pressure was on."

"Liquid?" I asked, feeling stupid.

"Cash out. Sell the investment in the company, which usually means either a forced sale or taking it public. We had investments in a half-dozen medical supply startups that were doing all right, but our biotech companies were blowing through so much cash and were still so far away from a product that there was no chance of taking them public."

I struggled to remember something Lorraine had said about a sale or acquisition of a biotech.

"Isn't there some kind of merger?" I asked.

"Fenton Biomedical. Yeah, we'll sell some stock there, but that's only one of six biotech companies. Not enough to save the fund unless we get real lucky somewhere else."

"So, this pressure to cash out—this is why you think Marquesson killed himself?"

"Fear of failure." Kit shrugged. "A guess, that's all. I can't pretend to understand what would make any human being fling himself from a balcony. All I know is that I didn't push him."

"What did you do?" I asked softly.

"I left him in the hotel room and caught a cab on Atlantic Avenue. I was headed toward my office in Cambridge, but I ended up here," he said, gesturing to the river.

"Got any witnesses who saw you in the lobby?"

"Not yet," he said.

I made a quiet note on my pad.

"You don't believe me?" he asked.

I jotted down his question.

"Could you stop writing for a second and answer me?"

I halted, but did not make any attempt to put my pen away. "It's not my job to start a story believing anything."

Kit searched my face. "But do you actually think I'm capable of pushing my partner, a friend for eight years, off a balcony, for the insurance money?"

After the way we broke up, I thought him capable of anything. "Like I said, I don't start off believing one way or another."

He was no longer looking at me, but peering at the river with a saddened gaze, toward the Longfellow Bridge. There was a long silence.

At last, he said, "You never in fourteen years let me either apologize or explain."

"I think the scene explained itself, Kit," I said swiftly. We were talking about the day I walked into his apartment in the middle of the afternoon to find him in bed with the graduate student who lived on the second floor—a woman I knew. Liz. I'd borrowed quarters from her and lent her laundry detergent in the basement. I did not want to relive this moment. "Let's stay in the present."

"No. Let's not." His eyes met mine with a fierce intensity. "You wouldn't take my calls. You wouldn't see me. You wouldn't go to parties if you thought I'd be there. But Addy, now it's your *job* to listen to me."

I flipped my notebook shut and turned away.

He grabbed my arm. "Addy, please. I'm apologizing. I screwed up. Liz hit on me heavy. I was twenty-two and horny and not what you call true blue. But you were working at that stupid newspaper twenty-four hours a day—"

He was referring to the *FreePress*, the student newspaper where I'd gained most of my reporting skills. I was suddenly furious. He was so career-driven he'd subscribed to *The Wall Street Journal* as an undergrad, for godsakes, but I couldn't show a little dedication to my internship? "So it was my fault?" I asked. "Is that what you're trying to say?"

"No. I'm saying it was my fault. I screwed up. I hurt you, I pissed off Rory. Nothing good came from that afternoon. Nothing. But it was fourteen years ago and right now my whole life is on the line. So I'm asking you to not hold it against me. Not to think I'm capable of murder because at twenty-two I was capable of incredible stupidity."

I stared up into his soulful eyes and did not blink. "I see no connection between the two."

#

Still in silence, we climbed the stairs of the overpass and descended onto Charles Street.

But the air had been cleared. There was no denying the relief. I'd been insulted and wounded for fourteen years. Although I had not forgiven Kit, nor forgotten his absence at my brother's funeral, I no longer felt the need to wave my grievances over my head. I put down the placard, the message already proclaimed.

We made our way up the block to the Paris Deli, which was a narrow bowling lane squeezed between a Realtor's office and a travel agency. Inside there was a lunch counter along one long wall and a half-dozen booths along the other. Photographs of the Eiffel Tower vied with posters of the Acropolis.

After the lunch rush, it was quiet. Two middle-aged women with shopping bags sat together in the last booth. The one facing us stared at Kit. He ignored her.

We sat down at the nearest table. Kit checked his watch. "One thirty-five."

I pulled out my notebook and jotted it down. Thirteen minutes after Marquesson's death. Although unlikely at rush hour, Kit might have made it directly to the restaurant by this time even *after* pushing Marquesson from the balcony. I didn't mention the possibility.

Kit went to the counter. The menu offered everything from souvlaki to bologna sandwiches, but I had no appetite.

Kit returned with my extra-large Coke, which I sipped slowly, distractedly.

"You sure you're not hungry?" Kit asked. I half expected the lecture everyone else gave me, but he must have decided against it. He ordered a gyro, then hardly touched it.

I watched him, recalling the college meals I'd cooked in his apartment kitchen. I'd made hamburgers with mushrooms, and tuna with curry, thinking they were the most exotic recipes in the world. He praised every attempt excessively but ate little. Soon, we switched to ordering takeout.

I forced my attention to the counter, where a young, narrow-shouldered Greek kept glancing at the clock, anxious to leave. "Was that guy here?" I asked Kit.

"He was here, I think, but in back, at the grill, with the father."

I looked toward the grill and saw an older man with thick, white hair, scraping at the grease with a knife. "The owner?" I asked.

He nodded.

"And neither one remembers you?"

"They never came to the counter. A woman waited on me. The daughter I figured, but he says he doesn't have a daughter."

"No women at all?"

He nodded.

"Why would he lie?"

"Maybe he's got some kind of temporary visa. Or maybe she's one of his relatives working here without a green card. I think he's afraid of Immigration."

I glanced at the counter. "You mind waiting here, while I go talk to him?"

He shrugged as if to say, *You're the reporter, how can I stop you?*

I strode to the counter, leaning forward and waving for the older man's attention. He left the grill hesitantly, handing the scraper to his son.

I identified myself as a reporter for the *News-Tribune*. He introduced himself as Jimmy Xifaris and matter-of-factly asked what I wanted. He handed me a menu and I realized that he meant lunch. He appeared pleased that I might become one of his customers.

Even after I handed the menu back and told him I was working on the Kit Korbanics story, Xifaris's deep brow did not furrow. I noticed his accent wasn't all that heavy, either. He'd been here long enough to have his working papers in order. "You want to know if he was here?" he asked, calmly.

I nodded.

"Like I told his lawyer, I wish I knew." He glanced past me and noticed Kit in the booth, but even this did not throw him off. His eyes returned to me just as calmly, and he waited until I finished writing before he continued. "I wish I had worked the counter that day, so I could say for sure."

"You think maybe he was here?" I asked.

His arms went up as if allowing the possibility. "Many people walk in and out of here in a day."

"But the woman who waited on him?"

Here his brows met, a crease deepened. "This is where it confuses me. Where the story makes no sense. There have been no girls behind the counter but my niece."

"You have a niece?" I replied, perhaps a bit too excitedly.

He touched my hand to stop me from writing. "I have a niece, but she went back to Greece six months ago to get married."

Marquesson had fallen from that balcony only two weeks ago. I noted the time disparity in my pad.

"The poor husband," Xifaris was saying. "Damaris is no wife. She could not even keep the counter clean. And so emotional. Snapping at customers. I promised no more girls work here after Damaris."

"Damaris's last name?" I asked, thinking that he would balk. But he didn't. He grabbed a napkin from the dispenser and a pen from the top of the cash register. He wrote her name, Damaris Lefkas, and then, with a new thought, he asked me to wait while he went to the back room to get her address. He returned with a full piece of paper, where he had included not just her address in Matala, Greece, but her new husband's name and their phone number.

I thanked him and folded the paper in half, closing it inside my notebook. Our booth was empty; I found Kit waiting for me outside on the street, staring at the passing traffic.

As I swung open the door, he turned to me, eyes blue and level. "So?" he asked.

"No witnesses here," I replied.

Book II
The Angle, June 20, 1991

6

The Grand Jury deliberated only two-and-a-half days before indicting Kit Korbanics on murder in the first degree, the premeditated act of pushing his business partner from an eighteenth-floor balcony at the Harbor Inn Hotel and Convention Center.

Gerard, who'd brought his laptop along with him to the courthouse, messaged the information to me via modem.

Yeah, right, he jumped. GJ indicts your man. Murder One!!!!

I stared at my computer, the acceleration of my heart making the words shift on the screen. The indictment sealed my future, catapulting my profile to more certain prominence. At the same time, I felt winded: Kit Korbanics, charged with murder.

I was irritated at Gerard's unabashed enthusiasm. He would not be the only newsman to react to today's events with such single-minded glee, but it was typical of him to add the exclamation points.

He must have used his laptop to message the editors as well, because within minutes Mark Schneider materialized in Financial with Lev Grabowski behind him.

The two marched through the aisle oblivious to the department. Ed Holland, the banking reporter, who sat up front, did not exist. Lorraine, on the phone behind me, tracking down a technology story that had been offered the possibility of Page One, was no longer of consequence. A Harvard MBA would stand trial for the incredibly violent and public murder of his business partner. At the moment, there was no other story in the city.

I had been plodding through a survey of Greater Boston elementary schools, checking on the account Kit had given me the day before—trying to locate an educational interest in either Arthur Fiedler or the Esplanade. Now I pushed aside the stack of phone books, knowing I might never have time again for such a low-percentage shot.

As Lev and Mark skimmed past the busy reporters, the disparate activities ceased. Ed Holland rolled his chair away from his desk and angled toward us. Even Lorraine cut short her phone call and turned to the huddle of editors standing over me.

Reporters responded not just to the bulk of Lev Grabowski's presence, but his air of command. He could be thin and diseased, and we would still follow him into battle. In death, he would draw us to his casket, where we would mill about, searching his waxen face for some sign that he liked our most recent stories.

"Murder one," Mark said. His boyish features were aglow. In the newsroom, male reporters and often editors went jacketless, but not Mark, who coordinated the patterns of shirts and ties with thought and spent much time running to the dry cleaner. But today, his jacket was off, his French cuffs rolled to the forearm, and the knot in his necktie uncharacteristically askew.

Facts had to be gathered, photos and sidebars assigned, headlines sized. Even Lev, who had thirty years or more of Grand Jury indictments under his belt, basked in the emergency lights.

Newsmen lived for this rush, the challenge of beating the clock and being the champion of the information. They lived in modest homes and drove modest cars, but at times like this, their power was not middling. Like high school kids in charge of the yearbook, they had a controlling position on the subject of the hour.

You could fuel the computers with the electricity in the air—and yet I sat at my desk, where it was all being generated, unable to just ride the current. Somewhere along the Esplanade, in the searching of eyes and scribbling of notes, I had held my own court on Kit Korbanics's soul. And now that I was no longer trying so hard to prove to myself he was guilty, I was overwhelmed by the one question no one in the newsroom had yet asked: What if he were innocent?

But at that moment, with Lev and Mark standing over my desk, I would do nothing to minimize my own story. My profile subject was no longer merely under investigation, but officially charged with murder.

Looking up at them, I asked, "You want me to try to get through to Korbanics?"

Before Mark could answer, the phone at my desk rang.

I picked it up. Gerard. I handed the receiver to Mark.

"Korbanics is going to be in court all day. Gerard will cover the bail hearing," Mark relayed.

"You think he'll get bail?" I asked.

He put the same question to Gerard and stood silent, peering over the cubicle half-wall into City, as he took in what must have been a protracted response.

"Gerard's already talked to the DA," Mark informed us. "He said Korbanics has come in several times for questioning. Been cooperative. Handed over documents. The evidence is considered circumstantial, so—"

"He has no priors and many ties to the business community—I doubt they'll be able to hold him," Lev interrupted.

Mark put his hand over the phone. "We need to talk strategy on the profile," he said to me. He ended his call with Gerard and swiftly redialed Nora, the City editor, and asked her to round up the Photo editor and the Graphics czarina. They were to meet us in the conference room in fifteen minutes.

In the meantime, Lev was deploying his troops. Seeing Lorraine at her desk, he barked, "You get to the biotech community. Find people who knew Marquesson. Get their reaction to this indictment. Or better yet . . ." he pivoted toward Ed Holland, who was in his at-the-ready posture, back erect, eyes alert, eager for Lev to know he was part of the available infantry, "the financial community. See what they say about Korbanics now that he's officially indicted. See if anyone breaks ranks and casts him off as a ne'er-do-well."

Ed, who had been in the middle of some sort of failing savings and loan story, rolled back to his desk with a look of determination on his face. He'd do both assignments without complaint. This was his opportunity to get in on the Korbanics story, to jump off the business page onto Page One. Even Lorraine, who didn't usually react so swiftly to orders, turned to her phone and began dialing.

Instantly, Lev was on the move, turning the corner of Financial into the open newsroom with Mark striding to keep up with him. I'd grabbed a yellow legal pad and followed closely at heel in my own urgent gait.

In the conference room, Lev took his regular seat at the head of the table. I parked myself in a chair to his right, leaving a few empty spaces for Nora and her contingent.

Mark was already at the whiteboard, eyes scanning the ledge for a marker. He would never sit down. These "strategy sessions" were his forum, where he showed his talent. He would break a complex writing assignment into components and juggle around the pieces until reporter and editor had the illusion of control.

He found a marker on the floor and wrote SOURCES in green capital letters. Below he drew three, swift columns, titling them in nearly illegible hand: The first was the *pro* column, the second *neutral*, and the third *against*. I dutifully copied this diagram on my legal pad.

Lev's secretary arrived at the door to drop off an interdepartmental memo. He read it silently and passed it to Mark. "Promotion wants to start radio advertising by Wednesday drive-time," he said in a grave tone.

"Tell them Tuesday," he said to his secretary, who instantly departed with the message.

Then he turned to me. "Tuesday at the latest. Mark has to see the lead and top of this story."

A lead and top would give editors an idea of what the angle, or "approach," of the story was. Editors would have a rough idea on a headline and Promotion some notion of what to put in the ad. I nodded as if this deadline were no problem, but I felt myself grow cold. Five days. This gave me just five days.

Mark was scrutinizing the memo. "Full-scale advertising, huh?"

"They're planning to sell a lot of papers with this one," Lev replied in that same grave tone.

"This was major shit before, Addy," Mark said. "But now it's really major shit. Businessman indicted for murdering his partner. And not just gun shot. We're talking rage enough to throw another human being from a balcony."

They were both looking at me. I nodded again to show I understood.

"A victim with Marquesson's scientific credentials makes this a national story," Mark continued. "*The Wall Street Journal* could send a reporter. The *New York Times* might do a piece. We're not just competing with the *Herald* anymore."

"I get it, Mark. I'm not going to screw up."

Mark and Lev exchanged a look: *Defensive, isn't she?*

"Okay," Mark said, moving on. He struck a businesslike tone. "You're going to write in first person, letting readers know right away there's a former association with Korbanics. You don't have to spell out your sex life, but you have to keep reminding the reader throughout the story that you come to this story with your own inside knowledge."

I scribbled the orders on my legal pad.

He returned to the whiteboard, writing "Addy's insight" in the middle, *neutral* column.

"You're going to give the reader the close-up, the perspective he can't get anywhere else. But you've got to bend over backwards, I mean a complete backbend, to make sure you're seeing things straight," he added.

I looked at him squarely.

"Not clouded by fond memories," he continued.

Or by painful ones, I thought, as I straightened up.

"Estella Rubin is shrewd," said Lev. "She's got a defendant who's a highly personable whiz kid and no alibi. Her best hope is to convince the public, through you, that this indictment is an outrage and that Korbanics is just not the kind of guy who could commit murder."

"I realize the defense has its own agenda," I said.

After watching Mark write Korbanics and Rubin under the *pro* column, Lev said, "Addy should have a firm handle on the state's evidence to balance all the bullshit Korbanics and his lawyer will be telling her. She should go down to the court this afternoon and sit with Gerard. The prosecution is expected to give some forensic evidence at the bail hearing."

Mark, who was writing "prosecution's evidence" in the *against* column, waved off Lev's suggestion with his free hand.

"She doesn't have time to sit around in court," he said, turning around. "She can read the transcripts later at home and talk to forensic experts if she needs to. She's got only five days for interviews, and that's if she works all weekend."

"I'll work all weekend," I offered.

This had been expected. No one offered praise.

"Like I said, you got to bend over backwards hearing all sides of this story," Mark continued. "You got to talk to as many sources as you can. We're taking a big risk on a first-person piece like this. We've got to be able to say it's fair."

"It'll be fair," I said, levelly, but I wondered if he meant *fair*. There's fair and there's *fair*. I had the impression he meant *tough*.

I told him about my interview with the Paris Diner owner who could not confirm the official alibi. I mentioned having procured the phone number of the counter girl, but that I had not gotten anyone in Matala, Greece, to pick up the phone.

"Have you spoken to Marquesson's wife?" Lev asked me.

"I left a message on her machine this morning."

"Try her again," he said briskly. "His wife has been saying all along it wasn't suicide. This is a vindication for her; she may talk."

Mark wrote "the widow" after the prosecution's evidence in the *against* column.

"What about Korbanics's old girlfriend? The one the *Herald* said dumped him?" asked Nora, who had just appeared at the door with the Graphics czarina and the Photo editor. "What's her name?" She looked at me to supply the answer.

I'd never seen Kit's girlfriend until I spotted her photo in the paper, but Rory had mentioned her name enough times. She was some sort of scientist, but had changed careers. At one time, Rory thought Kit would marry her.

"She's an artist. Has a studio at one of the Newbury Street

galleries," Mark recalled. "Joan Something."

"Warner?" I asked, vaguely.

"Yeah. That's it. Gerard hasn't been able to get through to her lawyer," Lev informed us.

"I know," Mark said. "But Addy used to have quite a gift—getting people to talk to her."

I was thrown by this compliment, this acknowledgment that I had skill. And then, in the most miraculous turn of events, Lev considered this. For the first time in a long time he looked at me as if I might have value. "Maybe she can still pull it off," he said.

So as not to overplay this brief moment of support, or perhaps to avoid the pathetic lapdog reaction reporters have to his praise, Lev immediately turned to Nora, who had taken the seat between us, and ordered her to get a police reporter to do a legal chronology of the case. He also wanted the Cambridge-beat reporter to get a reaction piece from Marquesson's old colleagues at MIT.

While Nora was writing this down, the Photo editor, a man named Kelley, took a seat to my right and gave me a list of optimal times to try to arrange a session for his photographer to meet Kit at his town house.

When he was finished, Nora touched my arm. "So come on, tell us. You know this guy. You think he did it?"

Mark was looking at me intently, and I felt suddenly that Lev, with his sea-green sensors, detected new weaknesses. I was acutely aware that my access to Kit Korbanics was not just a coup, but a vulnerability. I was bruised fruit, ripe for picking.

Even the Photo editor and the czarina were silent, waiting.

I said, in a flat tone, "I'm a reporter, Nora. I think anyone is capable of anything."

Lev and Mark exchanged a look. I'd given the right answer.

#

Back at my desk, I was overwhelmed with self-doubt as I struggled to open my bottom drawer.

This assignment required that I be smarter and tougher than I'd been in over a year. And now I was wondering if yesterday on the Esplanade I'd started to go soft. By the end of the interview, I had been thinking less of fingerprints and financial motives, and more of the look in Kit's eyes.

I told myself that Kit could be a master of projecting false sincerity—a chronic liar and a cheat. I had to be careful. Months of chemical dependency might have robbed me not just of nutrients, but of my powers of discernment.

The drawer swung open and I was faced with a haphazard heap of notebooks and legal pads that had jammed the free flow of the metal guides.

I grabbed two fresh notebooks to take to my interview with the ex-girlfriend Joan Warner. A source that close to the subject would give the profile both depth and validity. I hoped to God I had the wherewithal to get her to spill her guts.

In the past, I'd been in awe of her. A woman who had held Kit Korbanics's attention for over two years. Now it occurred to me that maybe Kit did to her what he had done to me. Maybe she, too, had walked into his bedroom and found it fully occupied.

I was standing there, notebooks in hand, staring at the mess of my drawer, when the ringing phone jarred me. It was a first-grade teacher from Samuel Adams Elementary in East Boston, returning my call.

She informed me that she had taken her class into town two weeks ago. The group retraced the journey in the popular children's book set in Boston, *Make Way for Ducklings*, from the Esplanade to the Public Garden.

I asked her if she could be certain that it was June 4th.

She told me that she had confirmed the date with a bus

charter receipt.

"Do you remember stopping at the Arthur Fielder statue by any chance?" I had a sudden image of Kit's expression, the directness of his eye contact, the frustration as I prodded him for more detail.

"Yes. Well, you see I'm a musician myself, a pianist, and a big fan of the Pops summer series. I stopped to explain the statue to my class."

"Do you remember seeing anyone at the statue? A businessman?" I asked.

There were hundreds of businessmen on the Esplanade that day. She couldn't possibly remember one from the other.

"But did you see anyone around the statue?"

"I was paying more attention to the kids than to anyone around me."

"How about the time? Do you remember what time it was?"

"Let's see. We had our lunches at about twelve-thirty," the teacher replied. "It was maybe a half hour or so after that."

One o'clock. I didn't have to check my notebook. I could see it clearly, as if I were reading the time in bright red numbers, over Kit's shoulder, from his digital watch.

7

At the Fitzgerald Gallery on Newbury Street, a thickset man who looked more like a construction worker than an art dealer sized me up immediately as a reporter. Almost as soon as I got through the door, he informed me that Joan Warner had no works on display, and although I had not asked, he added that she no longer rented the studio upstairs, either.

From Rory, I'd learned that Kit's girlfriend was a scientist whom he'd met through biotech. But actually, this artsy part made sense to me. I could see Kit being impressed with that in a woman. Kit had been so straight in college because he'd known from birth, I think, that he wanted to work in the world of high finance. Money required conformity. But a part of him had been drawn, perhaps awed, by the more offbeat types: a journalism major like myself, or a fine arts student who skipped her morning classes and violated all sorts of rules.

By phone, I got Lorraine to check the database for show listings and was able to track Joan Warner to a gallery in Newton Corner. Although this was only fifteen minutes west of the city, I had to stop first in Brighton to pick up my car, an old but serviceable Volkswagen Jetta that I drive as little as possible, usually only on suburban assignments.

At the Newton gallery, I found several of Joan Warner's works, but more important, I found her business card stuck into the corner of a canvas. The painting was a series of spheres at various angles. It looked like something from a physics class.

Her studio was in Waltham, which borders Newton on the northwest, and was only a short drive away. My first job out of college was at the Waltham bureau of the *News-Tribune*, so I knew the terrain. Felton Street was a one-way road along the river on the South Side, an industrial road in the midst of the city's downtown.

I was led to an old mill building that had been reconfigured without really being rehabilitated. The concrete exterior needed paint, and midsize trucks and loading dollies dominated the parking lot. But I did find signs for an antique store and a frame shop on the lower level and guessed that the art studios would be upstairs.

Climbing the wide, wooden stairway, I landed on what appeared to be the loft—a vast space with high ceilings and newly constructed walls painted a bright white. Sunlight streamed in on an enormous canvas, the size of a bedroom wall. The subject, a pair of doomed tropical fish swimming in globular water, appeared to be a Joan Warner original. I walked past it, around a half wall, where I found a brown-haired woman, her back to me as she worked on a clay bust.

Even without the canvas, I knew it was Joan Warner. She had what Kit Korbanics would want from a woman: She was almost as tall as he was and had the full-figured appeal of the graduate student I'd found him with the night we broke up. When she turned, I could see that, while older than I, she had an airy prettiness to go with the soft, curling hair. She wiped her hand on her smock and smiled. "Are you looking for someone?"

"Joan Warner," I said.

The smile did not fade, but a look of caution came over her face. "You are?"

I struggled here. If I identified myself as a reporter as I should, she would back off immediately. If I said I was an old friend of Kit Korbanics's, I could gain some ground, or depending on their breakup, alienate her completely. "Addy McNeil. I found your work in Newton Corner," I began tentatively. Then, with a new thought, I sidestepped around her, as if to get a better view of the canvases against the half wall. "The gallery owner gave me your business card."

The caution disappeared as the smile reestablished itself. "Look around," she said. "If you're interested in anything, I can give you a price list."

I thanked her and she turned back to her clay mound, dipping her hand into a pail of water on the floor before she began reworking it.

I studied a dozen canvases, nearly all unframed. The scientific background was in evidence from the linked atoms of one work called *Life Itself*, to the biology-like preoccupation with fish. Mostly she worked in oils, alternating from the brilliant colors of the atoms to a monochromatic depiction of a fish swimming against an insurmountable tide. Again she appeared to be making an environmental statement by featuring identifiable pollutants such as tampon applicators and syringes. I murmured favorably and she glanced over her shoulder to see what had caught my attention. "That one's already promised to the Harbor Cleanup Coalition."

I tried to look disappointed before moving on. In the corner, behind another canvas, I found a half-finished sketch of human forms. One, turned in profile, looked as if it might have Kit's jawline. The other was completely nebulous, but for some reason it made me think of my brother. "Did you know Rory McNeil?"

"Yes." She looked puzzled, but not put off. "I met him a couple of times. Nice guy. I was sorry to hear about . . . you know." She looked off, uncomfortable. Then she frowned. "What did you say your last name was?"

"McNeil. I'm his sister."

"Oh, I am sorry." She was flustered now. "Really." She wiped the clay from her hands a second time as she approached me. "Is that how you found out about my work?"

There was no flicker in her eye, no doubt of my sincerity. I wished I could go on merely as Rory's sister for I had obviously gained ground here. Legally, I could not use anything she said, if she didn't know my identity as a reporter. "No, not exactly."

She waited.

"I don't know if Rory ever told you anything about me?"

She shook her head sadly, as if reluctant to confirm that I wasn't always foremost on my brother's mind.

"I really am intrigued by your art," I said. "But it's not the real reason I'm here."

The look of caution returned to her face.

I looked at her levelly. "I'm a newspaper reporter."

She did not immediately retract, so I plunged on. "I'm assigned to write a profile on Kit Korbanics." I tried to make it sound as if this task had been foisted upon me. "I could use your help."

She backed up toward the clay mound, but although there was a tightening of her expression, there was no outrage at my pretense. She was not going to start shrieking for me to get out, or call for one of the truck drivers. I was not just a reporter, but a sister of someone she knew who had died.

I suppose I should have felt ashamed about this, using my brother's death to this advantage, but for once, I felt no guilt. There was no periphery for me at the moment, only focus. My strategy was to keep talking, so I told her about meeting Kit at the Eliot and later at the Esplanade, and how one minute he seemed so angry and another so innocent. I told her about Estella and her reputation for manipulating the press. I played up how concerned I was about being used as a tactic, and how I had to make sure I didn't get played.

She frowned through much of this, her fair, unplucked brows arching. She kept glancing past me to the stairway, hoping, I suppose, that another artist would wander in and rescue her. But no one did. At last, when I finally ran out of things to say, she looked at me directly and said, "I can't help you, Addy. My lawyer has told me to keep my mouth shut."

"Yes, but does your lawyer know how aggressively Kit plans to use the press?" I asked.

"I don't think my lawyer cares about what Kit does with the media," she said.

I tried another tactic. Without ever using the term "libel law," I went on to explain that now that Kit was officially charged, he was a public figure and she was protected from any legal repercussions. I begged her to talk to me on background and said I would not put her name in the paper unless her lawyer okayed it.

"I'm not afraid of Kit suing me," she said, softly.

I met her eye. "Then please help me."

There was silence.

"I only have five days to talk to people." And with a sudden inspiration, I gestured at her sketch. "Five days to put together a portrait of him. Five days to figure out where all the light and shadows go."

She thought about this a moment.

"I need your help," I repeated.

I'm not sure if it was this artist-to-artist appeal or simple weariness that got her, but at last she agreed to at least listen to the questions. And then returning to her sculpture, she forgot she was only supposed to be listening and began answering them with terse yes and no responses.

Yes, she had initiated the breakup. No, it had nothing to do with the murder charge.

Rather than stand there like an attorney cross-examining her, I took a seat at a small stool, putting myself next to the water pail at her feet as she continued to pull and pinch her clay. "Why, then?" I asked.

She stood, one hand on her sculpture as she stared past it to a snapshot on the wall that she must have been working from. After a moment she told me that they had been together for two years, and that her life had changed a lot since they first started going out. Although she'd always dabbled in art, she'd been working full time as an immunologist at Fenton Biomedical when they met.

I jotted this down. The company Lorraine was so interested in. The one the French pharmaceutical company was acquiring.

"Do the venture guys usually hang around the lab?"

She smiled. "No. But Kit was different. For a money guy, he was incredibly committed to the work we were doing—"

"On what?"

"On Fenton's immunophilins program. The small molecule drug to treat multiple sclerosis. MS. You might have heard about it. We made a few headlines when we identified the protein receptor."

This sounded vaguely familiar. I nodded.

She continued, unprompted. "Anyway, Kit used to drop by the lab late in the afternoon. He was there the day I'd gotten back some great results on data on a compound I was testing. I was testing potency and the results were beautiful, truly beautiful, and I needed to retest immediately. Verify them. But I ran out of T-cells and the blood bank at the hospital was closed for the weekend. Kit volunteered his own blood. He actually sat there and let me bleed his vein. I'll never forget it."

"Generous guy, huh?"

The fond look in her eye disappeared. "In some ways."

Sometimes, it's best not to ask questions. I remained silent and she began to elaborate on her own.

"Yes, Kit could be extravagantly generous—especially with money and with things. He rented me studio space on Newbury Street. I was able to establish myself as an artist in an incredibly short time because of him. I have to admit it. He used all his connections, called on every favor owed him, to get my artwork shown." Her tone darkened. "But after a while, it started to feel like a bribe."

"A bribe? What do you mean?"

She didn't answer. "He was never really generous inside. His focus was always on himself, his career. The success of the MS drug. It was really a selfish thing. Profit for The BioFund. Nothing else really mattered."

"Why did you say bribe?" I pressed.

"Going out with Kit, I knew about the kind of upper-level decisions a person in the lab shouldn't know." She looked at me then, as if just remembering I was a reporter.

"What kind of upper-level decisions?"

But she'd already realized she'd said too much.

"About the merger?" I probed.

She looked at me strangely. "About product," she said, after a moment. Then, she laughed. "It's too technical to go into. But I should have stayed in academia. That's what Kit always said."

"But from immunology to art, that's an unusual career change, isn't it? I mean you must have devoted a lot of your life to graduate school?"

"I got burnt out," she said, swiftly. "We were all working such crazy hours trying to get that compound. And in biotech, money is always an issue. It all becomes so desperate. People start to lose perspective. They begin to forget the means and focus exclusively on the ends."

So why didn't she pursue a job in academia? I wanted to know.

She looked off again. "Maybe I'll go back someday, but at the moment I'm disgusted with science. I'd always wanted to pursue my art, and like I said, Kit was very supportive." There was no gratitude this time. She seemed to resent him for it.

I asked her if there were other women.

She laughed. "I wish. That would have been easier to deal with. Simpler. I could compete with other women."

I was awed for a moment by the magnitude of such female confidence. Still, I could not quite get at the reason for the breakup, which seemed vague even to her. Mixed up in her mind somehow with her career change.

Certainly she must realize how it looked, the timing of the breakup, I pointed out.

"The *Herald* got it wrong. We broke up at the end of April," she said. "And oh sure, I got the hard sell from Estella to go back to Kit so he could have a devoted supporter in the wings. She told me I owed it to him. But I refused to become one of her tactics. I didn't owe Kit anything. In fact, he owes me. I've compromised myself enough for him." Her look of annoyance gave way to pain, and I guessed that she still loved him.

I probed for more. "Did you fight a lot?"

She didn't answer but continued on her own train of thought. "We lived in different worlds with different values. I decided that I couldn't live in Kit's world, where the ends are everything."

I asked her about these "ends" she kept talking about.

"The drug. The merger. Money. I decided I didn't need his

high-priced studio." She sounded as if she were trying to convince herself and began gesturing emphatically at her canvases. "I've been much more productive here, where I can afford my own rent. To tell you the truth, I think Kit was getting bored with me toward the end, but was too involved in the chase to be troubled with a breakup," she said.

I gave her a quizzical look and she explained that by *chase* she was referring to the desperate need to find cash in biotech, the pursuit of a buyer for Fenton. During the last six months Kit had taken an active role as negotiator, trying to get Lavaliere Pharmaceutical to bail out the MS drug project.

Still, this sounded like an evasion to me. "But you didn't fight?"

"Yes, of course, we fought. At the end of a relationship, when two people are desperately trying to revise each other, there's always a lot of fighting."

"Over anything special?"

Her eyes darted away from me. She looked at her clay bust as if it troubled her.

"Was he ever violent?" I asked.

"No," she answered swiftly.

I hesitated, then plunged on. "Do you think he could have killed Francis Marquesson?"

I expected her to avoid this question and prepared myself for her to end the interview. Maybe even throw me out. But she didn't. She didn't look annoyed, but rather, reflective. After a moment, she turned to me, her voice low and confiding. "Listen, the first thing you have to understand is that there are also other things in my life. And I don't want this part in the paper. Not even on . . . what did you call it?"

"Background," I answered.

Still, she hesitated and I put down my notebook to show I was ready to comply.

"I have a five-year-old daughter." She motioned to the clay bust, and I realized the childlike form was intended to be a little girl. "Her father, whom I had been with when I was doing postdoc in Japan, never met her."

It always amazed me how people opened up to me, as if they forgot I was a reporter. Maybe Mark was right about it being a gift. I nodded for her to continue.

"He didn't even know about her. But he found out five months ago and showed up in Boston. I felt I owed it to her," she gestured at the bust again, "to try to make that relationship work."

Her expression was a sort of dutiful sadness. I'd been right about her still being in love with Kit. It occurred to me that much of what she said about Kit was probably an attempt to talk herself out of loving him.

I expected her to duck the Marquesson question, but then, without any more prodding, she continued on her own. "If you're asking me if I think Kit Korbanics could have killed someone, I'd have to say that men, in general, are ruthless. Men like Kit are so driven, they don't care who they hurt if they get in the way . . ." Her voice trailed off.

I had picked up my notebook again and was writing as fast as I could, knowing I couldn't ask her to repeat anything or she might realize how this statement could be used—how that theoretical tone would not come through in print.

This thought must have occurred to her, too, because her tone changed again. This time she was businesslike, matter-of-fact. "But if you're asking me if I think Kit did kill Francis, the answer is no. What kind of fool would do the job in the middle of a big biotech conference with the press around? And it's not his style to throw someone off a balcony." She looked at me levelly. "You say you knew Kit in college?"

I nodded.

"Ever go out with him?

I could not lie to her when she'd confided so much to me.

"Well, then," she met my eye, one woman to another, "you know he's neither as honest nor as violent as you'd have to be for that kind of murder. If he wanted Francis dead, he'd be slick about it—God knows, he has access to enough labs to get his hands on a compound that could murder Francis in a more subtle fashion. Traceless. Or more likely Kit would simply buy the murder, hire himself a professional."

I'd stopped writing and she motioned for me to record her last words.

"Kit's too smart to have done it that way. And you can use that with my name on it if you want to. I don't care what my lawyer says."

8

Although some people in the substance abuse program appeared at every meeting at every location, this lunch-time "nooner" drew a different kind of crowd than in Brighton where I usually went. Here, in the lecture hall of a downtown teaching hospital, the group was small. Not ten people were huddled together in the first two rows of this cool, blue amphitheater, with its cloth-covered walls and matching carpeting.

I had taken a seat alone in the third row. Several people looked over their shoulders at me with my plastic bound report on my lap. It was frowned on to bring office work to these meetings, but the bail hearing report had been delivered to the paper by courier late this morning and the copy boy hadn't gotten it to my desk until I was about to leave.

Under normal circumstances, I would have skipped the meeting, but I was under oath to Mark to make at least two of these a week. And I was going from here to an interview with Kit in his town house, so I needed to be prepared.

Except for the occasional patient who was sent down in his street clothes, the people at this meeting tended to be further along in recovery and more fully employed than the Brighton crowd. The usual attire was silky dresses and fine wool suits. They were bank tellers and administrative assistants, loan officers and lawyers. Many, like me, had been addicted to medications that were prescribed, but the majority had gotten into cocaine at the end of the eighties, and blown their lives and careers.

Although I supposed I should be able to relate better to these people, truth was, I found the meeting uninspiring. This high-tech arena, with its television monitors and recessed lighting, was more conducive to a lecture on the physiology of drug dependency than the honest revelation of human weakness.

A man named Lawrence, an architect, stood at a lectern between multiple blackboards to lead the meeting. There were no posters with catchy slogans here, just a chalk diagram on one board that appeared to be left over from a medical class. It looked like carbon rings.

There would be no confessions of house hoists or car thefts. The big issue was usually divorce: the division of assets, and the rebuilding of relationships with estranged teenagers.

Today, Lawrence was asking people to share "dependency" problems.

We of the addictive personality are supposed to be prone to overindulgences of all kinds—moderation not being among our internal settings. At my first meeting, Dennis had told me how "vulnerable" we were in the first year of recovery and cautioned me against cigarettes and drinking, gambling and sex. Any vice that held allure.

But now, Lawrence's big "revelation" was that he had come to rely too much on accolades from work. I immediately suspected this as a sneaky way to inform us he was some kind of big deal at his architectural firm. But he went into detail about how he'd gone off the deep end, spending ten hours a day on blueprints for an Israeli train station and neglecting his wife.

This was turning into what Dennis calls "the recovery whine," where every aspect of life is seen as a potential dependency. When a woman in the front row began to confess an unhealthy compulsion for French croissants in the morning, I pulled my satchel from the floor onto my lap.

This leather bag, a small suitcase really, is my life. A jumble of toiletries—the neutral lipstick I've started to wear, brushes, hair ties, the month's feminine essentials—float with my wallet, keys, pens, notebooks, and the bills I mean to pay. Everything is always there, but nothing smaller than a fist can be found when I need it. There are dark corners and folds where important slips of paper and wrappers of Lifesavers hide.

But the bag easily accommodates the thick press packets and other large documents I collect. Now I used it as a tent, reopening the court transcripts under its cover and reading at a surreptitious angle.

I'd seen Gerard's story about yesterday's bail hearing in this morning's paper, and I'd also caught some of the television coverage last night. But both reports had compressed the issues, focusing mostly on the conclusion: The defense had prevailed and Kit *had* been released on bail.

Now as I read, fast at first, then more slowly, I was getting into details that had either been omitted, or I, in my haste, had somehow missed. I came to a dead halt at the full power of the prosecution's evidence.

On page five of the transcripts, the prosecutor, a woman named Leanne Cutler, presented what she called the negative evidence: a wastebasket turned upside down on the balcony. At first, police thought it was a step stool dragged out of the room by Marquesson to hoist himself over the rail, but the sophisticated laser—the alternate light source—used by the forensic specialists picked up no footprints on the wastebasket's bottom.

What else could it be but a prop dragged to the balcony by someone trying to stage a suicide? I looked up from my satchel to find Lawrence's eyes on me. Slipping my hand out of the bag,

I allowed the leather sides to close around the transcript report and shifted my gaze to the woman with the croissant problem. I forced myself to listen.

She was in telecommunications, something to do with car phones. From the back, I could see the padded shoulders of a suit jacket and the simple coiffure of a female executive. I couldn't see how big she was, but she was complaining about having gained thirty pounds since she'd given up cocaine.

The woman directly in front of me leaned over her shoulder to murmur, "We're all just so vulnerable."

I nodded my agreement, but I wasn't thinking about our dependency problems. My mind was whirring with images of Kit alone in that hotel room hunting about for a wastebasket before he fled.

I found myself back in my satchel, skimming the pages of the transcript. I stopped at the page where police gave evidence about the suspicious nature of Marquesson's fall.

This was the part that Gerard's story had focused on. A suicide bent on killing himself generally dives from a balcony, landing head first. Marquesson had landed on his side, indicating twisting in the air, struggling for survival.

And though I'd heard the rumor that Kit's fingerprints had been found on both sides of the sliding glass door, now I learned that police detectives had also found the glass door closed, an unusual gesture of tidiness for someone distraught enough to hurl himself over the balcony.

The blood must have drained from my face because the woman in front of me turned around again to ask if I was all right.

"Fine," I said, snapping my satchel shut and lowering it to the floor.

"Did you know someone?" she asked in a whisper.

From her grave expression, I realized the topic had changed. The telecommunications executive was shaking her head, and it looked as if her shoulders might be heaving. "It could have been me. It could have been any of us."

"I don't think the police really care where it's coming from. They probably figure the more coke-users it kills the better," the woman in front of me offered. She had a strong Boston accent and the hardened tone of someone who had learned to suspect everyone of everything.

I realized that they must be talking about synthetic coke. Although it was only two weeks ago, to me it seemed like decades since those five people had overdosed at the Mission Hill party. In my mind, the story had been eclipsed when Marquesson died three days later. But then, I hadn't related so closely to the victims as these people did.

For a moment, I thought the telecommunications executive might possibly have known one of the victims. If she did, she also might have an idea where the cocaine was purchased—a tip on the possible source. I leaned forward in my chair to try to get a look at her face, but her head was tilted down in mourning.

My hopes of getting a lead on Gerard's prized story were immediately dashed. From the lectern, Lawrence asked the question for me. Had she, Anita, known any of the victims? Anita shook her head sadly. "Not personally," she said. "But on some level, we all know them."

There was a moment of silence. Respect for the deceased. I felt like a heel: the opportunist in a support group. I made a note to avoid these middle-of-the-workday meetings when I was revved up in reporter mode, more a journalist than a human being.

Lawrence was standing up and stretching. People were rising from their seats and heading toward the lobby where a coffee maker was set up.

I remained in the lecture hall. I intended to finish reading the bail report during the break so I could pay attention during the second half of the meeting. I flipped to the final page, which dealt with the autopsy.

The medical examiner found that Marquesson's hyoid bone had been crushed. *Consistent with a strangling*, the medical examiner had written. *The defendant should be considered dangerous and held without bail*, the prosecutor had said.

According to the transcript, Estella objected that the prosecution was trying the case when the bail hearing was only about the defendant's reliability to appear in court. She went on to inventory a list of prestigious Boston business organizations to which Kit had ties. But other than referring to it as "fantasy forensics" she did not dispute the physical evidence.

I closed the cover and threw the transcripts back in my satchel. Lev had been right to insist that I immerse myself in the prosecution's case. For the first time, I felt scared at the prospect of being alone with Kit. I actually hoped Estella would be there to chaperone our dinner meeting.

I sat back in my chair and closed my eyes. When I opened them, the group was returning and the woman entering the row in front of me was staring at me, strangely. I must have looked as if I was throttling myself. Both of my hands were at the base of my throat and my index finger on the soft spot between the vocal chords where I imagined Francis Marquesson's hyoid bone had been.

9

The entrance to Kit's brownstone had tall wrought-iron railings and heavy mahogany double doors with an entry canopy. So imposing was it that the cabby who dropped me off insisted that the building was one of the city's business clubs. He waited outside, double parked on Commonwealth Ave., not quite believing I had the right address until Estella answered the door and I waved him away.

I was relieved to see her, even as her eyes darted past me into the street, checking for television cameras. She swiftly closed the door behind me, offering no greeting as she led me through the parlor to a living room, where the drapes were drawn on the large bay window that faced the street.

I heard a phone ringing in a back room. "Has it been bad?" I asked, knowing that reporters from every newspaper and radio and television station in Boston had been accosting Estella for interviews.

She gazed at me a moment, as if interpreting my outfit. I wore unfeminine reporter clothes—chinos and a pink man-tailored shirt, with a pair of cuff links I'd inherited from Rory. My hair was swept off my neck. Very little makeup, although I'd freshened my lipstick. She seemed to note that.

"Let's just say that he needs to get the unlisted phone number changed," she said wearily and motioned for me to take a seat on the empire sofa, as if she had been pressed into allowing my entry. But now, seeing her through Lev's eyes, I noticed the theater of her reluctance, the exaggeration of the sigh.

It felt weird, this privileged access I'd been granted. The coup of a reporting career, I had to remind myself. I wondered if Estella Rubin had ever asked Kit if he did it, or if she simply assumed that anyone who could pay her retainer was innocent enough.

I knew that Estella would only allow this kind of media exposure if she felt it could be controlled. I didn't know what Kit told her about our meeting on the Esplanade, but I realized that it was my job to let her think she had the upper hand.

Kit's living room was enormous, although dim today with the drapes drawn against the fading sunlight. Unlike most of the neighboring Back Bay town houses, this building had not been divided into apartments and converted into condominium units. It had remained unscathed as one three-story private home with the original features.

A veined marble fireplace and its elaborate mantel commanded the high-ceilinged room, its detailed plasterwork preserved through the years. It was the kind of place I used to rave about in the Saturday real estate piece I'd been forced to write. "Full of historical charm." At the moment, I manufactured no exclamations.

I took my assigned seat on the empire sofa. It had been newly reupholstered in a plump, wine-colored suede. I might have expected the suede, but I was weirded out by all this period furniture with its curves and inlays. Not to mention the knickknacks.

There had been no knickknacks in Kit and Rory's college apartment, not even a beer stein collection. And Kit was such a large, masculine figure, I'd envisioned him as a minimalist, with a few canvases and expensive sculptures thrown into an otherwise barren room. Here, there was an almost feminine array of Tiffany lamps, leather-bound books, and Austrian crystal.

Estella left to find Kit, who was upstairs in his study, and I pulled my notebook out of my leather satchel, dutifully recording these details and thinking how little I really knew about Kit Korbanics.

I was standing up, studying the clay dolphin between two urns on the mantelpiece. It was an abstract figure, a dull gray, contorted in what looked like a net.

My back to the archway, I felt Kit enter the room, the energy field vibrating as if a switch had been flipped to full power. I turned from the dolphin—Joan Warner's work, I imagined—to face him.

Standing beside Estella, who was petite, he at once dominated the room, a hulk amidst the fragile crystal. He was dressed in business attire that seemed as if it could not contain him, the jacket and tie long removed and the first few buttons of the dress shirt loosened, cuffs rolled to the elbows.

I focused first on the hands, the large knuckles, fingers swelled with the day's heat. The Irish ring with heart pointed outward looked tight enough to stop the blood. Against my will, I imagined those hands around a neck. I had to force myself to raise my eyes to meet his.

The images faded. There was no violence, no rage. Rather, Kit's expression was stoic, as if his broad shoulders were bearing up under the burden. Then, as he walked in to greet me, I saw what looked like bereavement in his face.

There was a moment when he seemed to be waiting for something. I realized that he had been expecting physical contact—a hug, or even a kiss—the way strangers kiss the mourners at a wake.

This threw me off balance. I opened my mouth to offer him my condolences, but didn't know what to say. A moment before

I had imagined him strangling a victim. I wasn't sure I could manage the empathy he so clearly expected.

I told myself there was no proper tone for a reporter. Sympathy would sound as if I were co-opted, as if I had decided all accusations were false. Anything else, and he might guess my thoughts, that I had fallen into enemy camp. "You look tired," I said at last.

"I'm worn out by recent events." He sank into the sofa, which was too fine and delicate for his frame. He shifted about uncomfortably until, at last, he sat pitched forward, elbows on knees and his chin on his fists.

He was a sorry figure, no question. I took a seat opposite on one of the matching rococo armchairs, feeling somehow relieved.

Estella took the other, spreading the pleats of her deceptively low-power rayon skirt over her knees. Then she began a methodical search of the compartments of her hide leather briefcase, which produced a tape recorder. She held it up to let me know she was recording.

I opened my notebook, but before I could decide on my first question, Estella went into response mode. The indictment was "an abomination," she said, with well-practiced indignation. The phrasing was no different from the canned statement she'd been releasing to the press. She went on with more legal diatribes about the perversion of justice. I wrote furious notes, as if struggling to get it all down, knowing none of it was usable.

Satisfied with my attention, Estella concluded her prepared text and slid into her matter-of-fact attitude, relaxing further into her armchair. She gestured for Kit to give his own response, telegraphing by eye contact the need for caution.

"I'm confident I'll be exonerated," he said, in a practiced way that seemed derisive, not of me, but of his own posturing. He leaned back, letting his hands drop to his lap, and I could see the frustration in his face, the jut of his chin and tremble of his cheek muscle.

"Why?" I asked.

"Because I'm innocent. That's why." His retort was swift. Estella shot him a cautionary look.

"And the DA has a bullshit case," Kit added, ignoring her.

"That's not for publication." Estella was upright again in the armchair.

"Let me rephrase that for you," Kit said, again magnifying the prefabricated quality of the lines. "It is disappointing that the state would bring a case on such flimsy evidence. I can only guess at the career considerations motivating the DA." He looked at Estella with a sour expression that challenged her rule.

"Which evidence do you consider flimsy?" I asked.

"All of it," Kit answered.

"But specifically?"

"We will be challenging the admissibility of all the forensic evidence," Estella interrupted.

I hesitated. "I'm not questioning its admissibility in the courtroom. There are all sorts of technical reasons it might not be admissible. I want to know why you say it's flimsy."

Kit leaned forward again, elbows on knees, hands folded under his chin. "Let's answer Addy's questions head on," he said in the quiet, authoritative voice of a high-paying client.

If Estella felt chastised, she was too cool to show it. "By all means," she said, as if this were her standard operating procedure. Then, after a moment of repositioning the pleats across her knees, she added, "When we can."

"What I'm asking is if you have alternate explanations for some of the evidence. Like why the balcony door was shut—"

"I couldn't possibly know why he—" Kit began.

Estella rose her hand to silence him. "Addy, we're putting

together our case at present, and I'd rather not give away specifics just yet. But let me assure you, we will refute every piece of the state's evidence."

I met her eye. "When?"

"At trial."

"What—a year from now?"

"I expect to get this case dismissed. But if not, I'll push for a speedy trial."

"Six months?"

"Less. It would be unusual, but given the paralyzing effect this has both on Kit's career and the funding of the state's only growth industry, I think I can make a case."

As a reporter, I might have corrected this characterization. Despite the recession, I doubted biotechnology was the state's only growth industry, but I let it pass. "I have four more days to come up with a lead for this profile. A week and a half for the final copy. Certainly you're not going to go to trial in that amount of time. We both know the profile won't come out the way you'd like it to if I have no specific refuting of this evidence."

There was a long silence.

"We couldn't possibly have every piece of our defense together in a week and a half," Estella said. "You'll just have to explain that in the article."

I don't have to explain anything, honey, I wanted to say. I can write the profile to present Kit as a murderer or the victim. Surely, she must realize I needed facts to decide which way to go. I looked at Kit to see how he was responding, but his expression was unreadable.

Suddenly, a chirp resounded from Estella's briefcase. She pulled out one of those portable phones and put the receiver to her ear. After a moment, her expression changed. She stood and marched to the parlor to finish her conversation. Kit and I stared at each other.

"You're staying for dinner, right?" he asked.

I hesitated. He noticed. There was an uncomfortable silence.

"You cooking?" I asked, attempting a light tone.

"Very funny. I had Estella pick up takeout from the Siam Lotus. Do you like pad Thai?"

I had no idea what pad Thai was, but before I could answer, Estella returned, a buoyancy about her full skirt. Something had changed. She flipped shut her phone and began packing up her briefcase. When she finished this task, she turned to Kit saying she had to talk to him in private.

Whoever had called had not been totally unexpected. Kit immediately rose from the sofa, wearing an expression that appeared both hopeful and afraid-to-be-hopeful. Excusing himself, he followed Estella out to the parlor, where they whispered together, voices rising and falling, excitement swallowed by caution.

If I were Gerard, I might have pressed myself against the doorway and tried to listen, but I could never bring myself to slither that way. Legally, it's a violation of privacy, which means you can't use information gained in an I-Spy mode. More practically, it alienates the source forever if you get caught.

I felt that Kit trusted me. There were things he wanted to tell me. Estella was the impediment. All three of us understood that.

The parlor conference continued and at last, to occupy myself, I went to the bay window and peeked out of the drapery. A *Herald* reporter was outside, a tall, red-bearded guy I knew from Superior Court. It occurred to me that if this profile was the grand slam success it was intended to be, I might have my pick of jobs on any big city newspaper in the country. New York or Washington would be a considerable jump ahead for me in prestige and salary.

At last they returned. Estella wore a smug, sealed expression, and Kit looked amazingly invigorated. The tension in his face had dissipated, a semblance of boyishness returned. Estella moved next to me to get her own peek from behind the drape. "Oh, God, I better get out of here before the rest of the pack returns. Nothing for tomorrow's paper, are we agreed on that?"

"As long as you don't turn around and give it to another reporter on the record," I said.

She looked at me with a puzzled expression. "Gerard Hanley works for *your* paper, doesn't he?"

"I don't care."

A smile came to her lips as she grasped and apparently enjoyed the inner-office rivalry. She said she was taking no questions from any reporter but me.

"Speaking of which, when are you going to tell me what went on with that phone call?" I asked.

"Not yet, but I think I'm getting closer to your deadline. Can I give you a lift anywhere?"

"She's staying for dinner, remember?" Kit responded.

"You're going to have a party without me?" Estella said, in mock disappointment. "Can I trust you alone with this vulture?" Her jocular tone did not mask the seriousness of her concern.

"Of course," he said. They exchanged another glance. Estella was clearly hesitant.

"Come on, vulture," he said to me, as he guided Estella to the door. She went reluctantly with repeated glances over her shoulder, a meaningful warning in her eye.

She stopped at the door, shifting the shoulder strap of her briefcase as if she might decide to put it down and stay. But Kit already had his hand on the door, ready to usher her out. I realized that he, too, was eager to see her go.

Through the leaded glass window, we watched her wave off the *Herald* reporter who followed her the half block toward Berkeley Street, where her car was parked. As she opened the door to her white Land Rover, she cast one last look in our direction before slipping into the seat. This was not lost on the reporter, who turned to see what she'd been looking at. He, too, was frowning at us when Kit double-bolted the front door.

#

"So you wanted to see the house?" Kit asked, after the Land Rover sped off. The blue eyes met mine. "My *environment?*" He was poking fun at me, employing the term I had used with an inflection that made it sound as if I viewed him as a foreign species. I was amazed at the change in him, a new light-heartedness.

I gestured for him to lead the way. The second floor of the house was devoted to guest rooms, except for a large library with quarter-paneled oak and a bay window, and an attached study, where Kit obviously worked.

On his desk was a neat pile of what looked like science journals. One was thick as a phone book. *Aldrich*, I read. *Catalog of Fine Chemicals.*

I picked up the brochure next to it, a slick, marketing brochure of pharmaceutical drugs—long names I didn't recognize.

"The future of pharmacology is structure-based design," he said. "Drugs developed logically. They go right to the protein and relieve the symptom without as much blind trial and error. Small molecule synthesis. That's what The BioFund was supposed to be about: funding the future."

I dropped the brochure on the desk to be able to take this quote down. This fervor, which Joan Warner had mentioned, still surprised me. I always thought Kit a pragmatist. Or more, an opportunist, like me.

Up on the third floor, the original servants' quarters had been converted into a suite. The rooms in back, on the alley-side, had been turned into an upstairs gym with treadmill and Nautilus equipment. The front rooms had been combined into an enormous master bedroom with his and hers baths and dressing rooms.

Kit showed me the view from the bedroom bay. Commonwealth Ave. is divided by a mall, a walkway from Mass. Ave. to the Public Garden, adorned by statues of revolutionary war figures. The soldier directly in front of us, with his snapped saber, was John Glover, Kit told me. A commander from Marblehead who had led his marine regiment to the battlefields of New York.

Way in the distance, I could see George Washington on horseback, guarding the Public Garden. Kit had a funny smile on his face as he pointed all this out. I got the feeling he was playing with my curiosity. He clearly wanted to tell me about the phone call, but was waiting for me to ask.

I did not pounce right away, fearful that Estella's cautions would still be fresh in his mind. Instead I asked him about the renovations, and he went on with some enthusiasm about his architect and her three different sets of blueprints. I wasn't really listening. I had pulled away from the window and was peering into the opened "hers" closet, empty except for a pair of Kit's running shoes.

He pointed out the window, to the mall again. "That was our jogging route," he said.

The "our" was obviously meaningful. For a moment I wondered if he meant Joan Warner. I gave him a puzzled look.

"Rory used to meet me after work. We'd cross over to the Esplanade and go all the way up to the B.U. Bridge."

Rory had only started running a year before he died. My mother, no exercise fan, was convinced that the running had caused the irregular heart rhythms. "You and Rory were running together?"

"Not every day—his schedule was erratic—but a couple of times a week."

I had not realized Rory maintained this kind of weekly contact with Kit. "When was the last time—I mean, that you ran together?"

"About a week before he died."

"How was he?" My tone had changed. A part of me desperately hoped that my mother was right. That it was the running that had killed Rory. At least that was an answer.

Kit looked at me levelly. This was something he had thought about before. "Healthy. Not winded or weak afterwards." It was clear he'd been over this in his mind, looking for signs he might have missed. "Can I ask you a question?"

I nodded.

"Was there an autopsy?"

"Yeah. Pulmonary edema caused by acute cardiac arrhythmia."

"But what caused the arrhythmia? Did the doctor *say* it was stress?"

I assumed he was returning to the Benson thesis, the involuntary suicide again, which I hoped to dismiss. "No. The doctor said a couple of people die of it in the hospital each year for no apparent reason."

A shadow crossed his face as he wrestled with something. After a moment, he put his hand on my arm as if to brace me for his next question. "Do you think there is any possibility of foul play?"

"Foul play? What do you mean?"

He turned away. "I'm not sure what I mean. I just know Rory was unhappy at that law firm he worked at."

"They're not *that* sleazy," I said, trying to make a joke of it.

But Kit did not laugh.

"Did he tell you what he found out about the firm?" Kit asked.

I had a sudden flash of Rory that day he came to the newsroom, the tension in his face, my own impatience. I told Kit that Rory had been trying to tell me something on the afternoon of the day he died.

Kit was silent, as if deciding whether to press on. At last he said, "You know that I used to throw Rory legal work from time to time?"

I recalled Rory had been grateful for this gesture.

Kit continued, "The last time we ran together, he warned me away from using the firm. He told me he'd been in one day, putting together his hours on a case. He was on the computer and wandered into the wrong screen, ending up in the accounting program. Anyway, reading through it, he realized that two hundred thousand dollars was missing from the escrow account of one of his clients. Turns out the partner, Quinn, needed money to pay federal taxes he'd forgotten about for five years and decided it was all right to *borrow* money from the clients."

I felt a thorough revulsion, followed by deep sadness. My brother had had to *work* for these people.

"Anyway, Quinn tried to convince him that he was just about to return the money. But I think he was freaked out Rory would tell someone."

"You mean like the Mass. Bar?" I asked.

"Maybe. But I was thinking of the client. A guy named Henry. Rory introduced me to him once when we ran into him at a Celtics game. A rough character. Not likely to take the news well."

I probed his expression. "So what are you saying, Kit?"

He averted my eyes. "Nothing. I guess."

"You think Quinn might have . . ." It was too ludicrous for

me to say aloud. Criminal defense lawyer kills associate? "Couldn't he just put the money back and deny anything ever took place?"

"If he *had* the money," Kit said in a low voice.

"So you're thinking Quinn might have killed Rory to shut him up? Like poisoned him or something?" My tone was incredulous.

"I don't think Quinn would have actually done it himself," he said, and then as if shaking it off, "I don't know, maybe I'm crazy. It's just hard for me to believe that anybody's heart stops for no reason."

"The doctors say it happens more than you think. At least two dozen cases a year. Mostly young men. Just like mostly young boy babies die of crib death." I said this with sudden vehemence. As difficult as it was for me to accept my brother's bizarre death, this suspicion of Kit's only made it worse. Rory had been trying to tell me about this the day he died, and I had blown him off.

Brenda Starr, I could hear Rory's voice. *You missed a good story.*

Kit had been reading my expression intently. Suddenly, he looked sorry he had brought it up, sad that he had distressed me. "Forget it. Don't listen to me. I'm turning into one of those everything-is-a-conspiracy people. I think I'm just having a tough time all around."

He looked off through the window, at the fabulous urban view he no longer saw. After a minute, I asked, "Do you mind if I ask a question?"

"You mean for a change?" He smiled now.

"How come you didn't come to Rory's funeral?"

His mouth fell open slightly and his cheek muscles tensed. *Yet another false accusation*, his expression seemed to say. "Didn't your parents get my letter?"

"What letter?"

He shook his head at all the things that could go wrong in his life. "I wrote them a note explaining it to them. A couple of days after I went running with Rory I left for Japan to raise capital. I didn't find out until I got home—about two weeks too late."

"I didn't know," I said, trying to sound as if it hadn't mattered much.

He wasn't fooled. "Addy, please believe me, if I were here, I would not have failed to pay my respects. I may have been lousy to you, but I think I've always been a decent friend to Rory."

His plaintive tone took me aback. I remembered all the times Rory had said as much. And there was every possibility that my parents *had* gotten a letter from him and not mentioned it. I'd made it clear Kit Korbanics was not a preferred topic. "I believe you," I said, quietly.

#

"We haven't talked much about your personal life," I said. We were downstairs in the kitchen, an unimpressive galley that contrasted sharply with the money put into the rest of the house. Except for the microwave, which was new, the appliances looked like they dated back to the 1970s. Until recent events, I imagined Kit Korbanics had nearly all of his meals out.

He was pulling take-out boxes from the refrigerator. He stopped and scrutinized my face. "You mean Joan Warner?"

I nodded. "Did she inspire the his-and-hers baths upstairs?"

He put the cartons on the counter, taking a minute to carefully choose his words. "As fascinated as I was by Joan Warner, I always knew she was short term."

The refrigerator door swung shut. I felt oddly satisfied with this answer. "Why was that?" I asked in an indifferent tone.

"She was an idealist, a flake really. She was miserable if

things didn't go right in the lab. Couldn't compromise on anything. Even after she got into art, she complained. No one understood her art. The world was too commercial. At first, I found her attitude refreshing, but after a while . . . well, business is what the world's about. You're a reporter, you know that."

"You were together a long time," I said.

"A couple of years," he said dismissively. To me, that seemed a lifetime.

He continued, "The *Herald* has tried to make out there was a connection between the murder charges and our breakup, but the truth is, we were overdue. Although I suppose it would have been nice to have her stand by me." The bitterness had returned to his voice.

I was leaning against the counter as I jotted down his answers. I let the notebook hang in my hand. Kit's expression had grown dark again, struggling to suppress rage. The enormity of his situation reached across his face, his brow twisted; he seethed at the injustice. A moment of pure contortion, and then it was gone. He reached up to the cupboard above me and pulled out two plates.

I decided to level with him. "I met with her."

He put the plates on the countertop and searched my face. "She probably told you the same thing then," he said, at last.

"Pretty much," I said.

"Did she go into any of her complaints about me?" He tried to sound casual, but I sensed anxiety.

"Not really," I said. *Apparently you didn't cheat on her the way you cheated on me*, I wanted to add, but didn't. "Sounded like she's still in love with you."

He met my gaze and held it. "It doesn't matter. I'm not in love with her."

I looked down at my notebook, as if double-checking something else he had said. After a minute, he began spooning food from the cartons onto the plates. As they warmed in the microwave, he ran to the cellar to choose a bottle of white wine.

I was left alone in the kitchen. There was a door, heavily bolted, to the alley. I looked through the pane of glass onto a small deck that descended into asphalt. A white Porsche was parked in back. Even in college, Kit had been into fast cars, although then it had been a Volkswagen Scirroco. He'd lent it to Rory and me when we had to go home to Worcester for my uncle's funeral.

Kit returned from the basement with the bottle. I told him that I didn't drink, so he poured seltzer into my wine glass.

Since there was no table in his kitchen, and the vast empty dining room was awaiting ordered furniture, we wound up in the living room, sitting side by side on the uncomfortable suede couch.

"The indictment is complete and total bullshit," he said, before I could even take a bite. "Addy, you have to believe that."

His eyes met mine and I felt his aloneness, his need for friendship. Close to him like this, I could feel his body heat, smell his soap. Clean but leathery, it must have been aftershave. I steeled myself. "Tell me why," I said gently.

He struggled again, I could see it in his expression. "Can you imagine what if feels like to be charged with murder? At first I was numb, and then I was in such a rage that I was incoherent. For the first time, I really did *want* to kill someone. I wanted to strangle Leanne Cutler. I wanted to wring the neck of everyone on the Grand Jury. The only thing that gets me through—through this pure torment—is that this indictment is so outrageous, so bizarre, that the prosecution's case has to fall apart." His eyes met mine. "And that luckily, I have someone I can trust to tell *my* side of the story."

"I can't tell a very convincing story if I don't know what's going on," I said. We both knew I was referring to the phone call Estella received.

His smile reappeared, the knowledge he had and would not give.

I lightened up on my interrogation. During dinner, when it was hard to take notes anyway, I asked him about his family, whom I'd never met. I knew little about them except that they lived in New Hampshire. Kit seemed relieved by the distraction and filled me in on growing up in North Conway, where his parents owned a couple of convenience stores, and where he had skied his way through high school.

He went on to tell me about his freshman year at Boston University, when he decided on a finance career, and later the two-year internship at Copley Securities, which was the reason he got into the Harvard MBA program. A principal of the securities firm was on the admission's committee.

I filled an entire notebook waiting for the moment Kit would decide to answer my real question, and at last had to borrow a legal pad from him to continue. We took a break to clear the plates.

I stood at the kitchen sink, running warm water over the plates, while Kit took the take-out cartons outside to the trash. Returning, he reached around me, plunging his hand into the water and nudging me aside. "We don't let reporters do the dishes around here," he said.

"Finally, a bonus to the job," I said, surrendering the plate.

He quickly shut off the water and headed us back to the living room. We sat on the floor this time. Kit poured himself another glass of wine and continued his story. He lay on his back, on the Oriental, his eyes closed as he took me through his move to New York, where he worked for two different investment banking firms. He told me how he had lived the exorbitant New York lifestyle, making and spending money at a frenetic pace.

I sat not three feet away from him, back against the sofa, the legal pad on my knees as I took notes. I had stopped asking questions and was allowing Kit to ramble.

His eyes, still closed, winced as he recalled an incidence of politics at his investment banking firm, causing an important deal he'd been negotiating to collapse. That weekend he had gone to Boston. Through a client, he met Francis Marquesson.

"How could I not be impressed with Francis Marquesson?" Kit sat up on his elbows to ask, though certainly this was rhetorical. At the time, which was more than a decade ago, Marquesson was a hot scientist in Boston—his name often linked to important DNA discoveries.

I did not attempt to answer. I was hoping that if I allowed him his own agenda, his own schedule of information, I would be rewarded for my patience.

When Marquesson approached Kit in 1983 about the venture capital partnership, he had jumped at it. Their union seemed ideal: Kit knew the capital markets and could put together the fund; Marquesson knew the startups and could judge the viability of the science.

Kit picked up his wine glass and drank deeply, returning it to the table empty. "But Francis was a lot like Joan—he pretended otherwise, but ultimately, he was disgusted by the business world."

"So you threw him off a balcony," I said, with a wave of my hand. I instantly regretted my flipness.

But Kit gave me a sideways look, obviously amused. "That's right. Right in the middle of the biotech conference, I said enough of this, and threw him off the balcony."

We stared at each other a moment, and I was aware, again,

of the warmth of the room. Kit sat up and leaned forward, putting his hand on my shoulder. "Addy, I didn't kill Francis. It's not something I would do."

I looked into those blue eyes so intent with their purpose. They begged to be believed, and even as I felt myself drawn in, I halted. Kit had a magnetic quality that I could not deny, a manner of pleading for intimacy. I straightened my back against the couch, its scrolled leg at my shoulder blade. "What was that phone call to Estella about?" I asked.

"Vulture," he said, letting his hand drop from my shoulder.

"You sit here, staring into my eyes and think I'm going to be charmed into believing everything you say?" I asked. "You want to convince me? Then give me facts to work with."

"I wish I could," he said.

"I wish I could write a twenty-point headline exonerating you, but I can't—especially not after reading the transcripts from that bail hearing. I can only believe that it's bullshit if you explain *why* it's bullshit."

"I can *prove* it's bullshit."

"Then prove it. "

He glared at me, forcibly curtailing his speech.

"Tell me why the wastebasket doesn't have any footprints on it—or why the medical examiner is so sure Marquesson was strangled first."

"I can't tell you that," he said, turning away from me. "But . . ."

"But what?"

Kit's eyes were down now, studying the intricacies of his Oriental. "This is off-the-record information," he said after a minute.

"Off-the-record information, what the hell does that mean?" I held my arms out as if beseeching the gods.

"It means you'll be able to use it in the profile because it will be court record by then, but you can't make it public now, or funnel it to that Hanley guy."

"As long as you can promise this information doesn't get to him or anyone else any other way."

"It won't," he said. "And you can't ask Estella about it until I get a chance to talk to her first."

"Deal," I said swiftly.

"She's going to be pissed."

I waved away her annoyance.

He looked at me squarely. "We found the way bills."

The pen had fallen between my fingers and I let it drop to the Oriental carpet. "The one establishing your alibi?"

"The very one. Zara Cab has a way bill that shows one of their cabs picked up a passenger at the Harbor Inn Hotel at 12:40 P.M., with a drop-off on Beacon Street at the entrance to the Esplanade fifteen minutes later. The times match up within minutes of what I said in my statement to police." His blue eyes blazed with victory.

I felt a lightheaded pleasure—a desire to hug him in congratulations and pat my own back. My instincts had not been so wrong, after all. *Kit had an alibi.* But I checked myself again. My mind, which often worked with a delay mechanism, flashed back on his usage of the word *passenger*. "These way bills, they establish that *you* were the one in the cab?"

He had reached for the wine bottle and began refilling his glass. "No, Ms. Prosecutor, but Estella got the name of the cab driver and her assistant talked to him early this afternoon—that's what the phone call was about. He thinks he can identify me."

I felt the buoyancy of his hope, the relief from his nightmare. "I guess congratulations are in order then." I picked up my glass, lifting it as if to toast.

But as Kit drew nearer to touch his wine glass against mine, I became aware again that I was off balance. I recalled Dennis's cautions, and even though it was seltzer, I took only the smallest of possible sips.

10

I stood in front of the bulletin board in Detective Anthony Legere's office giving due attention to his collage of photographs: pasty males with gaping wounds in their chests; unidentifiable forms decomposing in the woods; and women with their dresses hiked up around their hips. One had a black X taped over her exposed areas. "This is lovely," I said.

Anthony, entering the office, grinned sheepishly. These photos were his trophies: the dead bodies he personally had found at crime scenes. Somewhere in the last ten years, Anthony had cultivated this habit, this black humor to defend against the daily perversity. "Chief is after me to take them down," he said.

"It would be a *real* shame."

"Ellie doesn't like them, either." Ellie was his wife. She'd been my roommate when we were both fresh-from-college reporters at the *Waltham Transcript*, a small, six-day daily. I moved on, landing a job at the Waltham bureau of the *News-Tribune*; she stayed at the *Transcript* and became its Lifestyle editor. I'd called her last night when I got back from Kit's. She arranged the interview for me this morning.

Not being a police reporter, I had no personal connections on the Boston force. You'd need to be married to a detective directly involved to get any information about the Marquesson case before it came to trial, anyway. So I turned for help here in the suburbs, where I'd first started out. Besides, Anthony had a statewide reputation for his forensic expertise.

Anthony always seemed more educated than the average cop, with a B.S. in criminology from New Haven College. But it wasn't just his technical background that distinguished him. Other detectives told me that he had an art, an instinct for reading a crime scene. Of all the people in the world, I felt I could trust his interpretation of the evidence.

"You look different. You lost a lot of weight or something, *babe?*" he asked. Anthony, with his studious demeanor, was not really a "babe" kind of guy. When I'd started here, copying down crime news from the daily police blotter, I made a big commotion when one of the desk sergeants called me "babe." After Anthony and I became friends, it became a joke between us, and then a bizarre endearment that lasted through the years.

"I'm starting to put it back on," I replied.

He nodded in a manner that allowed the information to pass without either acceptance or challenge, and I guessed that the topic of my weight loss would come up tonight over dinner with Ellie. If I looked markedly different with my shorter hair and thinner frame, Anthony was completely unaltered, as if he had not lost nor gained anything during the last ten years. He was, as I remembered him at twenty-two, exceedingly fit, with state-trooper-like posture and dark hair, a millimeter longer than the average cop's, absent even a strand of gray.

"How's your family holding up?" Anthony had never met my brother, but he had come with Ellie to the funeral.

"It's still tough for my parents." I was thinking of the previous weekend: Father's Day, a particularly grim Sunday dinner. "I try to get out to Worcester as much as I can."

"Good daughter," he said.

"Yeah." I looked down, putting an end to this topic. I sat at one of the three empty desks that were pushed together in the middle of the room.

Anthony's office was the same as I remembered it ten years ago, even though he'd been promoted. He still had to share this windowless square with the department's other two crime scene detectives, now his underlings, who had been ordered to vacate for this interview. And the file cabinets, lined up along the far wall, were still overflowing, with adjunct file boxes squeezed into the surrounding floor space. The daily grit of crime scene work was considerable in this city.

"So how did you manage to get this Korbanics guy to agree to a profile?" Anthony asked, taking a seat at the metal desk facing me.

I explained the Rory connection and left out the part of having dated him.

Anthony marveled at my luck. "Ellie thinks maybe you'll get a book out of this. You going to do a book?"

I shrugged dismissively as I opened my notebook and began scrounging through my satchel for a pen. At this point, I was just hoping I could keep it together for a newspaper profile. "If I do," I said, as I retrieved one of my chewed-up Bics, "I'll give you a credit in the acknowledgments."

He smiled. The phone at his desk rang; he answered it and was headlong into a conversation. His responses were terse and technical and his tone lost what little cop quality it had as he became the scientist. After a few minutes, I decided he was talking to the medical examiner.

In a little while, he put down the phone and let me know he only had a half hour before he had to leave to meet the medical examiner. They were trying to convince the parents of yesterday's victim about the importance of the autopsy.

"Victim of what?" I asked.

He looked at me, obviously displeased that I had not been following news events in his jurisdiction. "What? You're not reading the paper anymore?" he asked.

I frowned at him, unapologetically. "I can't read *every* paper, *every* day."

"I mean your own paper. It was on page three of your *own* paper."

I hadn't gotten to page two of my own paper this morning. Gerard had called first thing this morning to give me the latest developments from the prosecutor's office. I was left with only enough time to scan the headlines before driving out here.

"We think the synthetic cocaine has made its ugly little way to Waltham," Anthony said.

Although Waltham had its corporate wealth along Route 128, it also had its share of poverty and heat-of-summer stabbings on the South Side. I immediately pictured the stretcher arriving at one of the dilapidated multifamilies on Charles Street, but Anthony dispelled that notion.

"We had an overdose. A Brandeis University student. Last night. Her parents are Orthodox Jews and don't believe in autopsies. We have to try to change their minds." He glanced at his watch, a heavy gold piece of jewelry Ellie must have bought for him. "You got questions? You better ask them."

But my mind was now racing off in a new direction. There hadn't been an overdose from synthetic cocaine since the Marquesson story erupted and its reemergence would create havoc in the newsroom. Gerard would either be diverted from Korbanics or forced to give up the reins of what had once been his biggest chance for a Pulitzer nomination. This thought filled me with a dark, mean hope that I could increase his suffering. I could pull ahead of Gerard right here. Remind him of the days when I was always out front. "Can you give me the inside on this synthetic cocaine thing this afternoon, if it turns out?" I asked.

"Even if we get the go-ahead, the blood work will take a

couple of days to come back from the lab. Besides, I got to answer to Ellie, remember? Even for you, she won't let me have a Boston paper scoop the *Transcript*. I'll get you a special invite to the press conference, though."

That last part was a joke. Everybody and their mothers would get invited to the press conference. "Off the record, how sure are you that it's the synthetic stuff?" I asked.

He smiled again. "Off the record, I'm not telling you."

"Can you at least say if there were signs of burning in the nostrils?" I persisted. On one of the victims, the chemical combination had been so volatile the powder actually seared the nasal membranes.

"I can tell you what was in your own paper," Anthony answered.

I gestured for him to continue.

"No burns," he said. "Whoever's making the stuff plays around with the recipe. It's not consistent. Sometimes it's mild enough that it takes a whole gram to be fatal. Only once it's been strong enough to burn the passageways. Now I'm finished talking about it, okay?"

I nodded reluctantly, not wanting to let it go. An overdose of a Brandeis student seriously upped the social scale of the victims, who until now had been mostly low-rent urban types. The news must have come in late last night and been quite sketchy for the story to have been buried on an inside page. If an autopsy confirmed the synthetic cocaine, the story would go Page One.

As satisfying as it would be to do an end run around Gerard, I knew it was a wasted effort to try to get Anthony to budge. Besides, I didn't have time. The priority was to sort out my confusion about Kit. If I blew the profile, with my once-in-a-lifetime privileged access, I'd never make the page. There'd be no spot for me under anybody's banner.

Since our dinner last night, I'd gone over and over scenarios in which the cab company's production of the way bill could turn out to be a coincidence instead of an alibi. After all, in a city the size of Boston it would be a miracle if one of the cab companies *hadn't* picked up someone in the hotel area on Atlantic Avenue the afternoon Marquesson died. A drop-off on Beacon Street was not that unusual, either. "What's the deal with this laser thing they used on the wastebasket? Is it foolproof?" I asked.

Anthony nodded his head with obvious respect for the technology. "It's called Alternate Light Source. It's electrostatic, lifts from any surface. When matter touches, it leaves a trace. If Marquesson had stepped onto that wastebasket, the ALS would have picked it up."

"So in terms of crime scene evidence, how would you rate that?"

"Depends," he said.

"On what?"

"On what else we got."

"No footprints on the balcony ledge either." This was one of the late developments Gerard had called to tell me about this morning.

I expected a look of surprise or appreciation of this tidbit, but Anthony made no comment.

I reiterated the information I knew he'd probably memorized, the fingerprints on both sides of the glass, the closed sliders to the balcony.

"And the hyoid bone was crushed, right?" he asked.

His enthusiasm had grown, and I found myself wanting to temper it. "But they didn't find any fingerprints on Marquesson's neck," I replied. This was another bit of information Gerard had somehow gotten out of the prosecutor's office yesterday. "They can do that now, right? Get fingerprints off skin?"

"Sometimes," Anthony responded, "there's better luck with young skin and females. More emollients in it. Besides, the victim was splat on the sidewalk, right? A tough surface to print."

I felt a hope I had not acknowledged fade, and I was thrown off by my own, surprisingly deep sense of disappointment. We were quiet for a few minutes. I didn't have to ask Anthony if he thought Kit did it—I knew.

The phone rang, but Anthony didn't answer it. Instead he looked at his watch. "I'll let Chloe get it. I only got five more minutes for you before I got to go."

As hard as I tried, I could not forget the tenor of Kit's voice, or the look in his eye: clear, blue, unwavering. "What if Korbanics had an alibi?" I asked, suddenly.

"But he doesn't. That's the thing. That's the reason he's indicted, *babe*." The babe here was jocular, an attempt to lighten the tone.

"But if he had an airtight alibi," I continued, "one that confirmed he was somewhere else. Then could you explain the physical evidence another way?"

Anthony was silent, and I could tell by his expression that he was intrigued by the question, like a new challenge on a crossword puzzle. "This is all theoretical, right?"

"Right."

"And not for attribution. Last thing I want to do is shit on someone's evidence."

I looked at him levelly. "Promise."

He stared at the beige cinder-block walls for a moment in an unseeing way. Then his expression focused with an intense look of concentration that lasted several moments. At last his eyes returned to mine, settled and resolved. "It's conceivable that this guy dragged out the wastebasket himself, and what, it was wicker, right?"

I nodded.

"He's a certifiable MIT genius. So he figures out wicker won't support his weight. Instead, he flings himself over the rail."

"But no prints on the rail," I reminded him.

Anthony waved that away. "At a classy hotel with a view of the harbor in the tourist season, they've had how many guests over the last few weeks? There's bound to be a mishmash of prints on the balcony rail. No big surprise if they couldn't isolate Marquesson's. I'm sure the defense will make that point."

I was reminded of my gross inexperience in covering a murder story. I had fallen prey to a common problem among green reporters—allowing myself to be overly impressed with information because it came in a government document. I bought into the authority figure, pretty much accepting the evidence as fact because it came from the prosecutor. My only consolation was that on some level I must have understood that because I had come to Anthony for help.

"How about Korbanics's prints on the sliding glass door?"

Anthony's brows met to form an unbroken line across his forehead as he considered an alternate explanation for this. He began slowly, "Well, the guy acknowledged from the start he was in the room. It was a suite, wasn't it? Supposedly for business conferences?" He waited until I confirmed this.

"The defense could come up with some client who will testify he was out on the balcony earlier with Korbanics," he continued. "If they're lucky."

I marveled at Anthony's insight. Kit had said as much.

"Otherwise, they'll get Korbanics to testify he went out there alone for air." He smiled, obviously pleased how quickly he could come up with a theory. "You know, to think big business thoughts. Or about how much money he's going to make."

"But the crushed hyoid bone?" I asked.

Anthony's expression indicated this was more of a problem. "So how airtight is the alibi?"

"Pretend he was here having coffee with you and the chief," I replied.

He narrowed his eyes, thought a minute. "I suppose that the victim *could* have crushed the hyoid bone when he fell," he said at last. "It's unlikely, but you can bet his defense will haul in some medical expert to testify that it's possible. Unless they're morons. And they're not. He's got that Rubin woman, right?"

Anthony did not like defense lawyers; the roll of his eyes when I nodded indicated that Estella was no exception. "This guy tell you he's got an alibi?" Anthony gave me a penetrating look.

"No," I lied.

He scrutinized me with an expression that let me know he didn't feel compelled to believe everything I said. "Because unless they're complete morons they'll fabricate some sort of alibi. Don't go soft on this guy just because he knew your brother."

"I won't," I said quietly.

Chloe, the department assistant, was at the door, a pink telephone slip in her hand. She waved a distracted greeting at me and informed Anthony that Bill, the medical examiner, had called to say the meeting was off. The victim's parents had canceled for today. She had a list of other available time slots in the afternoon to check against Anthony's schedule. He pulled out a day organizer from his top drawer and searched for a thirty-minute unit he had free.

As I sat there, waiting while Anthony and Chloe tried to negotiate a new time, I wondered if I *had* gone a little soft. Was the woman who sat in front of me at the substance abuse meeting right? Were we all just pathetically vulnerable? I didn't

think so. Kit had confided things in me he should not have confided. He truly seemed to be speaking to me from the heart.

"Well, so switch 'em around," Anthony was arguing with
Chloe. "Tell him the Thompson autopsy Monday can wait. The
odds of foul play on that one are remote."

Foul play. The term suddenly jerked me from my thoughts,
reminding me of the questions Kit had raised about Rory's
death. *It's just hard for me to believe that anybody's heart stops
for no reason.*

"You here, Addy?" Chloe had gone and Anthony was
studying me again.

"Anthony, how many autopsies you been to?" I asked suddenly.

"You kidding? I could do it alone by now, I think. Probably
do a better job. Bill's sloppy sometimes. I always got to remind
him to slow down."

"Really?" I picked up my pen from the desk.

Anthony had been speaking casually and now he realized
that I was, after all, a reporter. "No. Not really. Bill's a pro."
He was backtracking; we both knew it. "He's got one of the
best records of all the medical examiners in the state."

"But other medical examiners, they screw up?" I asked.

"Babe, we all make mistakes. We just don't admit them to
you," he said.

Another thought had occurred to me. "Seriously, Anthony,
you ever know a medical examiner to miss something?" I
asked.

He hesitated.

"Like long ago. Or in another state?"

"Oh, yeah." His tone became relaxed again. He could talk
about mistakes made outside his territory with impunity. "Oh,
yeah. Like years ago in New Hampshire, I heard an ME missed
a bullet that was lodged underneath the guy's armpit. Missed it

completely. Body was exhumed later."

Now his eyes narrowed. "Why you so interested in autopsy mistakes? You got a tip there was a screw-up in Marquesson's autopsy? It was done downtown, by the top medical examiner in the state with probably a half-dozen detectives looking over his shoulder."

"I know." My mind was whirring, but I did not dare admit to suspicions about my brother's death. "I'm just curious. That's all."

"You thinking there was some kind of screw-up with the Marquesson autopsy?" he repeated. "You heard anything?"

"No, I haven't," I said in a firm tone, trying to stop his speculation. "If I had those kind of sources, would I be hanging around Waltham taking your time?"

"Maybe." He searched my face, trying to get a read on the information he knew I was withholding. Behind him, the bulletin board broadcasted the gore that he so often saw, the possibilities that must run through his head.

"It's not about Marquesson." I felt like a fool. He had real victims to draw chalk around. I grabbed my notebook and stuck my pen in its wire rings. "It's nothing."

He was watching me intently as I rose from my chair. I thanked him for his help and told him to tell Ellie I'd try to get together with her when I was finished with this assignment.

As I headed for the door, he touched my arm. "Nothing is ever nothing with a reporter," he said. "You got more questions, *babe*, you give me a call."

11

My parent's home is a medium-size colonial, distinguished from the others in their upper Burncoat Street neighborhood on Worcester's north side only by my mother's meticulous gardens.

The VCR I'd wanted to buy my father was out of stock on Father's Day. Now, a week later, with the box in my car, I decided to make the trek again. Mostly so I could bring it to him. But I had other reasons.

I'd worked all day and into Saturday evening interviewing colleagues of Kit's in the venture capital business as well as a personal secretary who claimed to adore him but had quit her job. She also tightened up and twisted the rings on her fingers every time I asked about Kit's working relationship with Francis Marquesson.

After a morning of roughing out a half-dozen leads of the profile, none of which was satisfactory, I was ready for a break. I'd also been frustrated by more futile attempts to reach Damaris, the Paris Deli counter girl. I was beginning to wonder if they even had telephones in Matala, Crete.

The house smelled of roasting onions and lamb, but my mother was not in the kitchen. I found my father sitting in the adjacent family room. He was alone, the television dark and silent, with no visible signs of reading material anywhere near his lap.

"What are you doing?" I asked, as I scanned the room for the best place to put down the heavy box. The television, an updated Japanese model my brother had bought for them the Christmas before he died, was on a simple cherry stand in the corner. There was no shelf for electronic accessories. I laid the box on the green-carpeted floor beside it, my eyes still on my father. He was rising from his easy chair with feigned energy, as if I had simply caught him in an off moment between chores.

"I was waiting for you," he said, smiling. My father, Thomas X. McNeil, Esq., was seventy-one. Although still practicing law five days a week, he had slowed down in the year since my brother's death, handing over more cases to his associate and taking every other afternoon off.

Once a tall man, my father had lost stature over the years and no longer towered over me. We embraced gently, as if aware of each other's fragility. "What do you have there?" he gestured at the box.

"VCR. Happy Father's Day again, Dad."

"I told you you should forget about it," he said, but his face gained a new light. He was not a big television watcher, nor a film afficionado, but gadgetry of any kind fascinated him and, if nothing else, the challenge of connecting the thing would help keep his mind engaged.

We were bent over the box, tearing apart cardboard with a kitchen knife and casting aside Styrofoam, when my mother walked in, wearing both her apron and her gardening gloves.

I always thought my mother, a sturdy woman of German extraction, would have made a great pioneer. I could envision her with one of those brimmed hats covering her blond hair, sitting on the covered wagon, steely against the elements as she headed for new territory. Now in her late sixties, she was still physically strong, with broad shoulders that seemed impervious to the aging process. Rory had had her untiring stance. They said I took after one of my father's sisters, a tomboyish wisp who had died in her teens of influenza.

"The white peonies did not survive the winter," my mother announced. "But the pinks took hold and it looks like we have our first little buds."

My father applauded her success as I stood to lift the VCR on top of the television. With my back to her, I could feel my mother's eyes on me, making their assessment. "You look better," she said, when I turned.

"I've gained weight," I replied.

She slowly began circling me to see if this was true. "A couple, three pounds, maybe," my mother concluded. Not since I was born a month premature had I ever satisfied her weight requirements, but now she sounded genuinely pleased. "Your color looks better, too."

My mother placed great stock in a person's color, often predicting with accuracy whether one of her friends, hospitalized after surgery, would survive. Although I had never told either of my parents about my insomnia problem, my mother had sensed my wanness through the phone lines. For months, I had lied about working Sundays to avoid coming home to see them, or rather, to avoid having my mother see me. One Saturday, on the pretext of coming to Boston on a shopping trip, she decided to make a surprise visit to my apartment. She found me still sleeping at noon.

I was too groggy to come up with any other lie than an attack of a stomach bug. I think my mother was so truly startled at my color and my weight loss that she began yelling at me. I mean, a no-holds barred, name-calling blast of anger. "Irresponsible . . . immature . . . selfish brat," it all came out in a torrent that exhausted her.

Eventually, she sat down on the edge of my bed with her hands over her face, shielding herself from the view of her ema-

ciated daughter and the strewn clothes and clutter that illus-
trated the loss of control in a life. "What will I tell your
father?" she kept asking me. "How will I tell him you are?"

I'd been to a dozen substance abuse meetings before the full
impact of that encounter hit me. At the time, I had been so
dulled by the drugs and then so defensive that I had not understood the fervor of her reaction. Finally, it was Dennis who
helped me realize what terror the sight of me must have inflict-
ed on my poor mother, who had only recently learned that
grown-up children can die for no reason at all.

"Four pounds," I said to her now. She accepted this esti-
mate without challenge.

"Look, Edie." My father pointed to the new VCR sitting on
top of the television.

My mother replied by telling me I was much too generous
and that I should save my money to buy decent furniture for
that apartment of mine. With that, she began stripping off her
garden gloves and heading toward the kitchen. "You can peel
potatoes for me if you like," she said, over her shoulder.

I rose, eager for the chance to talk to her alone. Despite her
abrupt manner, my mother was, in many ways, the easier of my
parents to deal with. While she did not hesitate to criticize you,
she also did not wilt if you criticized her in return. She had a
stoic air, as if most things she could survive.

My father, a probate lawyer for almost fifty years, had
enough fight in him when he was younger, waging and winning
political campaigns, to serve on the City Council in Worcester
when I was in elementary school. But he'd been weakened by
illnesses even before losing his son. Ten years ago, he'd had
double-bypass surgery. Two years ago, he'd had his prostate
removed.

My mother became curt and more direct as the years
passed, as if she realized there was little time left to waste. But

my father became gentler and gentler. He no longer criticized his children because he no longer chose to acknowledge failings in them. Much of the family dynamic revolved around protecting him from anything that might upset this vision.

I left him now, happy with cables to sort and a manual to read, and followed my mother into the kitchen, a modest rectangle with scrubbed white cabinets and speckled countertops. The room had a small bay window that looked out on my mother's perennial garden. Except for the immature peonies, it was a spring garden much past bloom. Carefully planned and well weeded, it was an inspiration of order and control. The pachysandra formed a tidy exterior border; the sedum crept over the rocks as intended without taking over the adjacent bed of faded iris and spent daffodil.

She pointed out a few nubs of pink beginning to bloom above the nearest rock. "French thyme," she told me. "I planted it last year in memory of your brother. This is its first bloom."

"It's beautiful, Ma."

She shrugged off the compliment. "*You* should garden. You need the sunlight."

I ignored this and spread yesterday's *Worcester Telegram* over the round table at the window. My mother had left the bag of potatoes, with the peeler beside it, on the chair. She moved to the sink and began washing green beans, her back toward me. I was silent through my first few potatoes.

"Mom, did you ever go through those notes to see if Kit Korbanics sent a letter after Rory's funeral?" I finally asked. Over the phone, she had promised to check on this for me.

She snapped off the ends of the green beans. "So many notes and letters from his friends." This meant she hadn't gotten to it. Gardening devoured her this time of year.

I could see Rory, just as he'd be at the table, his eyebrow

raised in good-natured mockery. *A little too busy taking dirt samples, are we, Mom?* he would say. Our eyes would meet in sibling understanding.

I was overcome, then, by a sharp sense of loss. The white of the half-peeled potato went gray as I sat there, I don't know how long, motionless, missing my brother and the jokes we used to exchange at my parents' expense. Most likely, he wouldn't be at the table, but out in the family room, growing irritated with my father as they argued over the VCR installation. But when he came back into the kitchen, he would seek my eyes, knowing that I was the only person in the world who truly understood how tedious my father could be when it came to any kind of home project.

So absorbed was I that I didn't realize at first how long my mother was silent. The tempo of her bean snapping had slowed to a halt. "Your father cried last week after you left," she said.

I felt this in the hollow of my stomach, a cold feeling I'd become accustomed to in the last year. Each holiday was like some sort of emotional test: How are we going to handle Christmas without Rory? Okay, what will Easter be like? But Rory had died in mid-March a year and a half ago, so this was the second time around for Mother's and Father's Days. I had let myself believe that it had gotten easier.

Deliberately, I pushed away the image of my father in tears, and struck a matter-of-fact tone. "That's why I wanted to get the VCR out here. Keep him occupied."

My mother murmured and began snapping beans again, which was as close as she would get to conceding that maybe it hadn't been such an extravagance. After a moment she, too, made a return to the matter-of-fact. "So you've seen Kit?"

"Several times, Mom. Can I check your files after dinner for the note?"

She scrutinized the last bean before tossing it in the disposal. "You think he did it? Such a thing?"

"I've got two more days to try to figure it out."

She shook her head. "You working crazy hours again?"

"That's what you do when you get this kind of assignment."

Her eyes met mine. "Yes. And then every assignment will become this kind of assignment. You'll be working every weekend again, giving up your life."

You'd think she'd be content that I was off Serax and gaining weight. But my mother was not one to savor victory long. "Would you like me to quit? Is that it?"

"No, Addy. I'd like you to learn to balance things a little better, that's all. You have two speeds. On and Off. There is more to life than reading your name on the front page."

"More to life" meant settling down with a husband. This was an old topic. I did not take the bait.

"Have you heard from Danny?" she pushed on.

Danny was a photographer I had been going out with last year when Rory died. The relationship, which consisted of Danny inviting me to follow him around when he shot Larry Bird at Celtics games, had only lasted a couple of months. I hadn't heard from him since he got a job at the *Los Angeles Times*.

"You know, he's three thousand miles away. It's been over a long time."

I said this in a tone that conveyed simple realism, a fact of life that did not plague me. But while I didn't particularly miss Danny, I had found his easy dismissal of me disturbing. I seemed to have scored an impressive number of romantic failures with newspaper photographers, whose star-quality egos both drew and repelled me. Over and over, I'd been surprised and hurt by their self-centered free-spiritedness.

My mother had moved to the stove, where she was dumping the colander of beans into a metal pot. She tended to frown all the time, even out in her garden, where she was happiest. It was a habit of concentration, which made it impossible to decide how much something was really bothering her. "Those potatoes ready?" she asked.

I rapidly finished peeling what remained. All the time I could feel my mother's eyes on me. She had not exhausted her inquiry. "How about that Dennis you're so friendly with?"

"Ma, he's a friend, nothing else," I replied. I could shut her up forever by telling her he used to be a cocaine dealer.

"Nothing else," she muttered. She had never bought the notion of platonic relationships. "Why not? He's not married, you said."

"He's my sponsor, Mom. Not my boyfriend. There's nothing between us. He's a *friend*."

She was silent, again, both her hands on the speckled counter as she leaned forward, peering at me. The frown now meant something. "How much time are you spending with Kit?"

I put the pot down with a deliberate clang and turned back to her. "A lot of time, Ma. It's part of my job. It's my assignment. I'm not looking for a boyfriend."

Her mouth settled into a thin line. "I know he was a good friend of your brother's. And very charming. But remember, he was trouble for you once. Don't let him become trouble for you again."

"Mom. The man is up for murder."

"That's the least of it," she replied. To her the fact that he'd hurt me so badly in college was more of a crime.

There was no question I'd inherited my ability to hold a grudge from my mother. No point trying to argue with her about it now. "Look." With both hands, I patted my hips. "I've gained weight. My job is back on track. You have to have faith in me, Mom. This is progress."

She acknowledged my progress with a reluctant nod. Then, concluding our conversation, she passed by me to the wall oven, where she opened the door to probe a thermometer into the leg of lamb.

#

Over dessert, a store-bought lemon pie that my father barely touched, he told me about a scholarship fund that had been established at Suffolk University in Rory's memory.

We were in the dining room, a formal room with small windows that overlooked my mother's amazingly green front lawn and a bed of yarrow. The wine-colored drapes were pulled aside to allow in the late afternoon sun, giving the room a pinkish cast. My father sat at the head of the table. Even with all the leaves removed, it was too long for us. Instead of sitting across all that length, at the opposite end, my mother was at my father's right elbow; I at his left.

"It's to go to a student who combines an interest in law with some display of musical talent," my father explained. Rory had been a promising classical guitarist when he was in high school. My mother, in particular, had been disappointed that he had drifted so far away from music when he got into law school.

My mother got up from her seat and went into the kitchen, where beside the counter she kept a two-drawer metal filing cabinet for bills, insurance policies, and other important papers. Metal glided on rollers, then efficiently slammed shut. She was back in minutes, offering me the official documentation.

On top was a letter from the law school dean at Suffolk University, updating my father on the recent tally of contributions and promising to send information when the university had selected its first candidate for the scholarship.

The Rory McNeil Scholarship. I felt a mix of emotions; I was pleased at this proof my brother's life had meaning, but as always, there was the accompanying slap of reality. Yes, he was officially dead. "This is great," I murmured.

"Read what it says," my father said, gesturing to the clipped papers beneath the letter.

In memory of Rory McNeil, and his contribution to criminal law. This scholarship seeks to foster the education of like minds, who will bring the same kind of dedication and integrity to the profession . . .

It occurred to me midparagraph that, of course, law universities don't routinely set up scholarship funds when one of their alumni dies, and that there had to be a committee of some sort behind this. I raised my eyes to meet my father's. His subdued expression was gone; he looked almost playful, withholding the information.

I glanced at my mother. Together, they must have envisioned this as good news to spring on me. A surprise to liven up the dismal day. "Who did this?" I asked, thinking of Kit. I had no trouble believing he was behind this grand gesture on Rory's behalf. And certainly, he had the resources.

My father dispelled this notion. "Keenan and Quinn," he answered.

For a moment, I thought I misheard. But my father, eyes welling up with emotion, was waiting for a response, so I said something about how pleased Rory would be. But I was too stunned to sound convincing. I noticed that my mother, who had begun clearing dishes, stopped behind my father so that she could scrutinize me without him seeing there was anything wrong.

"A real tribute," I said, and my mother, breathing again, began picking up silverware. Neither of my parents held my opinion of Keenan and Quinn. They considered it a renowned criminal law firm at a prestigious downtown address.

The look on my father's face, the pride in Rory's memory—the remains he could cling to—was so painful, I could not face it. I elbowed a teaspoon off the table so I could bend forward and pretend to search for it. I couldn't stop thinking of what Kit had told me about the escrow fund. What would motivate an embezzler to set up a scholarship to memorialize the associate who had caught him in the act? Eulogize the subordinate whose revelations he had to fear? It was too hypocritical to be true.

"Richard Quinn told me that the firm felt it essential that there be a lasting memory to the fine work Rory had contributed to the firm," my father said, his voice heavy with respect for the man who was at the head of such a downtown firm. "Either your mother or I have to go to the office sometime this week to sign trustee papers."

I had to sit up again and meet his eyes, grasping my mother's sterling. I was forced to see the depth of my father's gratitude in his expression. How dare Quinn do this? This man, this person who, at the very least, had accelerated Rory's death by overloading his circuits with the knowledge of his depravity? What could possess Quinn to now step in as the kindly benefactor, extracting gratitude from my father, the dupe in all this?

And then it was clear to me. If any of us had had any lingering suspicions about Rory's death, this would squelch them. Richard Quinn had no doubt deduced that it was good public relations for the firm as well. Not a few prosecuting attorneys graduate from Suffolk University.

My mother had returned with a pot of coffee and pitcher of cream, which she set in front of me. I had no need of a stimulant at the moment, but poured myself a cup, knowing that passing on caffeine would surely raise her suspicions.

My father began telling me how Keenan and Quinn was planning a special ceremony for the first award of a scholarship that we would all attend. Richard Quinn had floated the possibility of media coverage.

"You think you could get your paper to do a little story on it?" my mother asked. Her eyes shimmered at the possibility of a couple of paragraphs eulogizing her son's fine legal work.

"I'll do my best, Mom," I promised.

After our coffee, I insisted my mother let me do the dishes, mentioning the violets I had noticed bleeding from our neighbor's front lawn onto ours. She searched my face as she wiped her wet hands on her apron, but I maintained a cool mask, and the draw of the garden was too strong for her to withstand.

I began packing the dishwasher. From the dining room window, I could see out to my mother on her knees, dragging her three pronger through the grass. In the family room, my father was at work behind the TV.

Wiping my hands on my shorts, I made my way to the file cabinet. My mother kept files on everything and everyone. When she clipped a story from the newspaper for you, she slipped it into your file. When mail came to her home instead of to your apartment, she saved it in her organized fashion. I did not check the "Adelaide" file, which was probably brimming with "Dear Abby" columns. I went right to "Rory," a file ahead of the seed catalogues, to search for Kit's note.

My mother, the faithful pruner, had rid the file of old college admission test scores and the like. Sympathy notes and letters were stored in a thick manila packet marked "correspondence."

I pulled the packet from the drawer and overturned its contents onto the kitchen table.

When young people die suddenly, the world responds with deep-felt sympathy. There were almost a hundred notes and letters from people with both very close and very distant connections to my brother. I had intended to try to get home in time to catch a seven o'clock substance abuse meeting, but sitting down at the table, I resigned myself to a long and patient search.

Toward the end of the pile, I found what I was looking for. Inadvertently lodged inside a store-bought card sent by one of my uncle's neighbors was a long, handwritten note on Kit's letterhead. Dated April 2, 1990, there were two paragraphs of condolences and then praise for what a good friend Rory had been. Finally, it concluded with the explanation of his absence from the funeral: He'd been in Japan for two weeks raising capital at an international biotechnology conference. He hadn't even learned the terrible news until he'd gotten home. Word for word, it was what Kit had told me at his town house.

I extracted the note and threw it on the counter. As I returned to the drawer to put the packet back, I noticed several loose papers in the Rory file. The first was his death certificate. Then, behind the already-refiled scholarship documents, I noticed another official-looking document, four pages stapled together.

It was Rory's autopsy.

My father had successfully connected the VCR to the television and was now shouting to tell me how wonderful the new remote was.

I lifted the report quickly, folding it into quarters to slip it stealthily into my shorts pocket.

When my father entered the kitchen, I was kneeing the file drawer shut. I picked up Kit's note from the countertop and showed it to him.

"Oh, so you found it." Even a brief glance at it caused his eyes to well up again. "He was always a good friend to your brother."

He took a minute to read the opening paragraph. He

stopped, unable to go further, and handed me back the note. "I don't care what the papers say. I can't believe that boy killed anyone."

12

In the late seventies, when the honchos at the Hoighton Group, a syndicate based in Chicago, decided to buy the *Boston News-Tribune*, they already foresaw the 7:00 A.M. to 3:00 P.M. blue-collar workday as a dying lifestyle in Boston's affluent target-market suburbs. The separate afternoon paper, which had flourished during Massachusetts' industrial boom, became a thing of the past, and with it the morning deadline. For that reason, the paper placed a higher value on the news staff staying late than on coming in early. At 8:25 A.M., the newsroom was a desert of vacant desks and softly purring computers.

City was empty except for the dayside desk—the half-dozen copyeditors who insert updates into later morning editions. Sports, in the far corner, would not come alive until well after lunchtime, and even here, where the Financial department worked business hours, Lorraine was the only other person who was in.

I'd just thrown the morning's *News-Tribune* on my blotter and flipped off the plastic lid of my coffee when Lorraine wheeled her chair over to my desk, her eyebrows raised above her glasses' rims at my uncharacteristic arrival.

"New insomnia strategy," I explained. Rising at six had been Dennis's suggestion. The idea was to shift around my sleep pattern and confuse my body out of its 1:00 A.M. panic routine.

After last night's dinner with my parents, I was willing to try anything.

From Lorraine's expression, I knew she wasn't interested in my insomnia. Her big tweed chair twitched at the carpeting— she had information to relate.

"What?" I asked.

She leaned across me to point to the newspaper on my desk. On the front page was a two-column picture of Serina Wassermann, the deceased Brandeis student. It looked like something from a high-school yearbook. "Do you think that twit ever sleeps?" Lorraine asked.

I did not have to read the byline to the accompanying story to understand she meant Gerard. Quickly I scanned the three-deck head:

A freshman life

cut short

by synthetic drug

Still standing, I sidestepped Lorraine to flip the paper open to the jump page. Inside, the profile of Serina Wassermann covered two full pages and included a photograph of the girl's parents looking sadly bewildered. There was also a picture of a college-age girl who, according to the cutline, had been Serina's roommate during the summer session. "She just got caught up with the wrong people," the pull-quote said.

"How the hell did he do this?" I asked.

"Worked all weekend. They say he was here until nine o'clock last night with Mark, who came in just to edit it." Lorraine rolled her leviathan chair away from my desk to give me an opportunity to sit down.

"That's not what I meant," I said, although now I recalled seeing Gerard at his desk when I was in Sunday morning. I stood up and began to pace. "They weren't supposed to know

for sure if it was synthetic cocaine until today." Anthony had-
n't even gotten a go-ahead on the autopsy when I talked to him.
Blood tests could not have come back to the lab by Sunday.
There had been no ambiguity about that.

"Oh." Lorraine now understood all that I had missed.
"DEA got involved in the investigation. Didn't you see that in
Sunday's paper?"

It must have been on an inside page. I hadn't had time for
a thorough read of the paper between revising my lead and
going out to Worcester. I just shook my head.

"Anyway. DEA found some other student, not her roommate, but someone a couple of doors down in the dorm who
had a snow seal with cocaine residue on it. An agent Gerard
knows did the tests and gave the results to him—on the
record—yesterday afternoon. He beat the *Herald* and television. The talk radio programs are all quoting from Gerard's
story this morning."

Even though I knew I couldn't possibly have taken on this
assignment myself, even though I would have had to turn the
information over to City if Anthony *had* given it all to me on
Friday, I still felt a surge of childish jealousy. It was as if all the
praise that would be heaped on Gerard today would necessari-
ly be stolen from me. All the small-time hatred I'd managed to
squelch in the last week raged irrationally and with such venom
that for the next few moments I dared not speak. I was afraid I
might say something so out of bounds that even Lorraine, who
detested Gerard, might be compelled to defend him.

I dropped to my seat, staring at the inside sprawl across the
two pages. From just glancing at the subheads, I could see that
Gerard had managed to cover this poor girl's entire life, from
her academic precociousness while in elementary school to her
newly acquired, part-time job at a Moody Street furniture store.

Gerard must have interviewed at least a dozen people who

knew her, including a neighbor in her hometown of Beverly who had hired Serina to baby-sit her twins the summer before. Gerard had shown that he could handle the city's two biggest stories at the same time, and as a bonus, had proven to the editors that he could pull off in one single weekend the kind of in-depth, long-range profile I required two full weeks to complete.

"Is it any good?" I asked weakly.

Lorraine adjusted the bridge of her glasses on her nose as she prepared her analysis. "A lot of information," she conceded. "But the prose is stilted. You can tell how disjointed his thoughts are. Rush job. Reads like it."

Even knowing how loyal to me Lorraine was, I felt better. What she said was true: Gerard, despite his advantage of energy, tended to write the way he talked—jumping all over the place with a lot of starts and stops. This failing had doubtlessly nixed the numerous awards for which he had been nominated but had not won. I could take a small step toward generosity. "Wonderboy should be proud of himself, all the same."

Lorraine acknowledged this with a bow of her head, and for a moment we were silent. Almost immediately, we became aware of voices in the background. Judy Owens, the Financial editor, had arrived with a donut bag, and a couple of other reporters straggled in behind her. There was a chitchat of greetings and the thud of newspapers thrown onto desks.

Still unread, my brother's autopsy report was in my satchel. I had brought it to work with the idea of making a copy so I could get the original home to Worcester before my parents realized it was missing. Now it occurred to me that I should get to the photocopy machine before the City room got busy.

"You got your lead for the profile together yet?" Lorraine asked.

I shook my head. "Tomorrow."

She rolled backward to her desk, picked up a stack of documents from her blotter, and rolled back to my desk with them on her lap.

"The BioFund companies."

She pitched me the top document, a glossy-covered folder that I caught against my stomach. "What did you find out?"

"Not much. These are more pitch materials than prospectuses," she said, putting the rest of the pile on my desk. "They're projections of imaginary revenues designed to attract investors. And a little out of date. One of these certain money makers has since filed Chapter Seven. Nothing is for real."

I looked down at the folder. It wasn't a prospectus, but a slick marketing packet. A graphic on the cover was a collage of three photographs side by side: the far right, two Petri dishes full of color and moisture; the middle, a graduated dropper extracting fluid from the advanced experiment; and the left, the finished solution, bottled in clear plastic and capped in blue. The logo above it read "Fenton Biomedical Corp."

"That one I want back tomorrow," she continued. "I'm going to do a follow on the merger and the MS drug for next week's column."

I asked Lorraine what she knew about it.

"It's supposed to be one of those smart drugs," she said, as she rolled her chair back to her desk. There, she picked up a printout of a clip from our database and read it aloud. "'A small molecule compound targeted to a specific protein in the body. Fenton's drug will treat autoimmune diseases by interfering with the protein that turns the body's cells against itself.'"

She looked over the top of the paper, quick to clarify. "But this structure-based design stuff is all very iffy. And the FDA Advisory Committee sent the MS drug back to Fenton for more data in March."

My expression told her I didn't comprehend.

"Major setback," she explained. "The kind of thing that

could have put a startup like this under. But Fenton has this brilliant entrepreneur guy as CEO." She searched the text of the clip for the name. "Raymond Beane. He engineered the agreement in principle with Lavaliere, the French pharmaceutical that's buying them. It's supposed to be final in two weeks. Great story for my column."

I looked down at the bright, orangey liquids on the Fenton folder. From what Joan Warner had said, perspective had been lost producing this drug. It occurred to me that this could be what Kit and Francis had been fighting about in the hotel room. "Does The BioFund have a major stake in this Fenton company?" I asked.

"Smaller than some of its other investments. The fund really took a bath on Stratagem, the company that went Chapter Seven. But Francis Marquesson *was* listed as a member of the Fenton scientific advisory board. I'll mention that in the column."

I stuffed the folder into my satchel. I was meeting with Kit later this afternoon.

"Did you ever get to talk to the widow?" Lorraine asked.

I'd left a half-dozen messages for Ann-Marie Marquesson. "She doesn't seem to be taking my calls," I replied. I hated calling the newly grief-stricken, but also disliked being stymied by an answering machine. Gerard's success with the Wassermanns reminded me that some people liked talking about their loved ones, that it actually helped their grieving.

"I know the feeling. Raymond Beane doesn't seem to want to take mine," Lorraine said.

I asked for clearance to photocopy the financial information in the Fenton Biomedical Corp. marketing packet. Already turning to her computer screen, Lorraine accorded it with a wave.

#

The copy machine stood in the exact center of the open newsroom, ostensibly to give everyone equal access to it, but practically to inhibit reporters from making photocopies for their entire families. Pulling out the staple to the autopsy report with my teeth, I slipped the pages into the machine.

I had just completed the autopsy and begun on the Fenton packet when I glanced over my shoulder to see Lev getting off the elevator. He was wearing a bright blue suit that made him look as if he was prepared to march in some sort of First Amendment parade. His step was light. He stopped at the reception counter, still untended at 9:10 A.M., and leaned over the stack of morning newspapers, grinning as he read the headline. Surely he had been informed of the story by phone last night and probably had cleared the point size of the headline, but now he was seeing it in print and it obviously brought him new pleasure. He picked up the paper and stuck it under his arm, briskly traversing the room to his desk, where he would probably sit down to type his congratulation memo to Gerard.

As is the practice at the *News-Tribune,* a tearsheet of Gerard's heralded story would be pinned to the bulletin board in the reception area so that lesser reporters could read it.

I closed my eyes for a moment and forced myself to imagine my own story up there: Showcased for its excellence. Talked about on talk shows. Congratulated in memo by Lev.

In six days my profile of Kit Korbanics would run on Sunday's Page One. I had until 11:00 A.M. tomorrow morning to put together my lead.

#

The cover sheet to an autopsy is not unlike an application for a credit card or student loan. The information is categorized and laid out in neat boxes, which I scanned, attempting a detached, clinical reading as I hunted for the kind of mistakes Anthony had mentioned.

I was back at my desk. Several of the reporters were now out on morning assignments and the department was quiet again. Judy was at a meeting, Lorraine and Ed Holland were on their phones, consumed in their own stories. With the illusion of privacy, I lost my journalistic distance. Soon, I was looking for a different kind of error in the autopsy report: a mistake in race, height, or date of removal as if after all this time, I might discover that Rory's death had been a mix-up, and it was actually *someone else's* brother who had died.

For a moment, I felt an irrational swell of hope. Under a section titled *External Examination of the Body*, the subject's weight was listed at 119 pounds. My brother, six feet tall, had been 170 pounds. Could this mean that the young man in the coffin had been someone else?

This is a common fantasy of mine: At airports and T-stops, I often survey the crowd for a glimpse of my brother and imagine our surprise reunion when I find out he's not really dead. Rory explains to me that he had to hide on a Caribbean Island and dupe my parents for an entirely forgivable reason, which now I imagined had something to do with the escrow fund and the criminal types at his law firm.

They threatened to kill me, Addy, Rory would say. I immediately adapted this by having him tell me the firm also threatened my parents and maybe me, too. This way my brother wasn't just saving his own life. His disappearance became a more heroic act and I could be less annoyed at him for putting me through the funeral and introducing me to panic attacks.

I reread the external examination again to make sure. "The body is that of a well-nourished, young Caucasian male, measuring 72 inches in length and having a scale weight of 119 pounds." There was nothing wrong with my eyes.

But then, as I noted the exact match of my brother's height, I was struck by a particularly grim thought. I skimmed down a few lines and found the examiner's notation of both livor and rigor mortis and realized that by the time of the autopsy, my strapping brother would have lost all his body fluids.

The image of Rory as a depleted, sunken shell flooded me, and I put down the report, unable to go on. I'd been wise not to attempt reading this last night, before sleep. My eyes burned and I felt a vast emptiness, an enormous, foolish hole where all that fantasy had been.

Why the hell was I putting myself through this? I pushed the report into the clutter of used notebooks and unread mail on the corner of my desk. I had a lead to write, an angle to decide. I didn't have time to hunt for nonexistent mistakes in my brother's autopsy.

After a minute, I forced myself to pick up the phone and had the operator put through another call to Crete. I wasn't up to an interrogative phone call, but it didn't matter. I'd come to believe Damaris would never answer the phone.

As it rang a dozen, tinny rings, I imagined the inside of an island beach shack with goats out in the yard. It occurred to me, not for the first time, that Jimmy Xifaris at the Paris Deli might have been lying to me after all.

At last, I put down the phone and turned to my computer, calling up my work from the day before. I chose the best of several tentative leads I'd played with:

> *Kit Korbanics stands at the corner of Beacon and Berkeley Streets pointing to the spot on the curb where he says the cab dropped him off fifteen minutes before his business partner fell to his death from the balcony at the Harbor Inn Hotel and Convention Center.*
>
> *"Right here," he says, as he consults his watch. Korbanics is timing this trip to reenact*

his alibi. "Five to one, that's pretty close."

A tall, strikingly athletic man, Korbanics wears relaxed clothing, running shorts, a Gore-Tex jacket, and Ray Ban sunglasses. But he is obviously tense as he awaits a Grand Jury decision.

He snaps at a question about the cab.

"It's just that there's a Grand Jury deciding my fate at the moment and this cab thing has me frustrated. I usually ask for a receipt to keep track of my expenses. Why the hell did I have to forget this time?"

I'd chosen this anecdote because I liked Kit's quote. I also thought that since it could be read two ways, it was neutral.

Now, however, I was struck by the sheer power words can wield. Subtle choices make a stronger impression than the facts themselves, particularly at the outset of a piece when the reader is searching for clues about the character.

Truth was, a profile, with its attempt to "reveal" the subject with the small details of his wardrobe and verbal inflections, was the most subjective piece of journalism there was. Two reporters could use identical facts about a person and come up with completely opposite portraits. Show a subject spending too much time at the mirror or speaking sharply to a subordinate and Mother Theresa could be made to look like a murdering sociopath.

It struck me now that "snapping" at a question was strongly pejorative. I reworded the sentence.

I also deleted the reference to Ray Ban sunglasses, which made Kit appear like a temperamental movie star. Tension itself implied guilt, so I personalized my description of his nervousness.

Kit Korbanics stands at the corner of Beacon and Berkeley Streets pointing to the spot on the curb where he says the cab dropped him off fifteen minutes before his business partner fell to his death from the balcony at the Harbor Inn Hotel and Convention Center.

"Right here," he says, as he consults his watch. "Five to one, that's pretty close."

A tall, strikingly athletic man, Korbanics wears relaxed clothing, running shorts, and a Gore-Tex jacket to this interview. We have known each other since college: I can see there is tension in his face as he awaits the Grand Jury decision.

He apologizes to me for snapping at a question.

"It's just that there's a Grand Jury deciding my fate at the moment and this cab thing has me frustrated," he explains. "I usually ask for a receipt to keep track of my expenses. Why the hell did I have to forget this time?"

A bit more fair, I thought. Next was the hardest part: the nutgraph. This is where the reporter pretty much spells out the angle, or take, of the story. It's a point or theme that will go a long way in defining the structure of the story as well as its conclusion.

I stared at the screen for what seemed like hours. At last I typed in:

A way bill from Zara Cab shows that one of its cars picked up a fare at about the same time Korbanics says he left the Harbor Inn Hotel and Convention Center, and the venture capitalist is hopeful. But he needs to find the cab driver or the counter girl he says waited on him at the Paris Deli on Charles

Street, to solidify his alibi. Otherwise, he goes it
alone against the prosecution's forensic evidence,
which both places him in the hotel room and indicates
that Marquesson's death was not a suicide.

I reread this several times. No question, this was the heart of the story. But I felt guilty, somehow, for so brazenly typing it. Kit wouldn't like it, I knew that. I told myself that it wasn't my job to please the subject. My job was to be neutral, to tell the truth to the reader.

I was reminded of what Dennis always said about truth only being a set of facts. On my desk were three notebooks filled with facts that could be played any number of ways. Dennis would say I needed honesty. *Honesty, the heart's appraisal.*

Behind me, I could hear that Judy had returned to the department. She was arguing with Ed Holland about whether Fleet Financial's new commercial mortgage program was a valid news story for Sunday or whether it was just another come-on for free promotion.

Honesty might be the key to drug rehab, I told myself, but here, the editors wanted only facts. If Kit had anything new for me when I met him later, I could revise this in the morning. Or even if he found a witness by the end of the week, I could do a rewrite. This was just to make a preliminary deadline, to satisfy Mark and Lev for now. Everyone understood that a late-breaking development would change everything.

I hit the key to save a copy of the file and make a printout.

Two phones began ringing at once. One of them was Judy's, and she cut off her argument to go to her desk to get it. The other phone was mine.

It was my mother.

"What's the matter, Mom?" I wondered if she had somehow found the autopsy missing, but it would be unlike her to go over her files during planting season. I glanced guiltily at the pushed-aside report.

"Nothing is the matter," my mother said, her tone scolding me for the conjecture. "Everything is fine. Mr. Quinn's secretary called again from the law firm. Remember we told you they needed one of our signatures on the trustee documents for the scholarship fund? Your father and I were discussing this at breakfast and we thought since you were in Boston anyway, you could save us the trip. You could be the signatory."

I did not relish the idea of going to Keenan and Quinn in the middle of a work afternoon, but I recognized it as a reasonable request, a duty I must perform. "When?" I asked.

She told me there was no rush, that I could fit it into my schedule. The secretary would have the papers available and I did not need an appointment. "Just sometime in the next couple of weeks, Adelaide."

Her objective met, my mother did not dally on the phone, and I was left thinking how odd it was that she should have timed her phone call just then. So direct and seemingly unaware, my mother had an eerie set of instincts.

With my attention forced back to the autopsy report, I sat useless, for I don't know how long, incapable of moving on to the next task. I wasn't so much thinking conscious thoughts as I was feeling disoriented—shaken up and misplaced, as if I'd been asked to write a story from someone else's notes.

And then slowly from the many fragments of thought, one dominating question emerged: Why, more than a year after he died, would Rory's law firm go to the trouble and expense of setting up a scholarship to memorialize him—an associate who had been with the firm less than six months?

I glanced at the paper on my desk, but I was no longer seeing Serina Wassermann's youthful face or Gerard's byline. I was thinking about the media column in the *Herald* that had made note of my exclusive access to Kit Korbanics. About the mention of it on one of the talk radio stations when the news had first begun to leak out. Maybe Richard Quinn figured that if I was now on the investigative crime beat, maybe I was someone he needed to worry about.

Ridiculous, I told myself. And egomaniacal. Still, I retrieved the autopsy report from the clutter. At length, I flipped it open and steadied myself for the remaining pages. Under the heading *Information Available at Time of Autopsy*, I scanned the paragraph that included the time and location of my brother's death.

> *It was reported that decedent became unre-*
> *sponsive at home and was taken to the hospital*
> *where he survived for approximately one hour.*
> *There was a history given of moderate drinking.*

These were details that Karen Oblonsky, the lawyer from Keenan and Quinn who had been with Rory, provided at the time. Since she and Rory had been on a date, about to go out for the evening, the moderate drinking didn't surprise me much, although it did occur to me now that a drink would provide an opportunity for poison.

I told myself I was crazy, out of my mind to consider such a thing and moved onto the "external" and "internal" examinations of my brother's body. I gleaned as best I could from the medical terminology that none of the organs appeared unusual enough to comment on. The liver was described as having a "smooth and glistening capsular surface," which I took to mean healthy.

The conclusion of all this was stated as: "Probable cardiac arrhythmia." I made a note to ask Anthony if all causes of death were preceded by "probable."

The final page was an addendum, a different form and type-face. The hospital had sent my brother's urine and blood to a separate, private lab for the toxicological report.

Here, under service requested, it said: "BA blood alcohol. Results: The blood is negative for ethyl alcohol."

It seemed odd that the result should be completely negative when Karen Oblonsky had reported they'd been drinking.

Beneath there was another note: "Check for drugs. Results: Negative."

There was no detailing of what drugs were tested for, nor a service request to search for other toxins. Perhaps it wasn't a mistake I was looking for, so much as a vast oversight.

I told myself that I should not jump to conclusions, but I kept thinking of what Kit had said that night in his town house, about his suspicions of foul play. I had allayed those suspicions with my confidence in the autopsy. Again, I had completely bought a document because it came with an official stamp—a document I had not read and now found seriously lacking.

I tried to tell myself that my brother's apparently healthy liver had precluded the possibility of poisoning, which was why no tests were done, but it had no calming effect. My adrenaline was running and I misdialed Anthony's number before getting Chloe on the phone.

Chloe connected me right through, and Anthony answered the phone midsentence, launching right into a jab about how there didn't seem to be a need for a press conference this after-noon now that the DEA had gotten involved and we could all just read about it in today's *News-Tribune*. His tone suggested that I had called to rub this in, as if I considered Gerard's coup to be my own.

Normally, I might have pretended it was, simply to jostle with Anthony, warm up the conversation, and disarm him before moving on to the real point of the call. But I could not formulate strategy today. "Anthony, when you conduct an autopsy, do you always check for drugs and poison?" I asked artlessly.

He hesitated a moment. "You got information Marquesson was poisoned?"

"No," I said, quickly. "This is another story I'm working on."

There was silence and I wondered if he had heard the falseness of my tone.

"Really. This has nothing to do with Marquesson," I repeated.

He seemed to be weighing his next response all the same. "We always check for drugs," he said, "but only poison if there is a suspicion of poison."

"What do you mean?"

"Like if we find the guy with a gunshot in his head, we don't usually start checking for poison."

I ignored his humor, plunging on. "But if it's a sudden, non-violent death, would you be suspicious of poison?"

"Probably," he said. The question, put this way, opened new avenues for Anthony to travel. It would not escape him that my brother Rory had died this way. And although he did not say it, I guessed he made the connection because his answers became more kindly and deliberate. "If the officer called to investigate this sudden death had decided it was suspicious, the body becomes part of the crime scene. The autopsy is viewed differently by the ME and some forensic guy like me gets involved in the process. But are we talking about an autopsy of a death investigated by police?"

"No."

His silence told me that this was a disadvantage.

I asked, "But wouldn't the ME see something suspicious?

Wouldn't he be looking at the liver or the other organs to see if anything is unusual? I mean, isn't that the whole *point* of conducting an autopsy?"

"Depending on the circumstances of death, the ME might be more inclined to search for a natural cause of death than I would be," Anthony explained.

"Are you telling me an autopsy could completely miss it if someone was poisoned?"

There was a long silence as Anthony weighed his answer. "Addy, this is off the record, right?"

"Sure."

"Poison is tough. On a molecular level, it can be put together a lot of different ways. If it was a common poison, Bill and our forensic chemist working together on a suspicion might find it. But if it's an unusual compound, it could frustrate everybody. With a poison, you have to know exactly what compound you're looking for or you're not going to find it."

I was silent, pondering this information.

At last Anthony said. "Poisoning isn't all that common. I mean usually only women use it as means of murder."

"I know," I said, darkly.

"Tell me, this sudden death of yours, was the subject in some kind of trouble? Because you know, Addy, people don't usually poison other people without a motive."

"There's motive," I said.

Anthony quickly digested this. "On the autopsy report, on the lab section, does it say anything about how long the specimens were to be kept?" he asked.

I pulled the report back into my line of sight, flipping to the final page. "Toxicological results pending receipt of information. The specimens will be held for four months and discarded."

"They're gone," I said.

"Then if you really think there might have been a murder," Anthony paused, giving me time to change my mind and decide there wasn't. "If you really think there might have been a murder," he continued, "you have to find other evidence."

"How do I do that?" I asked dully.

"How do you do a story?" he returned.

I didn't answer, so he answered for me. "You talk to people, Addy. You talk to as many people as you can and you try to figure out who is telling the truth and who is lying."

13

The young, meticulous woman sitting behind the pink, granite reception desk was new since Rory had died and did not recognize me.

I told her I was there to sign the trustee papers for the Rory McNeil scholarship. She had white hands with long, squared-off fingernails that she tapped on the desk, as if this helped her think. She sifted through an out-box, but couldn't find anything. At last I asked to see Richard Quinn and she dutifully picked up the phone and transmitted the information to Quinn's secretary while gesturing for me to take a seat in the lobby.

The lobby had been refurbished for a new decade. The overstuffed upholstery, glass and chrome of the eighties had been replaced with a more traditional look. Instead of the pillowy sectional, there was now a tasteful sofa and matching wing chairs. The artwork, which had been large and modern, had been removed and now the theme was nautical: over the sofa, an oil painting of an old clipper ship in a rough sea; beside the light switch, a brass barometer with its needle pointing to illegible numbers.

I hadn't planned on coming here this afternoon, but Kit had called me at the paper and said he'd be a half hour late for our appointment. Since I'd met my deadline, and the legal office was on the way to his town house, I told myself I might as well get it over with. I was hoping the reality of the law firm—its bookshelves of Massachusetts statutes, its secretaries answering phones—would quiet my mind.

Susan, Quinn's administrative assistant, was walking up the corridor to the reception desk with an accordion file in her hands. She saw me in the lobby and waved.

She was a large woman, almost six feet tall with a power-house frame. You got the feeling that this secretary stuff was a sideline, something she squeezed in between trips to the gym. I'd been surprised when she'd come with Rory's secretary to his funeral. For Quinn, Keenan, and the half-dozen or so associates who came, it was a matter of appearances to attend, but I knew that for a secretary or administrative assistant, it was a matter of the heart. I rose from the sofa to meet her. When she clasped me in an embrace, there was no getting loose.

"I'm so happy they're doing this. So happy." When she let me go and stepped back, I could see her eyes had filled. I was suddenly, deeply touched.

"I am, too," I mumbled, not knowing quite what else to say. The receptionist, distracted by all this, had let a ringing phone go unanswered. Reluctantly, she picked it up.

"Richard's tied up in conference and I didn't want to keep you waiting," Susan said, slipping the elastic cord off the file and pulling out a series of documents, which she laid on the desk. I reached into my satchel for a pen, but she grabbed one from a holder on the desk and handed it to me. The pen, a gold Cross, had the name of the firm engraved on the side.

I read through the first document quickly, which established the parameters of the scholarship in detail: who should qualify to receive it and under what circumstances the money could be revoked.

Susan stood at my side, close enough that I became aware

of her breathing, or rather, a lack of breathing as she read over my shoulder. "So unusual for them," she said and lowered her voice. "I mean they're not known for their generosity toward their associates."

I wasn't sure if Susan meant only to convey the standard disrespect an employee feels for her employer, or if she had another meaning, but my pulse quickened. Wasn't this a verification of my own reaction? Confirmation of the unusual beneficence of Keenan and Quinn?

I signed the documents and turned them over to her. She had large, blue veins that seemed to pulse in her forearm as she stuffed the papers into the accordion file. I hoped for another remark about how strange the whole thing was, but Susan seemed aware that she had already overstepped her bounds and was determinedly quiet.

"Is Karen Oblonsky in today?" I asked suddenly. "I'd like to say hello."

Karen Oblonsky had written my parents a beautiful two-page letter telling what a wonderful son they had; how he had been a gentleman to her in his last moments on earth, buying her a kite the weekend before he died when they had walked through Fanueil Hall, and how he had put it together for her in his apartment. In the letter, she'd said the experience of the seizure and her failure to revive him with CPR had been so painful that she could not bring herself to go to the funeral. She was profuse with apologizes and my parents, touched by the letter, did not hold it against her. Neither had I.

But now, with my new suspicions, I could not help wondering if there were other reasons she did not attend. I checked myself here, made myself think the suspicion through to the end. Did I really believe Karen Oblonsky was some kind of assassin of the firm, a lawyer who would jeopardize her career, her life, by offing a troublesome associate, a co-worker?

Get a grip, Brenda Starr, Rory would say. *Take a day off from the comic pages.*

I waved away my own request. "Never mind, she's probably busy this time of day. I don't want to bother her."

Susan was looking at me with an odd expression. Then she lowered her head.

"What's the matter?" I asked.

"Nothing," she said, gazing down the corridor a moment. "It's just that Karen isn't with us anymore."

"She move on to another firm already?" I asked. I thought she'd started at the firm at about the same time Rory had.

Susan did not answer but began gathering her accordion file, as if she hadn't heard me.

"Where did she move to? Do you know?" I persisted.

"I think she might have gotten out of law." Susan's eyes met mine for only a brief moment. She had said too much and was clearly uncomfortable. "I'm not sure where she is now, Addy. Really. I didn't know her that well. Richard's probably wondering where the hell *I* am by now. "She glanced down the corridor again. "I better get back to my desk. Take care of yourself."

There was no last meaningful look or even a nod good-bye. She had a rushed, purposeful stride that did not allow anyone to sidetrack her along the way. I was left before the pink granite, exchanging a look with the receptionist I didn't know about Susan's abrupt departure. The receptionist seemed both stunned and a little admiring, as if she wished she only had the courage to leave a few of the people around here in the dust. But then she was distracted by the phone, which had started ringing again, and I was left standing around, uncertain what to do next.

Two men in dark, ill-fitting suits, no briefcases, entered the lobby, one taking a seat while the other approached the desk.

Rory had assured me that most of the criminal clients he had handled were white collar: high-level bank employees who embezzled from their trust departments; financial planners who sold nonexistent stocks. But these men had a dangerous look about them; the air in the room seemed to tighten. The one approaching the desk looked at me hard and steady as he passed. His face seemed vaguely familiar, as if I'd seen it in the news.

The receptionist, too, felt the tension, and put down the phone, turning cautiously to the gentleman at the desk. He asked for Jack Keenan, the senior partner who handled all the highest-profile criminal cases, and within minutes, a secretary came through to guide both men down the corridor to an inner office.

I was reminded that, despite the classy-looking nautical motif, this was a firm that represented people with whom you did not want to share an elevator. A place where the senior partner embezzled escrow funds himself. And where young associates fresh from law school might decide, after only a short stint here, to *give up* law.

"You know, I'd still like to see Richard Quinn," I said to the receptionist. "Can you see if he's freed up from his conference?"

The receptionist obligingly picked up the phone to dial his extension. More experienced hands in the inner offices might have fended me off, but at that moment I spotted Richard Quinn in the corridor, leaving a conference room with a man who appeared to be a client. They were heading down the hall, away from me. I bolted around the granite desk and ran up to him, calling him by his first name, although we'd never been on a first name basis.

"Richard!" I repeated, making a play of familiarity that he could not ignore in front of his client. They both stopped and turned. The client regarded me curiously.

Richard Quinn, in his early fifties, was a tall, unhealthy-looking man whose expensive tailoring did not offset bad pallor and stained teeth. A quick lawyer who made connections, he immediately recognized who I was. "Addy McNeil." The tone was polite, but cool. He had included my last name to enforce the boundaries I had breached. "Nice to see you again."

His eyes had a bright, blinking quality, like a politician who's just been cornered by a television camera. It occurred to me that Quinn might think I was here on a story. I sought to reassure him. "I know you're busy. I won't keep you. I came in to sign the papers and while I was here I wanted to personally thank you for the scholarship." I shifted my attention to his client to include him in the conversation. "The firm very generously created a scholarship in my brother's name. It means a lot to my parents."

The man looked vaguely amused by this. Richard Quinn's expression relaxed. "Your brother was a fine attorney," he said.

Staring at me again, the client must have made the family connection. "Oh, you talking about Rory McNeil?" he asked.

Richard Quinn now seemed pleased by this unexpected interruption. He smiled, a flash of yellow teeth, and I wondered what he said to himself at night. Did he feel remorse when he was alone or did he tell himself it was all a coincidence that one of his associates had been driven to sudden death and another to *give up law*?

Quinn pivoted, addressing the man beside him. "Oh, that's right, Rory handled your case for a while, didn't he?"

The man nodded. "Yeah. Good guy. We went to a Celtics game together. With a friend of his. One in the paper now, up for murder. Korbanics. You know him?" he asked me.

I nodded.

"You think he did it?"

Richard Quinn stepped in to introduce us. The client was Henry Spalding, an antique collector. Had I ever shopped at the Tiffany Lamp in Somerville?

I shook my head. "Not much of a home decorator," I said.

Henry didn't seem to care. His interest was in the Marquesson murder. I could picture him eagerly following the day's lead story to the jump page and calling talk shows to offer his view. He had a rough, impatient air and callused hands. I couldn't imagine him holding a fine collectible.

"I don't think he did it," Henry continued. "He's not that kinda guy."

I nodded as if giving his opinion serious weight. But somewhere in the midst of this exchange, it occurred to me that this could be the low-life client of Rory's Kit had told me about. The one with the escrow money. The account Quinn had embezzled.

I was thrown off by this revelation and stood there a moment unable to speak. Quinn fiddled with his papers, glanced toward the receptionist. I had to get him before he could flee. "Richard, maybe you can help me. I was hoping to reach Karen Oblonsky."

The pleasure in Quinn's face quickly evaporated. His eyes darted to his client before meeting mine. "Karen Oblonsky," he repeated, vaguely.

"Your associate," I helped him along. "She was the one with Rory . . . you know . . . that night. I thought I'd write her a note and tell her about the scholarship."

"Of course I remember Karen, but she's been gone for quite a while now. I can't recall off the top of my head where she went, but she and Susan were quite friendly. I think Susan already wrote and told her about the scholarship."

"Oh," I said, feeling the stir of excitement that detecting an outright lie produces. Susan had said she hadn't known Karen very well. I kept my tone level and lied in return. "My parents wanted to contact her. They wanted to invite her to sit with them at the dinner ceremony."

"Very thoughtful, but if I'm recalling right, Karen's moved out of state." He blinked rapidly, as if this might help his recollection. "Texas, I believe. Yes, we lost her to a Houston firm—"

"Really?" I said, allowing myself to sound just slightly dubious. "I heard she might have given up law for some reason."

"No. No. Houston got her, I believe," Quinn said, feigning loss.

I became bold. "I'll tell my parents. What firm did you say?" I asked.

Richard turned to Henry. "What's the name of that firm in Houston that does so much estate work? The one Ed was with before he retired?"

The man gave him a blank look.

"That part of the country is expanding so much these days," Quinn continued. "That particular firm was very active recruiting eastern lawyers. I just can't remember the name."

"I'm sure if she's all the way out there, she's not going to come back to Boston for this kind of thing," I said. "You sure she's still with that firm?"

"Yes. Susan talked to her last week, I believe. Said she's very happy out there in the lone-star state. A lot of opportunity. You know, I can have Susan contact Karen for your parents, let her know about their invitation and get back to you with her answer. You're still at the *News-Tribune*, I take it?"

No, actually I'm with Sixty Minutes *now*, I wanted to say. I nodded.

"Mondays are terrible around here. Everything backed up from the weekend," Quinn said. "We're under the gun here on a deposition. You'll forgive me if we rush off?"

"Of course," I replied, knowing I would never forgive this man anything.

#

Tourists, unaccustomed to the narrow, illogical, twists of downtown streets, often think the distances in Boston greater than they are. In truth, it was only a mile walk from the commercial district to Kit's town house in Back Bay. I walked up State Street to Tremont and cut through the Common and Public Garden. I was oblivious to the greenery and rush of business suits headed across the lawns. I raised and discarded suspicions only to raise them again.

It was a sunny day, but humid, not the slightest breeze from the water. The stillness in the late afternoon brought out the bugs, and soon I was swatting as fast as I walked. By the time I'd crossed Arlington onto Commonwealth, my cotton blouse was damp through and my jean skirt twisted out of line. I rang Kit's bell, realigning my belt loops as I waited, desperate for his central air.

Kit buzzed me in. Having just gotten back from his extended session with Estella and the legal team, he was wearing a suit, a light wool gabardine that fit him well. But even with the air conditioning he, too, looked tired and overheated. He took off his tie and his jacket while I was standing there, hanging them both in the parlor closet as he began telling me of the day's battles.

Estella had hired a private investigator to hang around the Paris Deli to see if anyone else remembered a young girl at the counter. One customer, also Greek, said he didn't think Xifaris's niece had gone back to Greece that long ago. The P.I. had followed the lead I'd given Kit on Damaris's relocation to Crete. Apparently, she was no longer living there. The P.I. had traced her to a souvenir shop at a cruise line.

But when Kit's blue eyes met mine now, I could see they

were full of a day's disappointments. Late this afternoon, the P.I. had called from Athens: The girl had disappeared from the souvenir shop and was believed to be crewing in the galley of someone's private yacht, but no one knew whose. "It could take months to find her," he said.

Kit motioned for me to follow him and we went into the kitchen, where he opened the refrigerator and brought out a bottle of seltzer.

"How about the cabby?" I asked.

"Tomorrow morning," he said, grittily. "Assuming he doesn't run off on a yacht, too."

He found glasses in a rack by the sink and poured us each a seltzer. It wasn't until he put the seltzer in my hand that he looked at me closely. "Something wrong?" he asked.

I emptied the glass with one long swallow. "Hot," I finally said. "I'll need to talk to him, too." I was thinking of my lead.

He glanced at my notebook, which was thrown on the counter, unopened. "Yeah, but something else is on your mind."

"A little distracted," I acknowledged.

"You found a story *better than me?*"

I put my seltzer on the counter. "There isn't a story better than you in the city."

He smiled ruefully at this, but his eyes remained fixed on me.

Standing there in his kitchen, leaning against the counter, shirt cuffs rolled haphazardly, Kit seemed comfortably familiar. In the last week, he had begun to confide so much in me, so easily that the reason for the confidences, the profile itself, now seemed almost irrelevant. A little alarm rang inside warning me I was losing my distance. But it struck me that the whole concept of distance was an artifice, a theoretical barrier I had already breached.

"It's Rory," I said.

He pulled himself off the counter, his expression troubled. He put his hand gently on my shoulder and guided me into the living room to take a seat on the sofa. He sat beside me, leaning against one of the delicate scrolled arms to give me room.

Across that space of suede upholstery, it all began to spill out, from the spotty autopsy report, to the strange creation of a scholarship fund, to the disappearance of Karen Oblonsky.

Kit made the leaps along with me, as I left the paper and my photocopy of Rory's autopsy report and headed directly for Keenan and Quinn's law office. But when I stopped, he made me go over it again.

And as I heard myself tell the story a second time, guided at points by Kit's methodical questioning, it all came out sounding much more reasoned. I imagined this was how he queried the managers of his investment businesses, babystepping his way to the full profit-and-loss story, and I understood in that moment why he was so successful. Sharp, insightful, and always in control: Kit had no downtime. Personal disappointment did not factor. There wasn't a second when his synapses did not respond.

Kit did not ramp up my suspicions, but he did validate all my points as possibilities, and I was grateful for that. Clearly in his mind any alternate explanation for Rory's death was no less hard to believe than an out-of-the-blue cardiac arrhythmia.

"There's an easy enough way for us to find out if Quinn is lying about Karen Oblonsky," he said, when I finished. "If she's a lawyer in Texas, Estella will be able to find her in the Texas lawyer's directory." Then he got up and headed into the parlor.

I followed him to the hall closet, which he opened to search among a crowded field of men's coats. At length, he pulled out the suit jacket he'd had on earlier and, from an inner pocket, retrieved a portable phone. Apparently he had Estella's private line on autodial because he got her with the touch of a button.

She must have had more news for him because he wound up listening to her for a while. I sat there staring into the open closet of winter coats and sports jackets, wondering what I was doing. I was supposed to be asking Kit about Fenton Biomedical or Francis Marquesson, not about Karen Oblonsky. Getting favors from him like this only increased my indebtedness to him. *Not a good position for a journalist.* But standing beside him, his shoulder a few inches away from me, I couldn't make myself care about this breach. The truth was, at this point, he was the *only* person I could have confided in.

Kit asked me to repeat the spelling of Oblonsky for him, which I did. Estella must have asked him why he was trying to find this woman because I heard him say that she just had to *trust him*, that it was important.

Toward the end of the closet, I caught a glimpse of a soft-looking brown jacket. Pulling aside a stiff-looking Burberry before it, I found the doelike suede Kit had worn so much in college.

I heard Kit thanking Estella, then clicking off the portable phone. He was about to close the closet door when I stopped him. "I remember that jacket."

Kit followed my gaze to the hanger and pulled it from the rack, smiling now. "I should have thrown this out or given it to the Pine Street Inn, but . . ." He fingered a frayed cuff.

"You thought you were such a hot shit in that jacket," I said.

"I did," he said, apologetically.

"You lent it to Rory a couple of times, I remember."

"It was a big sacrifice," he said.

We laughed at this, and there was an awkward moment. He moved to hang the jacket back up in the closet. But for some reason, I didn't want to lose that old college jacket to the line-up of sports coats. Before I could think about what I was doing, I reached out and touched the suede. "You wore this on our first date . . ."

He gave me a curious look. "I remember," he said.

"You do not," I objected.

"I do." He did not look away.

There was a new crosscurrent of air in the room, like a blast of the central air conditioning meeting steam from a cracked window. I let go of the jacket and felt suddenly embarrassed. *What was I doing?* I put my hands in the pockets of my jean skirt and took a step backward.

"Listen, I'm sorry about Liz. I was mad at you for working at that paper so much. I was trying to punish you, I think. It was stupid."

I didn't say anything.

"Rory gave me hell the next morning—made it clear he thought I was an asshole for blowing it with you."

I didn't doubt this. Rory had always been protective. I felt a deep sadness. There was nothing quite like an older brother. No one else would ever care about me in the same way. Again, I felt my loss.

"He told me to leave you alone. And when you wouldn't answer my calls, I gave up," Kit continued. "It always drove me crazy, though. This breach we had, you and me. And this subject Rory and I couldn't talk about."

I looked at him levelly. "At least it didn't ruin your friendship with Rory."

He didn't deny this, but his blue eyes seemed to fill with regret about many things.

I took the jacket out of his hand and forced the hanger back into the crowded rack. I closed the closet door on the suede and the memories.

It was then I told him about Mrs. Bowdin at the Samuel

Adams Elementary School in East Boston. She said she hadn't remembered seeing anyone at the Arthur Fielder statue, but maybe if she saw him in person, it might jog her memory about that day on the Esplanade.

He thanked me in a quiet voice, full of gratitude.

I blew it off. "I gotta get some seltzer," I said, attempting a casual tone.

He continued to look at me.

I forced myself to turn from him and head to the kitchen. I felt weighted with emotion and in a haze through which it was hard to think. Yet at the same time, I felt myself traveling on that air current. I could feel Kit watching me as I walked away.

You are a journalist here, a journalist, I told myself. *A reporter who is supposed to be objective.*

But he is innocent, another voice said, *and wrongfully charged.*

I might have interrogated myself further, demanding to know where this came from. But I didn't bother to challenge the conclusion, which I had been forming since that afternoon on the Esplanade. *So what?* I asked myself instead. *So what if he is? That doesn't change anything.*

I found my notebook on the counter and flipped it open, trying to settle myself enough to read my scrawl. But my eye could not follow the line and my thoughts continued to jump. I had a sudden recollection of one of the Boston TV newscasters, who, in the process of doing a story about a man jailed for a Mafia murder, had become convinced that his subject had been set up. The newscaster had made the story his own personal mission, and although he took a lot of heat at first about objectivity, he had won the man a new trial.

You are not a famous TV personality, I told myself. *You are a newspaper reporter.*

I heard Kit's footsteps and felt his hand brush my arm.

A pathetic one at that.

"Addy," Kit's tone was plaintive.

I stepped away and knelt on the floor beside my satchel. As if to fortify myself, I grabbed the plasticized folder that held the Fenton financial documents. I knew I didn't have the mental acuity to deal with simple addition at the moment, let alone biomedical breakthroughs, but I had to press on. Standing up, I moved two arm lengths away. "I've got some stuff I have to ask you about," I said, affecting a businesslike tone.

His eyes checked the folder.

"This Fenton company—the drug they make. The merger. Was there any conflict about that at The BioFund?" I asked.

"The merger is key to the survival of the MS drug. We all agreed on that."

"So you and Marquesson weren't fighting about Fenton?"

"Do we have to go into this?" he asked, moving closer. "Right now?"

I looked up. Those blue eyes went right through me, penetrating the haze and confusion, reaching something inside. Gently, he took the folder out of my hand and tossed it on the counter. His arms went to my waist and I lost all peripheral vision. I could see only his face, the line of his cheek, the strong jaw. The cropped blond hair I knew once had curled.

His scent, a leathery spice mixed up in my mind with the suede jacket, overwhelmed me. When he drew me toward him, my heart did not leap or flutter. I felt strangely settled about the matter. I gave no pretense of resistance.

We had a deep kiss that at first conveyed a shared sadness, although I wasn't sure what we were commiserating—Rory's death, our missed opportunities, or the current state of each of our lives. It hardly mattered, because the tenderness gave way as the electricity took over. All that weighty meaning was lost in a more natural impatience.

His hand went under my errant skirt and he began stroking the inside of my thigh. It had been more than a year since I'd made love. I'd been dead with a grief that plunged me into some sort of underwater world where I didn't take in air or feel friction. Now, my nerve endings were reborn and for the first time in a long time, I was breathing.

Kit guided me up two floors to his bedroom. On the indulgent mahogany bed of his we began again, and soon I had pulled off my blouse and Kit was helping me with my bra. His mouth was all over my breasts and I was lost in the heat of his tongue. I began pulling at his belt buckle. I did not care about objectivity or about professionalism, I cared only about the taste of his skin and the oxygen I was taking into my depleted lungs.

And even when Kit pulled away, wrestling with a sticky nightstand drawer where he kept the necessary precautions, I did not allow myself to think about what I was doing. And soon, his tongue began probing again, teasing a line down my stomach, and the last thing on my mind was the consequences.

Kit became more demanding in his lovemaking, his tender pace becoming more and more urgent. I thrilled at this, and was overwhelmed by a wild desire to satisfy him, lose myself in this claim he was making on me.

I was gone, blessedly free of myself and my nonstop thought and analysis. I wanted only to stay where I was, on this peak with Kit, lost in all the rhythmic reflexes, the tension that was mounting.

And then, when we had collapsed into each other, I was still reluctant to speak and reenter the world where I had lived. Intuitively, Kit must have understood this. He did not speak either. After a couple of minutes, he got up, snapped off the central air conditioning, and opened the side window of the bay. Then he lay back down beside me, fitting his body comfortably around mine.

The breeze that had been absent that afternoon filtered in through the window, and I noticed that Kit took long, grateful breaths. After a while it dawned on me that he, too, had been living in an underwater world. And whatever risks I had just taken, diving in like that, I had not been the only one needing rescue.

Book III
First Draft, June 25, 1991

14

"When the hell are we going to see the copy on the Korbanics profile?" Arriving late, Lev yelled the question at Mark from the door of the conference room.

The editors leaning against the wall looked at each other in a here-we-go-again manner. From the very first item on the budget, Tuesday's news meeting had been a battlefield. The latest synthetic cocaine death had created a turf war between Gerard, who insisted that he do the follow on the drug source investigation, and the Suburban editor, a quiet man who raised his voice to argue that his Waltham beat reporters deserved priority in their own territory.

Mark, torn by his desire to have Gerard exclusively back on the Korbanics case and his belief that bureau reporters were mentally incapable of digging up information that wasn't printed for them on a city hall press release, had been forced to side with the Suburban editor. Now, he was eager to defuse Lev. He waved the printout I'd given him. "Right here. 'Kit Korbanics: Up Close and Personal.' "

His word choice startled me, an unexpected finger on my spine. I forced myself to remain impassive. I couldn't allow myself to think about how well I'd taken care of the "Up Close and Personal" part of the assignment.

"A solid lead?" Lev asked. I was sitting near the middle of

the table, but he looked right past me.

"Enough to satisfy Promotion," Mark said. He was on Gerard's other side and I could not see his face. Was something lacking?

I leaned across the table and said, "I might want to fiddle with it a little bit after the meeting. There's a development I'm waiting on."

"What kind of development?" Mark asked.

His tone was suspicious and for one brief moment, I feared that he might have guessed that the biggest development in the Korbanics case was that I was no longer ethically qualified to write about it. I had not only made love to Kit, I'd stayed over and agreed to see him again tonight.

Now I ordered myself to pull it together. What else could I do? Remove myself from the assignment and turn the story over to Gerard? I glanced at Lev, who had not taken a seat but remained at the door. He was all newspaper editor today: jacket disheveled, pencil stuck over his ear, a look in his eye that said he was running out of time. "Legal development," I said.

I had not heard from Kit yet, but I was hoping that if he and Estella had a successful meeting with the cabby, I could revise my lead after the meeting. An alibi witness would not only exonerate Kit, it would go a long way to eliminate questions that might be raised about my objectivity.

The room was crackling with conjecture. Lev put a quick end to it. He announced the meeting was over but told Mark and me to stay. Remaining at the door, he shifted his feet impatiently until the last assistant editor had filtered out.

Grabbing the printout from Mark, he advanced into the room and took his seat at the head of the table. He tipped back in his chair as he studied my paragraphs.

I looked at Mark. His head was bent, fiddling with the stay of his cuff link. Lev slid the pencil from the top of his ear and put the end of it in his mouth like a cigarette. I watched him turn it several times.

Then the chair pitched forward. "This way bill, have you actually seen it?" Lev asked.

"Not yet," I said.

"You don't have a photocopy?" Mark asked, looking up.

"I can get one. This afternoon."

"How about the name of this cab driver he's searching for?" Lev asked. The pencil was in his hand now, poised to write.

I racked my brain. Had Kit told me? Had I forgotten it? "That's the legal development I was talking about. Korbanics and Rubin are meeting with him this morning. An alibi witness. I'm hoping to get it," I glanced at the wall clock. "By this afternoon."

"So you don't have a name yet?"

I shook my head.

"This has to go to Promotion right now. No name. No way bill. We can't use this. The paper is not going to run radio ads about a key alibi witness who may or may not materialize," Lev said.

"Wait a minute." Mark sat straight, alarmed. "If this is going to be Korbanics's defense, however flawed, we want to be first with it, don't we?"

"Word is Rubin is trying to drum up popular support so a judge will be more amenable to a dismissal. I don't want to hand it to her. A lot of people stop reading after the first six graphs. Addy wants to put something this high up, she needs proof."

Mark was looking at Lev in an odd way. "Can't she just qualify it? Say Korbanics *claims* to have a way bill from Zara Cab, but hasn't produced a photocopy or a witness?" Mark asked.

This was done all the time, but Lev was shaking his head. Something was up. Mark knew it. He glanced at me, trying to gauge my perceptions. I had an awful feeling in my stomach. Could someone have seen me leave Kit's town house this morning? Could Lev know?

Mark reminded Lev that Gerard had already done a story saying that Korbanics had taken a cab from the Harbor Inn Hotel to the Esplanade and that Rubin was searching for witnesses.

"What's so different about this?" I asked.

"Searching for witnesses, not that he had them in hand," Lev said, gruffly. "To let Rubin hint she has proof, you better have proof."

Mark was staring at the tabletop in silent disagreement. I didn't know how to respond. Lev was taking an unusually hard line, rejecting my lead, a good lead. He was being unfair, but what I'd done with Kit had gone so far over the boundaries that I could not defend myself.

There was no washing it off, a night of lovemaking. How could I return to Kit tonight? And yet, I desperately wanted to see him, to be electrified by that current he radiated, lose myself in the heavy, leathery scent of his skin.

Lev was staring at me. But when I met his eye, I was relieved to see that his suspicions were centered on Estella Rubin, not on me. I'd seen Lev worked up like this before, furious at an attorney trying to manipulate the reporter with a flow of partial information, timed expertly to damage the opponent's next move.

The worst part was that he was right. Estella Rubin was known for this kind of ploy. Here, I knew Kit was telling the truth, and yet I couldn't make the case. I couldn't talk about "gut feelings" or "instincts," not when I'd come from the subject's bed. "If I get this affidavit later, say tomorrow or something, can I revise my lead?" I asked quietly.

Mark gave me a quick, darting glance, surprised. Reporters always argued about their leads. I had easily capitulated. He seemed concerned about how Lev would answer.

Lev gave me his professional grit look: *I'm hard on everyone, but I'm fair.* "This is a newspaper, Addy. You get real news developments, you can revise your lead up until deadline."

Mark made a notation on his yellow legal pad. Lev said that while he wanted to see the first draft by Friday, he would be willing to come in Saturday if I had any major last-minute developments in the case.

I was touched by this offer, struck by Lev's utter fairness. Fair was something I could no longer claim to be.

To Lev, I promised to produce photocopies of any documents mentioned in the story. To myself, I vowed to break it off with Kit. I needed to regain my balance. I *needed* to be fair.

I would meet Kit at his town house, but only to explain. I must have at least a veneer of professionalism. I owed it to myself and to the newspaper to distance myself from my subject—at least until after the trial.

#

I let myself into Kit's town house through the kitchen door that faced the alley.

The message on my voice mail said that he wasn't sure what time he'd be back from Estella's office, so he'd left a key for me under the brick on the back stoop. This clandestine entry into Kit's home gave me an unanticipated quiver.

You're here to break it off, I reminded myself. Late that afternoon, there had been another development. Ann-Marie Marquesson had finally responded to my voice mail messages. Her lawyer had contacted Lev and an appointment had been set up. I would interview her at her Cambridge apartment the next afternoon. A gift from heaven. An affirmation of my decision.

The kitchen was dim and cool in the afternoon heat. The Fenton folder was still on the counter from the night before. I picked it up and was reminded of the way Kit had taken it from my hands and thrown it aside. I quivered again, feeling his hands at my waist.

I told myself that I'd come here to be fair, to explain myself to Kit in person. But I also wanted to feel my heart race when he walked into the room, feel his intense blue eyes on me, stripping me of thought, of clothes.

I'd been preparing my speech to him all afternoon and imagining his response. But now, as I stood in his kitchen, I found myself closing my eyes against his chest, feeling his breath on my cheek.

I felt a chill through my shoulders and shuddered. What had I done? Slept with a source, become involved with a man on trial for *murder.*

But he's innocent, the voice said. *Wrongfully charged.*

That doesn't mean I had to sleep with him. Or think now of connecting my future to his.

I stuffed the Fenton folder into my satchel and spotted the copy of my brother's autopsy. Originally, I'd hoped to show it to Kit, but now I knew I had to avoid all discussion of Rory. It only drew me closer to Kit. I had to deliver my speech and get the hell out of here. Maybe drive to Worcester tonight, return the report to my mother's file cabinet, and put the whole thing out of my mind.

I heard Kit at the front door. My spinal column tightened reflexively. For a moment I considered bolting out the back. I told myself I owed him an explanation and made my way through the large, empty dining room toward the parlor.

Standing under the tall archway, Kit had a ragged appearance, tie and jacket already removed, shoulders sloped and wearied. When his eyes met mine, they were the color of a dulled, evening sky.

His blankness of expression continued for a long, terrifying moment and I suddenly feared he didn't want me there. That I wasn't the only one who had decided to break it off.

Then he threw his jacket over the antique umbrella stand and his arms went around me. His kiss was sad and sincere.

I stepped backward. My heart was pounding. I reached for the opening line of my speech, but the pathways to my brain were blocked, the synapses immobilized.

There was bad news in Kit's face.

"What?"

"The cabby didn't show," he said.

Blood began draining out of my stomach.

"Not only did he not show up for our meeting," Kit continued, "but according to the cab company he hasn't shown up at work for two days." In his face, I saw something close to despair. "And when we went to the address he listed on his W-2 form, it was empty."

"You mean he wasn't there?" I asked.

"No, I mean, there was nothing in the apartment and the landlord said he'd kicked the guy out for not paying his rent for the last six months."

There was now a hole where my stomach had been. Fear rippled though the emptiness. "Nobody knows where he is?" I asked feebly.

"Nobody." Kit put his arms around me again, this time as a support.

I pulled away. "How about your detective firm?"

"Oh, they're on it. Estella and I were there this afternoon, too. It's just that after they lost that woman in Athens, I don't have a lot of confidence that they'll find this guy right away."

"How about Mrs. Bowdin, the elementary school teacher? Did you get hold of her?" I pressed.

"Estella and I went to her school in East Boston this afternoon. She doesn't remember me."

"But this cabby—what's his name?"

"Warren Reid."

"He's probably still in Boston," I offered.

"Probably," Kit said, without conviction.

"No, really, if he doesn't have any money, how far could he go?"

He shrugged. "I don't know. The waitress didn't have much money either, but she ended up on a private yacht, somewhere. It's all a crapshoot with these agencies. I mean, hopefully, in Boston we stand a better chance, but who knows how long it will take?"

He walked around me to the dining room, and I followed him through that empty cavern to the kitchen. His gait was slow, beaten. This was not the moment to plead for distance, abandon him as Joan Warner had done.

Kit was innocent and wrongfully charged.

My pace grew rapid. I needed that cabby as much as Kit did, and I needed him a lot sooner.

In the kitchen, Kit was at the end of the galley, in front of the refrigerator, pulling out a liter bottle of seltzer. He opened it and nearly drained it in a long, plagued gulp. Then he took a second bottle from the refrigerator and offered it to me.

I shook my head. I was thinking of the places in Boston that an indigent cab driver might end up. I envisioned Warren Reid as a hard drinker, a man who drove his cab erratically and might one day lose his hack license.

And then suddenly, I saw the little square photo on the hack license that was always stuck to the visor. "Did you get Reid's picture from the cab company?" I asked.

"Yeah," Kit said. "We got a bunch of copies made for the detective agency."

"Got any left?"

He nodded and walked around me, through the long galley toward the dining room. I picked up my satchel from the kitchen counter before following him. If the cabby I'd already promised failed to materialize, Lev would think I'd been conned, that it had all just been a ploy of Estella's.

If I wanted to write anything remotely favorable about Kit, I'd better find the alibi witness. I began scanning the downtown bars in my mind, trying to remember which ones were closest to the cab garages.

In the parlor, Kit had retrieved his jacket from the umbrella stand and was searching his pockets. He pulled out an envelope and handed me the photo.

Warren Reid was not an unattractive guy, younger and cleaner-looking than I had imagined. My heart sank; he might not be an alcoholic after all, but just a kid who decided to hitchhike to Colorado to hang glide, or move with a girlfriend to a yoga commune in Vermont. "What do you know about him?"

"We know he remembered my twenty-dollar tip. He told the dispatcher about it. He also likes to party and reportedly is fond of cocaine," Kit added.

My first reaction was fear: This asshole cab driver was likely to do himself in snorting a line of the synthetic stuff before I could interview him. But my second thought was more productive.

I asked Kit if he had a photo of himself. He went upstairs to his study and returned with a professional still he'd had taken for press releases. I packed both photos in my satchel and told Kit I had to go.

He asked if I'd come back. I said it would be too late. I had to track down a source that could help, a cabby friend who knew where a wayward cabby was likely to hang out.

15

A night game at Fenway Park. The cab spent twenty minutes at a dead halt in Kenmore Square. Twenty minutes late to the church, I ran through the basement hallway only to come to another complete stop. The room was jammed with people tonight, as if everyone in Boston who had ever abused drugs had decided to make this meeting.

Blocking the door were three squared-off looking men in their early twenties and an emaciated young woman in a midriff. In the crescent of space between her exposed ribs and the enormous back of the man beside her, I peered into the room. It held almost fifty people, most of whom had to lean against the wall. Either the Brighton police had just done a drug sweep of a neighborhood, or all the recent publicity about Serina Wassermann's death had scared an abundance of people into recovery.

I could see that Dennis was the speaker, up behind the desk again, foot raised on the chair, hand on his knee, and a dark, brooding look on his face. This threw me. I hadn't expected to find Dennis speaking tonight. Nor had I counted on finding him distraught.

I leaned forward to try to get a better view. The girl in the midriff leaned her hip into the door frame to make room so I could step forward. Dennis looked disturbingly pale, as if he were the one in desperate need of help.

He pulled his leg off the chair and stood, arms folded, eyes downcast. I realized that he had ended his story and was coming to some sort of gritty conclusion. "The people who make the big money never even have to see the stuff," I heard him say. "I was the one who got those baggies to where they had to go. I used to tell myself, hey, people who want coke will get it *somehow*. I wasn't making the big money, the guys with the cash, the guys pumping the drugs in, they were the drug dealers. They were the criminals."

He twisted his thick silver and turquoise bracelet. "Now, I realize that they were the heart. But the heart can't get the blood to the body without the arteries. I wasn't an artery, but I was one hell of a capillary. Reliable. I got the stuff to the mirrors. I gotta live with myself knowing that. Knowing I helped fuck up people like you." He gestured to the crowd.

"Hey, you didn't fuck me up," a young man who might still have been a teenager, sitting in the first row, said. "I made the decision."

There was a general murmur of agreement on this, but it didn't seem to reach Dennis. He wasn't thinking about them at all.

I tried to catch his eye, but failed. Inadvertently, I brushed against the woman in the midriff's shoulder, and she turned, exposing an earlobe that had been pierced all the way up the cartilage. I apologized, trying not to stare at her ear. She waved it away, smiling too brightly. "We're going," she said, as much to me as to her three male friends. There was a lot of eye darting between them and I realized they were high. On cocaine, probably. I felt a shiver of fear as they marched out of the basement hallway.

"I thought that I could control what went up her nose, because I had the best coke. Why *would* Andrea go anywhere else?" The self-loathing was acute, painful to listen to.

He continued, "I don't know where she bought that synthetic shit, but it was powerful. There were maybe two lines missing from the gram when I found her. They said she died instantly." Dennis had never told me this before. Had there been an *Andrea* among the victims who overdosed from the synthetic cocaine? Had I read that name in any of Gerard's profiles?

When I got inside the room, a throng of people, three deep, was around Dennis, all wanting to offer consolation. I circled the perimeter of the room to the back and found a newly vacated chair beside Lil. "It's his anniversary," she explained.

In substance abuse parlance, "anniversary" usually is the positive marking of another year, month, or even week off of drugs. Now, however, I understood that "anniversary" referred to Andrea's death. *Of all nights,* I thought, then quickly chastised myself for my selfishness. I, of all people, knew how hard a one-year anniversary could be. On Rory's anniversary I'd wound up at the St. Margaret-Mary Hospital having my stomach pumped.

Another thought occurred to me: If this was the anniversary, Andrea had died in June. This was at least three months earlier than the first publicly reported death from synthetic cocaine.

I stood again, making my way toward the front of the room. I remembered the one and only time I had gotten up to tell my story. Everybody had wanted to congratulate me, offer their support afterward. I had only wanted to get the hell out of there.

Maybe Dennis did, too. I glanced at the clock. It was already after eight. I edged my way into the throng, forcing shoulders to part and barging my way past Lil and Christy, the girl with the bad boyfriend. At last, I was close enough for

Dennis to notice me. I saw what I thought was relief. "Let's get out of here," I mouthed. He nodded.

It took him a few minutes to extricate himself from the crowd, but at last he met me outside in the parking lot. He knew a bagel shop in Coolidge Corner that was open. I got into his cab, a boxy model with wide leather seats. This ancient Checker Marathon and the medallion had been purchased with coke profits. Dennis must think about that every time he turned the ignition.

#

The Bagel Man was not one of those new bagel places beginning to sprout up all over the city. There was no tri-color decor or Yuppie pastiche. We had crossed into Brookline, which had an authentic-enough Jewish population that Coolidge Corner had been featuring bagel shops before anybody dreamed of franchising bagels. There was a counter, some booths, and a lot of fluorescent lighting.

Needless to say, there was only one kind of coffee and it was served in white ceramic cups with saucers. I brought two back to a booth where Dennis was sitting, his head in his hands.

"You all right?" I asked, as I slid into the vinyl bench opposite him. We were at a booth at a window overlooking Harvard Ave.

"No," he said, oblivious to the foot traffic parading past on the street. "But I don't particularly *want* to be all right."

I understood. On Rory's one-year anniversary, I had wanted to wallow in it. As if anything less would have invalidated his life. But I also knew that wallowing turned into self-pity and self-pity an excuse to do drugs. "Did talking about it tonight help?" I asked Dennis.

He lifted his head. "I thought I could purge by talking about it. Confessing, I guess. But I chickened out."

From where I'd been standing, it had sounded like a pretty

full confession. My confusion must have been apparent.

"Oh, I told them about Andrea's death and that I dealt coke," Dennis said. "I've told everybody about that. But I left out the worst part." He gave me a grim smile. "Of course."

What could possibly be worse than selling coke, I wondered? Unless he actually shoveled it into Andrea's nose against her will. But I couldn't ask him this question, so I remained silent.

He gazed out the window, staring across the street where a line had begun to form beside the Coolidge Corner Theatre. "Do you ever find yourself surprised by how many people there are? The sheer number? I mean we're ants, everywhere."

"No, we're not ants," I said, although I had thought this enough times. Down in the bottom of the hole, people became ants and adversity a mindless foot. Pretty soon, the effort at the daily ant hill seemed foolish. "Ants don't do drugs," I added.

He smiled at this. "Yes, ants can probably stand themselves without doing drugs."

"I bet they sleep well," I added.

He took a sip of coffee and lapsed into brooding. Seeing Dennis like this made me wonder if my suspicions about Rory's death were just some new, more convoluted form of mourning. Hunting for Karen Oblonsky. Freaking out because she'd left the firm. Was it just a new way for me to wallow in it?

Although I'd crossed the line from reporter to lover with Kit, I wouldn't allow myself to cross the line the other way with Dennis. I would not play the reporter and try to draw the information out of him, despite my curiosity. If he wanted to confess, he'd confess.

There was a long silence. I tore the foil on the emptied cream packet. Dennis frowned in decision. "The worst part—" His eyes met mine.

"Yeah?"

He took more air, as if this might fuel the difficult flow of information. "The worst part is that I think I might have moved some of the shit."

It took me a minute, but then I realized that the *shit* was the *synthetic shit.* I tried not to show shock or excitement. My reporter instincts clicked in, despite myself. *Stay cool,* I ordered.

"I mean, I didn't know about it at the time," he continued. "It was back in February before I'd even heard about it."

"February?" I asked calmly. But I was stunned. The first news reports about synthetic cocaine hadn't surfaced until September.

"Yeah, this was before anyone had heard of the shit. A business associate of mine asked if I'd be interested in this little opportunity, driving a car. All of a sudden the guy has a new fleet of Chevy Malibus. Like God gave 'em to him. I picked up one that was parked along Memorial Drive and drove it out to a ranch house in Lincoln. A grand. Not even fifteen miles."

"What makes you think it was the synthetic stuff?" I tried not to sound too eager, too probing. I didn't want to scare the information away. But my mind had begun racing. *Gerard would be livid!* The source of the drug. I was getting the answer to the question that had stumped the DEA.

"The second time I did this, I got rear-ended in one of the Route 2 rotaries. I had to get towed to an autobody shop. Luckily, the cops didn't show up."

I nodded, foolishly.

"Usually, I just left the car parked in the driveway of this ranch house. They'd give me the cash and I'd be told to leave before they started to unload. This time, I kind of panicked, with the car stuck at an autobody shop and all. I got a friend to come help move the stuff from my trunk to his. That's when I noticed how the coke was packed."

He realized this required further clarification. "Usually,

coke is packed in about three or four layers of plastic with a desiccant between the layers to keep it dry. This time the stuff was in some kind of industrial glassware, packed in boxes with this yellow packing popcorn."

"Yellow packing popcorn?" For some reason, this struck me as funny.

But Dennis was dour. "Yeah, some kind of joke, a defect in the dye lot, but the Styrofoam was all yellow, like real popcorn."

I wanted desperately to be writing this down. Instead, I searched to discard all other possible explanations. "So maybe somebody just got creative."

"I doubt it. If it was the regular stuff coming from Bolivia, the creativity would be aimed at making it smaller and lighter. Not heavier and harder to conceal. I mean, I was high all the time back then. I didn't think about anything too much, but I thought that glass and that popcorn were really weird."

I nodded again. *Yes, weird.*

"This coke, this shit, didn't come from South America—it came out of some lab at night," he said. "Anyway, the garage needed to see the registration, so I had to go into the glove compartment. These cars are always registered to some fake corporation, twice removed from the real owner, but the corporations always have the same-sounding name. You know, Smith-Anderson Inc., or Whitehall Corp. Something kind of bland."

I was holding my breath, afraid that the wrong exhale might jinx it. *I might be getting the name of the corporation. The source of the synthetic drug.* "So what was the name?" I asked.

"Integration Technologies."

I silently repeated this name to myself, engraving it into my memory.

"At that time, no one knew about this stuff. It hadn't hit the streets, or if it had, it wasn't killing anybody. But afterward, after Andrea died, and after I started reading about the synthetic shit in the paper, I figured it out. Whoever was making it had to get it out of the lab somehow. Why not use part of the distribution network already in place? The guy I worked for knew a whole shitload of guys like me. He was a major artery. Why not use him?"

"You don't know that for sure, though?" I asked, I don't know why. I had interviewed enough experts in various fields to recognize Dennis was one of them. It was synthetic cocaine. We both knew it.

"I'm sure." His tone was final.

My eyes dropped to my coffee to avoid meeting his eyes. I didn't want him to see into my soul, see how opportunistically excited I was by this cache of information. He was suffering badly. I knew this. Knew I had to try to alleviate it in some way. "But, you didn't know about it then," I offered.

He shrugged. "I knew I was transporting coke."

"Yes, but you were high on coke yourself."

He waited to see what logic I would employ to make this seem like consolation.

"You were a drug addict and you thought coke was good for everybody."

He acknowledged this with another shrug.

I continued. "Not that I'm justifying what you did. But you've already dealt with that. You've made that confession. Now we're talking about the synthetic stuff. You didn't know. Shit, even the people making it probably didn't know it would kill people."

"But they fucking should have." He stared straight at me.

"Yeah, they should have. But they're going to burn in hell because they kept making and selling the stuff after *everyone* knew people were dying. But we're not worrying about their consciences. We're worrying about yours."

"Yeah," he said, unconvincingly. He seemed tired by my efforts to defend him.

I myself was struck by the strangeness of it all. Never in my life did I think I would be trying to make a coke dealer feel better about himself.

Dennis was staring out the window again, at the line of people feeding into the theater. His eyes were unfocused, his mouth a thin, bitter line, turned on himself.

I knew that expression well. I understood at my core. *Rory*. The feeling that there was no way to make things right with the dead.

Suddenly, it dawned on me that my own opportunism aside, tracking down the source of the drug might not be solely for my own gain. It was possible it could help Dennis. We all had different ways to make amends.

"You remember that I'm a newspaper reporter," I began.

"*News-Tribune,* right?" Dennis was not impressed, nor shaken. Perhaps he was too numb to realize the implications of all that he had said.

I sought to reassure him, anyway. I had slept with my source, was falling for the subject of my own profile, but I still had rules I would not break. "I would never use *anything* that you told me. I take the confidentiality commitment of the group seriously."

He nodded.

"I mean that. You're my friend. I would never, *ever* do that to you."

I was urgent about this, and it touched him. The bitter line of his mouth softened a little.

I thought suddenly of my search for Karen Oblonsky. It might be irrational. It might be completely futile. But it was *something* I could still do for my brother. Like my mother planting French thyme for him in her garden. Like my father laying winter evergreens on his son's grave.

"I will forget I ever heard the name Integration Technologies if you want me to," I continued.

Dennis waited. I sensed he was a step ahead of me, anticipating my next proposal.

I plunged on. "But if you let me, if you give me the go-ahead, I can follow up on that name. When I'm done with this profile I'm working on, I can try to trace it through Incorporation's at the Secretary of State." I was talking rapidly. "And if you agree to be an anonymous source, at some point later, I might be able to put together a story that could possibly halt the flow of that shit in the city."

He looked at me squarely as he considered all of this.

I did not let my mind whirl. I did not think of connecting the dots, making the story, making the page. Or even of Gerard and the thrill of beating him to a pulp. I thought of Dennis and the jeopardy I could put him in, both legally and from his friends in the "distribution" business.

"I don't know your last name. And I don't want to know it. I just want to be able to use the information you gave me tonight."

Dennis pushed his coffee away. His thoughts were clicking as he twisted his silver bracelet.

"There's something else."

I looked up.

"One of my old buddies is still, you know, part of the business. He said there hasn't been a shipment like that for a while. But the last trunkload he did, he only got a couple hundred dollars."

It was clear I didn't get the significance of this.

Dennis continued. "The reason, this guy said, was because there was less risk in transporting this synthetic stuff. Word is the drug is a designer model. It's made of synthesized shit, brand new chemicals that aren't on the controlled substances list. Technically, it's not illegal."

A lead of a lifetime. Maybe why DEA was buttoned-up tight. Too overwhelmed to speak, I had one thought in my head: If I could find a way to confirm this, Gerard would die of jealousy.

"But it's murder," I said after a minute.

He nodded. "How long you think this investigation will take?"

I had to be honest with him. "I can't start it until I finish the story I'm working on now. An investigation like this, unless I'm real lucky, could take months. Half a year even."

"Maybe I could go to the Secretary of State in the meantime?" he offered.

"No. I'll go. But you can help me another way."

His eyes met mine.

"I could use your help to finish up this other story." I reached into my satchel to get Kit's photo, and as I did, felt a single key thrown in the bottom of the bag. The back door to Kit's town house. I'd forgotten to return it.

Dennis took the photo from me and studied Kit's face. "The guy who pushed his partner out the window?"

"I don't think he did it," I said, giving him the photograph of Warren Reid, the disappearing cabby. "I've got to find this guy to prove it."

Dennis peered at me intently. "Why do you care so much?"

At some point, I would confide in Dennis, but at the moment, it was too much. I'd already crossed enough lines tonight. "He was a good friend of my brother's," I said.

This tie to my brother was enough for Dennis. He bent his head to study the frame. When he looked up, he smiled at me, and I felt guilty. I wished that I had told him everything, that I had been honest, rather than merely truthful.

#

I phoned Kit when I got back to my apartment.

Although Dennis didn't know Warren Reid personally, he had seen him around. Luckily, my first suspicion had been right. Reid was a big drinker, a party animal who was unlikely to have gone too far. Dennis thought he remembered seeing Reid hanging around a cabbies' bar in the Fenway, as well as the Plough and Stars in Cambridge.

"Dennis says he'll find him," I told Kit.

Kit was cautious. "And who is this guy?"

"A source," I replied. "Very reliable." Although I'd hinted around that I'd had problems after Rory's death, I had never spelled out the Serax problem. I didn't feel I could risk scaring Kit off by confiding that I attended regular substance abuse meetings. He'd been so straight in college, so intolerant of our friends who drank heavily or did more than dabble with drugs.

"I'll pass the names of those bars to my detective," he said. "If you don't mind."

He was less thrilled with my efforts on his behalf than I had hoped he would be. "You're really not going to come back?" he asked.

I smiled to myself, flattered by the genuine tone of his disappointment. I'd wait until tomorrow to give him my distance speech. It was past eleven, and I desperately needed sleep.

I told Kit about having to get up early and drive the autopsy report to my parents' file cabinet. He seemed to understand the need for protective deception. And my mention of the autopsy report jogged his memory.

"Oh, I almost forgot," he said. "I talked to Estella this afternoon about Karen Oblonsky."

"And?"

"She checked every current legal directory in Texas and even had her paralegal put a call into the Texas bar. There's no record of a Karen Oblonsky anywhere."

16

I was parched, desperately parched. I found a drink on my nightstand. A tall drink. But instead of being in a regular glass, it was in some kind of beaker. I drank it anyway and it coated my tongue with a bitter powder. I tried to spit it out, but had no saliva. Only then did I realize there was someone in my bedroom. A woman was sitting on my desk, but I couldn't make out her features. My throat began to swell; I couldn't find air. The woman at the desk was smiling at me, watching me suffocate. "Hey, you," she said with an amused, Texas twang. It was Karen Oblonsky.

My eyes flew open. I sat up in bed, panting. There was no one in my room. I was alone. I took a deep breath, trying, as Dennis had suggested, to feel it in the corners of my ribcage before letting it go. But the blood hurtled through my veins. The breathing was a fight, a battle.

I turned to the nightstand and opened the drawer. The knee sock with the bottle of Serax inside had rolled from its corner. I picked the sock up and shook it. The pills rattled inside.

I thought of Kit, suddenly, how he would despise me for such weakness, and dropped the sock in the drawer. Lying down, I closed my eyes and refused to think of the little bottle in the drawer. Instead, I thought of Kit, beside me, rubbing the nape of my neck. After a minute, I pushed that image aside, too, and forced a dozen more breaths.

#

The numerical code to disable my parent's security system was Rory's birth date: 10-05-55. I stood in the front hall, quietly punching the numbers into the keypad, optimistic that since the system was still armed for night intruders my parents might be asleep.

"Is that you, Addy?" my father called from the landing. It was 7:00 A.M. He appeared at the top of the staircase in the thick terrycloth bathrobe I had bought him for Christmas. He looked disconcerted by my appearance.

"I forgot the French thyme Sunday," I said. "I was up early and thought I'd beat the traffic."

"Oh," he said, still sounding befuddled.

"Where's Mom?"

"Getting dressed. We'll be down in a minute."

"Don't rush," I ordered. I'd hoped to get here a half hour earlier, before they were up, but had run into a repaving project on Route 9. My mind was racing with all the things I had to accomplish in one measly twelve-hour work day—not least of which was preparing for my afternoon appointment with Marquesson's widow. I wanted to get in and out of my parents' house quickly. The last thing I had time for today was an emotional side trip to Worcester.

In the kitchen, I went directly to the filing cabinet and slipped the autopsy report back into the neatly groomed file. I was shutting the metal drawer with my knee when my mother appeared, already dressed in her gardening clothes.

"I was just looking over the scholarship papers," I said, turning swiftly. "Did I tell you I went to Keenan and Quinn and signed that trustee stuff?"

"Yes, you mentioned that yesterday on the phone," my mother said. But if I anticipated suspicion about my fiddling with her files, I was mistaken. My mother had little concern over the proprietary nature of her paperwork. As usual she was regarding my waistline and making an assessment of my coloring. "Sit down, I'll make you some eggs."

"Not today, Mom." The kitchen faced east, and sunlight poured in through the bow window. I pointed outside to the barely perceptible cloverlike nibs of pink blooming between the rocks. "I just stopped by to dig up a little of that French thyme you promised me. You think it can last a whole day in my car?"

"You stopped by this early in the morning for plants?" my mother asked. Now her look was dubious.

"It's the only time I have right now, Mom."

"And you're going to tend to a garden in that little yard of yours?"

"Well, I wouldn't normally, but you're the one who made the big deal about planting it for Rory. I figure I can go out and water a few plants in my brother's memory every summer."

My mother did not offer her approval, although I could feel it emanating from her. Like a good general, she took victory and moved to exploit it. "If you are going to take care of things now, let's start with taking care of yourself. You're here and it's breakfast time. So for once in your life, Adelaide, sit down and eat breakfast." She gave me her grim, steely, there's-no-fighting-me-on-this look.

"Mom, I'm on deadline."

"That career of yours. It isn't the only thing in life, Adelaide." My mother's tone grew fierce.

Then my father's gentle arm was around my shoulder. "You would never have made the trip all the way out here if you were in such a rush. You're too diligent. I know that for a fact. Besides, I need to ask for your advice on something."

His tone was low key, but I could tell he was hanging on my reply. My mother's eye caught mine. *Don't disappoint him,* her look read.

I dropped my satchel on the filing cabinet and resignedly sank into a seat at the table, shifting the chair out of the direct sunlight. My father sat across from me, his spiritless eyes now full of satisfaction. My mother clicked away to the refrigerator where she began pulling out eggs and milk.

I glanced out the window again at my mother's meticulously maintained garden and realized I would also have to wait through some excruciatingly methodical process she had to divide perennials. I was really the most inept of liars.

"She's quite an artist, isn't she?" my father said, misreading my expression.

"Yes."

A regular Claude Monet, Rory would say. I smiled to myself. "So, what's this advice you want?"

"It's about the scholarship." My father reached for the paper napkins, which were in the middle of the table in a wooden holder that Rory made in Boy Scouts. My father shook the napkin open as if it were cloth, laying it on his lap. "I talked to a woman from Richard Quinn's office yesterday, a Susan somebody? You know her?"

Since that day in Quinn's office, I'd left half a dozen messages for Susan about locating Karen Oblonsky. I made a mental note to try her one more time when I got into the newsroom today. "She came to the funeral," I reminded him.

He had no recollection, but this information further boosted his esteem. "Very helpful woman."

In my recent experience Susan had not been helpful at all, but I nodded.

"Anyway, it was about an idea I had."

My mother stopped clattering the pans at the stovetop. "A wonderful idea," she added.

He smiled a modest acknowledgment of this praise. "That the first recipient of the scholarship be a native of Worcester—

from Rory's home town."

I imagined that my brother, who lived in dread of having to return to Worcester to work for my father, would have found this ironic. "That's a great idea, Dad," I said.

My father's smile grew broader. "She called back last night and said Richard Quinn endorsed the idea. And what I wanted to know from you is how we could get a little publicity from the *Telegram*."

A city councilman for ten years, my father had learned the ins and outs of publicity at the *Worcester Telegram* at least as well as its own copyeditors. But even before Rory had died, my father had fallen into this habit: He seemed to regard his own era, his heyday, as having passed. Now, he preferred to rely on his children. They were the experts.

So despite the fact that I knew he knew all this, I explained to him that the information had to be written simply and sparely in a one-page press release and mailed to the Metro editor. I offered to write it up for him.

"You think they'll print it?" he asked.

"A full law school scholarship? Local angle. They have to." A new thought occurred to me. "I'll send a copy of the release to the Accent department. In a slow month like July, they might assign a reporter to do a feature."

"About Rory?" He glanced over his shoulder to see if my mother had heard.

"Well, they'll definitely run a couple of graphs about the scholarship," I answered. "But they could get interested. And you know, you're not unknown in Worcester. They could decide to write it up as a story. A feature about the young lawyer whose memory the scholarship is in."

My mother was heading toward him with the eggs. When she put the plate down in front of him, their eyes met. They had a moment of sad, shared purpose that I understood at once.

This was what had motivated Serina Wassermann's parents to spend a day of their mourning with Gerard. *The memory.* Canonize the dead, if only for a day in newsprint.

#

Mrs. Marquesson was not much different than I had imagined. At least not when I first walked into her condominium. She lived on Harvard Street, a couple of blocks from the Square, and had the middle-aged academic look that Cambridge requires: longish hair allowed to go completely gray; attractive, aging face without makeup. Newly grief-stricken, she seemed solemn but not dazed.

I knew from Gerard that she was the one who had persuaded detectives to review their initial finding that Francis Marquesson's death had been a suicide. She had also appeared before the Grand Jury.

Estella Rubin believed that the widow had a financial motive to insist Kit was a murderer—a life insurance policy, one recent enough to be invalidated by a suicide. This was one of the things Lev wanted me to check out, since neither Mrs. Marquesson, nor her lawyers, had spoken to the press.

This interview was another coup for the *News-Tribune.* I might be asked to write up the material as a separate boxed sidebar to the profile on Page One if Lev didn't make me turn my notes over to Gerard for daily. I wasn't sure if Mrs. Marquesson had responded to my voice mail, or the rumor that Estella was putting together a case for a dismissal. Either way, I prepared myself for her to say awful things about Kit.

Mrs. Marquesson seated me on a white sectional in a spacious living room. The modernness of the overstuffed couch contrasted with the architecture, which was Harvard Yardish, an exposed brick fireplace, long windows and dark woodwork stripped of paint and restored. There were knickknacks everywhere: ship models, photos of two college-age sons in ceramic frames, candlesticks and bits of pottery, all artfully arranged to look as if they had just happened together by chance.

She went off to the kitchen to get me a drink, swishing down the corridor with one of those full, hippy skirts in a muted African design. I figured on an herbal iced tea, but instead I got a Diet Coke in a tall, iced glass. When she handed me a stack of cork-backed coasters to choose from, I noticed that the side table she hoped to protect had an expensive marble top.

I thought about what Kit had said about her at the Eliot on our first interview, that Francis's wife had "hovered" over him, calling all the time and managing the details of his life. It was midafternoon, a time she had chosen for our appointment, and I wondered if she worked at all, if she was an academic off for the summer or if she was on some sort of mourning leave.

Mrs. Marquesson took a seat on the facing side of the sectional, arranging her skirt as thoughtfully as I imagined she placed her knickknacks. She pointed past my head to an alcove, where the walls were covered with framed documents. There was a small desk that looked like some sort of French antique. "That was Francis's study," she explained.

I stood and walked over, feeling bound, out of respect, to explore. The wall adornments included another photograph, this time of the two sons together with their father, but mostly the frames held science awards issued by various foundations and universities. Central in the room, placed over the desk, was a framed news clip of the profile Lev had written about him years ago, when they were both younger men.

Anyone with even a remote connection to the editor or publisher will bring it up during an interview to try to buy favor and influence how the story comes out. But Mrs. Marquesson did not mention it, even though I had halted for some time in front of the framed news clip.

"The study is a lot neater now," she said, with an ironic smile, meant to convey that she was not so besotted with grief that she did not have a realistic view of her late husband.

There was a neat stack of bills held together by elastic on the desk, but it was otherwise perfectly clear. "Are you a scientist, too?" I asked.

She seemed amused by this assumption.

"You don't work at MIT then, I take it," I prompted.

"No. I work at the Sivanandu Yoga Center," she said.

"An instructor?"

She smiled again at the assumption. "Someday, perhaps. Right now, I volunteer at the desk Saturday mornings and they generously let me take all the classes I need. Do you do yoga?"

I shook my head and turned to another wall of framed science awards as if I were reading. But I was thinking that despite the Cambridge veneer of a modern, left-wing woman, Ann-Marie Marquesson was a traditional housewife. Her free time might be spent volunteering at the Yoga Center instead of at the Junior League, but she had apparently devoted her life to raising her two sons and making a home for her successful husband.

A wife without her own career. It seemed likely that there might be a large insurance policy to protect her if the breadwinning husband should die.

We had been waiting for her lawyer, who was late. But now the buzzer sounded and Mrs. Marquesson rose to answer it. Within a few minutes, an unbelievably young man in full Brooks Brothers regalia arrived at the door. For a moment, I thought he could be one of her sons, but from their interchange, I gathered he was, indeed, the lawyer.

He introduced himself as Robert Sweeney and proffered his card, which identified him as an associate. This could be either good or bad luck. Inexperienced, he might not know when to shut her up. Having to prove himself, he might interrupt her every utterance.

We reseated ourselves on the big white sectional, Mrs. Marquesson and her lawyer side by side, facing me. Like Estella, Robert Sweeney produced a tape recorder from his pocket.

I considered my lost-tape-recorder routine, but my conscience balked. I'd already gone through one major deception this morning at my parents' house, and I didn't feel like trying to trick a grieving widow. Besides, the point of this interview was not to make Mrs. Marquesson slip up, but to hear her out. To allow her to describe the demon Kit Korbanics. To provide balance to the profile. To provide fairness.

Instead of making an exaggerated display of disorganization, I decided to begin the interview with the question I thought Marquesson's widow most wanted to answer. I leaned back, crossed my knees as I positioned the pen on the notebook, and asked her to describe her husband's state of mind the week before he died.

I thought she would say how level-headed her husband was, or how optimistic, or how committed to his work, but instead, she took a deep breath, as if shoring herself up for a difficult revelation. "On Sunday, he was out of his mind with rage," she said. "Furious."

"With Mr. Korbanics?"

"Yes. I think my husband would have liked to kill Kit. I only wish he had."

I wrote this down swiftly, expecting Robert Sweeney at any moment to tell me that was all off the record. But he didn't. And when I glanced at him, he appeared unruffled. *Yes, these feelings are natural from a woman whose husband has been murdered,* his calm suggested.

"What was your husband so furious about?" I asked at last.

"A business dispute."

"Did the dispute involve any particular company?" I asked.

Here, she grew cautious, glancing at Robert Sweeney.

"I know there was a lot of controversy over the MS drug the Fenton Company was putting out," I pressed. "Was the conflict over the merger?"

Mrs. Marquesson darted another look at her lawyer. I was unsure whether I was traveling down the right corridor, but I plunged on, nonetheless. "Your husband was on the scientific advisory board there—"

"He was the original founder," she retorted.

I was startled by the information. Kit had told me the story of Marquesson's inability to manage his first company that day on the Esplanade. I should have made the connection. I should have realized by Marquesson's seat on the board that it was Fenton. My heart began racing. "Did your husband oppose the merger? Was that what the fight was about?"

Her look cut me off, chased me off the path. "He opposed Lavaliere's first offer in '89. It was insulting. Francis got Raymond Beane to see that. That's why they pursued the ancillary business in contract screening. Another idea of Francis's that Kit gave him no credit for."

She waited as I wrote this all down, then continued. "But this time, Francis was all for the merger. The share price was more than fair. In fact, Francis owned his own founders' stock in addition to The BioFund holdings. He stood to become a rich man."

"Mind if I ask, how rich?"

She gave a strange, eerie smile. "Close to one million dollars personally when the merger is finalized next week. You tell me why someone anticipating this kind of success, this kind of wealth, would kill himself?"

I stopped writing. Mrs. Marquesson glanced at my pen.

This was major information, something the prosecutor might or might not have wanted her to reveal at this particular moment. Lev would crown me. Gerard would die. I had a slightly sick feeling in my stomach. "Is this why the district attorney is so sure it wasn't suicide?" I asked.

"One of many reasons," she said with an air of victory.

Robert Sweeney was nodding approvingly at Mrs. Marquesson. Everything said had contained just the right combination of emotion and rhythm, I gathered. His tape recorder made a soft whirring sound on the table beside me.

But the widow paid no attention. She was now staring off toward the alcove of her husband's study, the wall of framed awards. Her steely expression made me think suddenly of my mother.

It occurred to me that such a devoted wife would *have* to convince herself that it was Kit, an outside enemy, who had destroyed her life. Like my parents, like the Wassermanns, like myself, all she had left was the memory. My mother planted thyme, the Wassermanns talked to Gerard, I hunted for Karen Oblonsky.

I told her that I understood that The BioFund was failing. "Could they have been fighting over that?"

"My husband was realistic about The BioFund," Mrs. Marquesson replied. "With the money from the merger, he was going to be independent enough to leave the venture capital business and go back to science, to the lab, where he belonged."

The cold finger touched my spine. Kit hadn't mentioned any of this.

"Francis was just waiting until the merger was finalized before making his announcement because he wasn't going to mince words with the press about the reasons for his departure."

There was heavy meaning in the air. A moment passed as

both Mrs. Marquesson and her lawyer waited for my reaction.

"Are you trying to say Mr. Korbanics killed your husband to prevent him from leaving The BioFund?"

"My husband was *the name*, the one with the credentials, and he was about to abandon the partnership. Can you imagine the headlines people like you would be writing after he left?"

I nodded.

"The capital investment community is very small, and relies heavily on reputation. And Kit was consumed with his stature in the capital community," Mrs. Marquesson continued.

"What exactly was your husband going to say to the press? Can you be a little more specific?"

"That Kit sacrificed scientific integrity for the bottom line," she said. "He was always making promises to the press before the research was on track. Pushing the data. Embellishing the potential of the most minor discovery at any of the companies."

I'd heard Lorraine make the same complaint of half a dozen executives in the biotechnology business. It seemed to me that charges like this might only enhance Kit's reputation in the capital communities. "You think your husband leaving The BioFund would enrage Mr. Korbanics to the point where he would commit murder, throw another human from a—"

"Oh, I don't think it was rage," she interrupted. "I think it was calculation. You see, Francis thought that Kit was amoral when it came to science. But he was wrong. Kit Korbanics is amoral. Period."

A dramatic statement. A front-page kicker. If Gerard got his hands on these notes, he'd have the editor box up this statement as a pull-quote. My pen, clutched too tightly, was bleeding ink on my fingers. I wiped off my hand on a fresh piece of paper. "So what set off the fight on Sunday?" I asked.

"I don't know exactly, Francis wouldn't talk to me about

it." Mrs. Marquesson sounded truly pained by this. "But he was so disturbed after their conversation, he called Kit back half a dozen times. Then he spent the whole night awake, pacing the apartment with pounding migraines."

Here, Robert Sweeney moved forward, placing a cautionary hand on her arm. I wrote in clear, large letters, for this characterization bolstered Kit's contention that Marquesson had been mentally disturbed, appearing unstable.

Mrs. Marquesson realized it too. "Francis was angry," she said, in a more controlled voice. "Not depressed. Not despondent."

I turned over another page. "The defense says that you're insisting it isn't suicide because your husband had a recent life insurance policy."

She gave the lawyer a can-you-believe-this look. "No one has tried to make a secret of that policy. I gave that documentation to the district attorney," Mrs. Marquesson said, calmly. "The district attorney didn't seem to think our personal financial arrangements obviated Kit Korbanics's own insurance motives."

I took meticulous notes. "Can you tell me how much your husband's insurance policy is worth, then?" I asked.

Her lawyer raised his hand. "No comment."

"That'll look terrible in print," I told them. "People will imagine more than if you give it a number."

They glanced at each other again. "It's not millions and millions of dollars if that's what you think," Mrs. Marquesson said. "We have assets, stocks and stock options. And proceeds from the Fenton merger. We didn't need a lot of life insurance."

"How much?" I pressed.

Sweeney shook his head telling her not to answer, but Mrs. Marquesson decided to ignore him. "It's a small, term-life policy. Two hundred thousand dollars. Just enough to let me take care of legal costs of the estate and get the kids through college."

"Thank you," I said. But my success in procuring the number I had sought did not produce the usual excitement. I had given her good advice. No comment would have been dramatic, making it sound as if she had a motive to accuse Kit, a big number she had to hide. With her husband standing to make almost a million dollars from the merger, two hundred thousand dollars would sound as if it wouldn't be worth lying about.

17

Back at my desk, the little red voice mail light blinked furiously on my phone. I hoped for messages: from Dennis that he had found the cabby; from Susan that she had an address for Karen Oblonsky; from Kit that he simply wanted to call. But I knew I could retrieve none of them now.

I threw my satchel on the floor and stood, one knee on my swivel chair, looking over the cubicle wall. Mark was nowhere in sight, but Lev was already on his way. Almost immediately, he swung into the Financial department, his shirt sleeves rolled up and those high-intensity eyes ablaze as he steamed toward me.

I dropped to my seat and began to forage for my notebook, preparing to give him a status report on my interview. Within seconds, he was at the edge of the desk, walling off my view of the rest of the department.

Lev's power was in his unpredictability. He did not begin his probe with questions about Mrs. Marquesson. "Mark tells me you think you have a lead on this synthetic cocaine story?"

"Yes," I said, surprised that Mark had transmitted this information so speedily. I glanced over at Lorraine to see if she was listening, but her back was toward me, head bent over her notes.

"Mark says you have a source in the business. You know,

we've had a number of addicts who've given us leads to nowhere," Lev continued.

"This guy isn't an addict," I said, defensively. "And he's not in the business anymore."

Still frowning over the useless waste of reporter time, Lev was not impressed. "Make it clear we don't pay for information."

"He isn't asking for money," I said.

Lev nodded, as if only half believing this. "Obviously, right now you've got to stay focused on Korbanics. But I don't see any reason why you can't jump into the synthetic cocaine story next week—provided you do a good job on the profile."

I nodded, trying to be cool. He had just conceded me another high-profile story. I had to act as if I deserved it, as if it were my due.

"So how'd it go this afternoon? What did Ann-Marie say about Korbanics?"

Something about the casual reference to Mrs. Marquesson by her first name, coupled with the sharp way he said *Korbanics*, gave me pause. "She said her husband wasn't depressed and didn't commit suicide," I began cautiously.

"What else?" Lev glanced over his shoulder at the wall clock.

"She said Francis had a fight with Korbanics, but her husband wouldn't tell her what they were fighting about—"

"That's all right," he said, cutting me off. "We can still lead with her contention that they had a fight. We're going to go daily with this. Those your notes?"

I flipped the page to the beginning of the interview, and offered him the notebook, expecting to have to turn it over to Gerard.

Lev looked at me for a moment as if I were an idiot. Then the gallop of his thoughts allowed him a clearer interpretation of my response. The disdain disappeared and there was a hint of warmth. "*You* are writing the story, McNeil."

I needed a few seconds to absorb this. I thought I'd only be allowed to write it up as balance for my profile or, if I was lucky, as a sidebar for Sunday's paper. "You mean for tomorrow?"

"I know you've got your hands full, but Gerard's busy on a piece about the Wassermann autopsy. This can't wait until Sunday. Did you happen to ask whether there was an insurance policy?" he asked.

"Year-and-a-half old and invalidated by the suicide clause," I told him.

Lev scribbled a few lines on the yellow legal pad, but his expression told me he wasn't ecstatic about this development.

"The policy's only for two hundred thousand dollars," I continued.

He looked up swiftly.

I was encouraged. "Frankly, I think Mrs. Marquesson's motivated more by her grief—"

He cut me off again. "Just stick to the facts." He was glancing at the clock again. "We can talk more about this at the Five O'clock. I've got to go call Gerard about the Wassermann thing. Plan on twenty-five inches for Page One."

Page One. Those two words ran through my blood stream like a B-12 shot. Editor says Page One. Reporter salivates. An involuntary response.

Lev left, striding out of the department as purposefully as he had arrived. The late afternoon sun produced a dazzling glare on the computer screens. Lorraine, who was closest to the windows, caught my eye as she walked over to lower three sets of blinds. "Page One?" she asked. I nodded.

She walked back to her desk, pulled something out of her drawer which she tossed to me. "Mark came by earlier and said to give this to you." I caught a square yellow envelope midair.

Slipping the photograph out of the envelope, I was confronted with a picture of Lev and his wife sitting beside Francis and Ann-Marie Marquesson at some kind of banquet table. Francis Marquesson had his wine glass raised in a toast. Lev's eyes were on Marquesson, as if he'd been listening to him—a rare look of admiration.

The cutline read: "Science Museum trustees elect new board." It was an official event that could have thrown the four of them together by happenstance, but the camera had captured a look of familiarity among them. This was why Mrs. Marquesson had responded to my voice mail. She knew she had Lev on her side.

Lorraine had rolled across the carpet in her swivel chair. She leaned on my armrest and lowered her voice. "Mark said they've been buddies since Lev did that profile on Marquesson years ago."

This explained why Lev had been so hard on my lead, so intent on preventing Estella Rubin and the defense from making a score. Lev had his own problems with objectivity. "I guess that doesn't give me much leeway in how I write this story."

Lorraine shrugged. "You'll do okay."

I shrugged back.

She took the photograph out of my line of sight and slipped it back into the envelope. "Just make sure your own friendships don't get in the way."

#

I used to love the eerie dusk of the newsroom at the dinner hour, when it was quiet enough to hear the tapping out of thoughts at the few working keyboards. But after the Five O'clock meeting, I was not in the mood to listen to anyone's typing. I had a twenty-five-inch story due by nine o'clock. And I knew none of those inches was going to come easily.

The department had cleared out. Lorraine had left for another spaghetti date with her MIT boyfriend. Only the section editor and a copyeditor I didn't know remained at their tubes. I sat down at my desk and scanned my notes:

> *Kit sacrificed scientific integrity for the bottom line.*
> *Kit was consumed with his stature in the capital community.*
> *It wasn't rage, but calculation. You see, Francis thought that Kit was amoral when it came to science. But he was wrong. Kit Korbanics is amoral. Period.*

Every quote of Mrs. Marquesson's seemed like a new burden, each one sensational enough to be boldfaced and boxed on Page One. I envisioned Kit reading them in the morning paper, sitting on the suede sofa in the living room, coffee mug on the table.

Turning to my computer, I told myself that my job was to remain detached, as if Mrs. Marquesson were saying all these things about someone I didn't know. My notebook was in the narrow space beside my keyboard, and I alternated my gaze from the written scrawl of the lined pages to the infinite darkness of my blank screen.

At last, I created the story file, which I named *Widow1*. I told myself that Mrs. Marquesson had trusted me. She was dependent on my sense of fair play.

Bullshit, she's Lev's friend.

That doesn't matter. It's my obligation to report the news.

I stared at the blank screen again, trying to summon the words for my lead. I thought of Kit and his slow, beaten path through the dining room the night before. For him, tomorrow would be another awful day.

I forced the image from my head. *Don't let your own*

friendships get in the way.

The message icon of my computer started blinking. I pressed the key and called it up. "How much longer for the lead?" It was from Nora. "Ten minutes," I typed back.

I stood and looked over the cubicle wall. Nora's back was turned to me. Lev had stopped by her desk, briefcase under his arm. As he left her desk, heading out toward the main door, he turned and saw me. He waved—a twist of the arm behind him, an offhand gesture as he marched out. Still, several copyeditors on the Rim turned to see who was commanding that bit of editor's attention.

I sat down, turning to my computer. The ticking of the wall clock reminded me I could agonize no longer. I blurted out the lead:

> *In the week before his death, Francis Marquesson*
> *was involved in a bitter feud with W. Christopher*
> *(Kit) Korbanics, the venture capitalist who is charged*
> *with murdering him, Ann-Marie Marquesson, the*
> *victim's wife, said in her first public interview yesterday.*

I made an electronic copy and sent it to Nora's queue before I could retract.

Then I began to play with the rest of the story.

> *The widow said she did not know the specific*
> *nature of the feud, but it was her belief it had to do*
> *with the future of The BioFund, the venture capital*
> *fund Marquesson and Korbanics partnered.*
> *"My husband was planning on leaving," she*
> *said. "And he wasn't going to mince words with the press*
> *as to why.*
> *"Kit sacrificed scientific integrity for the bottom line,"*

she added. "He was always making promises to
the press before the research was on track.
Pushing the data. Embellishing the potential of
the most minor discovery at any of the companies."

Mrs. Marquesson said she believed Korbanics
killed her husband to prevent him from saying these
things to the press.

"Francis thought Kit was amoral when it came
to science," she continued. "But he was wrong.
Kit is amoral. Period."

I stared at these lines. A powerful opener. They would not only lead the *News-Tribune*'s front page, they would also be picked up by the wire services, quoted on talk radio, repeated on TV.

I had to offer Kit a chance to refute this. If I had never met him before, I'd give him that much. I picked up the phone and dialed his personal line. It rang eight, ten times. Kit didn't answer. I tried Estella's number, but only got her machine.

I reread the quotes. They would convict Kit in the hearts of the reader, stay in the mind of his colleagues even if he were acquitted.

I'd had neither lunch nor dinner, but my nerves were stretched, my stomach taut. The copy boy stopped by my desk to ask if I wanted to order anything from North End Pizza. Urgently, I waved him away.

I flipped over a page of my notebook and stared dully at my scribbles: LF INS POL $200— The relative insignificance of Francis Marquesson's life insurance policy would ruin Estella's day, but in the context of this interview, it was the least of Kit's problems.

It was then I realized I'd been allowing myself to stray. Lev had asked me to focus on the insurance policy. The thrust of the

story wasn't supposed to be Kit's character. The news value of
this interview was in the revelation of the upcoming wealth
from the stock sale and the fact that Mrs. Marquesson had no
financial motive to lie.

I flipped back to my copy and erased the last two paragraphs. I would give Lev the story he wanted and allow Mrs.
Marquesson to defend her husband's sanity. But the character
stuff, the negative quotes about Kit, I'd save for the profile,
where it belonged anyway, and where Kit would have a chance
for a rebuttal.

In the profile, Mrs. Marquesson's quote about Kit "calculating" her husband's death, a fake suicide, would be balanced
by Joan Warner's observation that Kit was too smart to plan a
murder that way.

I revised the story. The new version went like this:

> In the week before his death, Francis Marquesson
> was involved in a bitter feud with W. Christopher
> (Kit) Korbanics, the venture capitalist who is charged
> with murdering him, Ann-Marie Marquesson, the
> victim's wife, said in her first public interview yesterday.
>
> The widow said while she did not know the
> specific nature of the feud, it was her belief it had to do
> with the future of The BioFund, the venture capital
> fund Marquesson and Korbanics partnered.
>
> She revealed for the first time that her husband
> was anticipating a sale of his founders' stock in
> Fenton Biomedical Corp., which he started in 1986,
> when the Paris pharmaceutical, Lavaliere Pharmaceutical,
> Ltd., completed its acquisition in the next couple of weeks.
>
> Mrs. Marquesson estimated her husband's profits
> from the upcoming sale at just under $1 million, and
> added, "You tell me why a man expecting that kind of
> wealth would kill himself."

From there, I went into her contention that her husband was neither "depressed" nor "despondent," and that she had no financial motivation to hide a suicide.

I revealed the insurance policy's insignificant $200,000 value in light of the family's other assets and anticipated Fenton stock sale. Not until the end of the story did I allow the charge that Kit killed her husband to prevent him from leaving The BioFund partnership.

I scrounged through my drawer until I found the notebook I'd used during my very first interview with Kit at the Eliot. Flipping through the pages, I finally found our discussion about Marquesson, which I paraphrased:

> *Korbanics, who could not be reached for comment yesterday, acknowledged in an earlier interview that he and Marquesson argued over the direction of The BioFund, but downplayed these differences saying that in a venture capital business, those arguments were a routine aspect of "the decision-making process."*

I spent an hour and a half refining and correcting before sending the final copy to the City queue. I was drained from the process, but satisfied with my compromise. I'd done right by the widow; at the same time, I'd protected Kit from the irreparable damage of her most damning comments.

As I grabbed my satchel from the floor to go home, the blinking light of my phone reminded me I still had not collected my voice mail.

Picking up the receiver and punching in my code, I hoped for good news from Dennis about finding the cabby. There were several dead clicks. Once I heard a person breathe before hanging up.

I doubted that Dennis would be too skittish to leave a voice message, but I made a mental note to call him in the morning, just in case. There was only one real message. It was from my mother.

She reminded me not to leave the French thyme in the back of my car overnight and to water it thoroughly before planting.

18

When I awoke the next morning, my mind was so dull that, for a minute, it felt like the old days when I used to triple on Serax.

The adrenaline rush of deadline had made it difficult to get to sleep, and then sometime before dawn, I began waking at twenty-five-minute intervals, each time thinking I'd heard the thud of the morning paper thrown on the porch.

The last time I checked, at about 6:00 A.M., it still hadn't arrived and I fell into the respite of a morning coma. Now the sun was bright enough behind the window shade to let me know it was late. Under my bed, I found my oversize *News-Tribune* sweatshirt, which I wore as a bathrobe. Pulling it over my T-shirt, I ran through the unfurnished corridor of my living room to the front porch.

Brighton, a working-class neighborhood, was rarely quiet. Traffic battled on North Beacon Street and the German shepherds two doors down barked nonstop. Now, on this bright, sunny June morning, when the kids who lived in the two-family directly across the street should have already been fighting over the Little Tikes trike overturned on the front lawn, there was a dead silence, as if everyone had moved out overnight.

I cursed my erratic paperboy. There was nothing on the porch except the paper bag of unplanted, unwatered French thyme. The little leaves were all brown, the nips of pink crushed and dry.

I sat on the front stoop and spread the little clumps of parched root and leaf on the slatted floor. Water was beside the point now.

My mother would be horrified. I told myself that the French thyme was her memorial to my brother, not mine.

From inside the house, the phone began to ring. Having worked so late, I was not expected until noon. I rose from the stoop slowly. It could be Mark calling to congratulate me. Lev might have posted a tearsheet of my story on the bulletin board.

The only phone was in my bedroom. Usually on the nightstand, it somehow had been relocated to the floor. I uncovered the receiver from under a pair of pants I'd been wearing the night before.

It wasn't Mark, but Susan from Richard Quinn's office. I had no chance to register surprise. "I've been trying to call you back, but you're never at work," she said hurriedly.

I made a feeble apology. She wasn't interested. "I've left the firm, so don't call me there anymore. In fact, don't call me at all. I'm going to give you this information because I think you should have it, but you've got to promise never to let Richard know where it came from."

I promised.

She halted before blurting out the rest. "The reason you can't find Karen Oblonsky in Texas is because she's not there. She's in rehab at a clinic in Westwood, trying to kick her coke habit."

#

I did not allow myself to waver, but quickly dialed Kit's private line.

I don't know how many times it rang, for I could hear nothing but my own thoughts, my frantic suspicions.

A woman addicted to cocaine would need money. She would be unstable and desperate.

The grogginess was completely gone, as if I'd just injected a liter of caffeine. My suspicions raced. The fits and starts of my thinking made me aware that I was not entirely rational. That Karen Oblonsky had a coke habit did not make her a murderer. That Richard Keenan had been caught plundering his client's escrow account did not mean he'd hire one associate to poison another.

And yet, it seemed to me that the state had brought charges against Kit with less of a motive. A five-million-dollar key-man life insurance policy on his BioFund partner paled beside Rory's ability to destroy Richard Keenan's legal career and put his life in danger from the client.

Kit answered with distance in his voice. Immediately, I gave him my prepared explanation, the duty of my job, my attempt to allow him a rebuttal even though I hadn't been able to reach him last night.

He said nothing, but allowed for a painful silence. I did not apologize. "I realize that you are a reporter," he said at last.

The inflection he put on "reporter" was not particularly flattering. Still, I was encouraged enough to press on: I told him I'd found out something bizarre, something to do with Rory, and I needed to talk to him.

There was silence. For a moment, I thought he might refuse me, but then he told me to meet him at The BioFund offices in half an hour. "I have a lot going on today," he said. "Don't make me wait."

#

The BioFund offices were in a newly renovated building in Lechmere Square in Cambridge. Across the river and down Memorial Drive—not a bad cab ride from Brighton. I got there before Kit and was asked to wait in the reception area by a middle-age woman who did not appear to be a receptionist, but some sort of upper-level assistant. She disappeared into a back room.

The BioFund had a small reception area, but there was a distant view of the Charles River, between two buildings on the opposite side of Edwin Land Boulevard. Along the Boston skyline, I could see the plain brick tower of the Mass. Eye and Ear Building, and beside it, the more modern stepladder of Mass. General, the hospital where Rory had died.

I needed desperately to talk to Kit about Karen Oblonsky. He was the only one who wouldn't think I was crazy. I had taken heart in the fact that he had agreed to see me. To juggle his schedule on such short notice meant that despite the morning's paper, he still cared a little. I didn't expect him to be happy about the story, but I hoped he would be open-minded enough to listen, to eventually understand that it was my job. That I had no choice.

I took a seat on an antique-looking divan in the reception area. Despite the view and expensive decor, The BioFund offices seemed to be lacking. From the look of the mahogany reception desk covered with stacks of mail, the receptionist had either quit or been let go. The magazines in the waiting area were two to three months old, reporting the bombing of Baghdad. From the inner office I could hear the copy machine chugging as if it were losing its breath.

Someone had thrown the day's paper on the Oriental rug beneath a side table and I reached over and drew it to my lap. It was the morning's *News-Tribune*.

My story, in the upper-right-hand side, had been awarded a three-deck head.

Marquesson widow says
husband to become millionaire
feuded bitterly with Korbanics
By Addy McNeil
staff reporter

My byline was on Page One, but for the first time in my career, I was absent the thrill of ownership. Instead of pride, I felt agitation. The headline somehow made the story harsher. As if the fight were over the money. And the prose itself seemed stronger, more powerful, set in typeface.

> *Mrs. Marquesson estimated her husband's profits from the upcoming sale at just under $1 million, and added, "You tell me why a man expecting that kind of wealth would kill himself."*

This was the last paragraph before the story jumped to the Metro section and the question hung with added emphasis.

I found myself reading it as Kit would read it—an act of betrayal.

In the back office, the copy machine shrieked to a halt. A woman swore loudly. Metal clanged, as if equipment were being kicked.

Kit arrived at the door, an Au Bon Pain bag in one hand, file in another. He was casual in chinos and a golf shirt. However, the look in his eye was markedly cold and businesslike and I was taken aback by the sheer intensity of it.

He waved the manila file and gestured for me to follow him through the corridor into the conference room. I took a chair facing the view of the river and skyline. Under the file, I noticed he had his own copy of the morning's *News-Tribune*. He threw them both on the glass-covered conference table and walked around to sit opposite me. Without looking at me, he sipped a cup of coffee he had extracted from the donut bag. Desperately, I wanted to bring up the Karen Oblonsky thing, but I knew this was no time to seek his understanding.

"Tell me, I'm curious," Kit began. "Is it that you don't believe I'm innocent or that it doesn't matter to you when you have a Page One story?"

His tone was so caustic that for a moment I thought I might lose all composure and cry. I could no longer look at him. The blue eyes were ice cold. "I told you I wasn't given a choice," I said.

"I suppose it would have been too much of an imposition on our friendship for you to have left out Ann-Marie's belief that I would kill her husband just to keep him from leaving the partnership?"

This touched a raw nerve. Suddenly, I was no longer guilty, but angry. "Do you want to know what she really said?" I did not wait for his reply. "She said you calculated the whole thing. And 'Kit Korbanics is amoral. Period.' And I cut it."

"That was generous," he said, dryly.

"Listen, I cut what were probably the most sensational quotes of the year in the most sensational story of the year to help you out."

"Compromising your journalistic integrity, I suppose," Kit said.

"Yes," I said.

Our eyes met. His blazed with anger. Mine refused to beg for any forgiveness.

"I had a job to do," I said.

We stared across the table at each other, for a moment neither of us flinching. And then he looked away. I realized he was afraid I would see how much he was wounded.

I remembered that look he had. I'd seen it years ago, in college, when I'd told him I couldn't see him. That I had to work another night shift at the *FreePress*. "I'm sorry, Kit. You don't know how sorry I am." My tone, suddenly full of emotion, revealed more regret than I had intended. Inadvertently, I had peeled away my protective layer.

Kit searched my face. Rather than shrinking from me, as I

half expected, he gave me a look that both forgave me and acknowledged that we were playing on an entirely new field. "We blew it before. Let's not blow it again," he said.

I had the urge to reach across the table and kiss him, but I didn't. Stay cool, I told myself. Professional. The moment passed. He picked up his coffee. I shifted my gaze to the view of Boston.

The flat top of the Mass. General heliport reached out to the skyline. Above it an emergency helicopter was trying to land. I thought again of Rory.

"She's wrong, you know," Kit said suddenly. It took me a moment to realize he was talking about Mrs. Marquesson. "We weren't fighting over the future of The BioFund. I expected him to leave. Francis and I both knew there was no future in The BioFund."

"What were you fighting about then?" I asked quietly.

He did not respond.

"Mrs. Marquesson said there wasn't any conflict over the merger."

"I can't talk about Fenton. I've told you that. I've got responsibility to the limited partners. You've got your career obligations, I've got mine."

"But if it could help your defense?" I pushed.

"The merger will be completed by the end of next week. Then, I'll be free to talk." He had a sly look on his face as he slid the manila file across the table to me. "If there's still a trial."

Inside the manila file was a photocopy of a medical record. *New Guilford Hospital Psychiatric Unit, Admission History and Evaluation.* I had to scan the page a couple of times before I realized it was Francis Marquesson's medical records.

According to the record, Francis Marquesson, then an MIT professor, had been admitted for three weeks in 1971.

"Identifying Data and Reason for Admission: depression, lack of appetite and affect."

On a second page was a past medical history, which indicated Francis Marquesson had been prescribed sedatives three months before that for "anxiety." Finally, there was a diagnosis of "severe depression," and in scrawl, a notation: "Suicidal tendencies."

"We need this information in the Sunday paper," Kit was saying.

Even with his friendship to the Marquessons, Lev was too much of a newsman to try to quash a scoop of this kind. The paper would run a teaser on Page One, or maybe even a Page One sidebar.

"How did you get these?" I asked.

Kit was casting around for something. He leaned his chair back to peer under the table. "Don't you want to write this down?" he said, and I realized he'd been looking for my satchel.

I followed his gaze to the lump of leather on the floor beside my chair and pulled out a notebook and pen. "Can I get a photocopy?" I asked.

"Yeah. The machine here is acting up, but I've got one at home in my study. I'll make a copy for you tonight."

"How did you get these?" I asked.

"It wasn't easy," he said at last. "If you notice, the records are both old and from out of state. They didn't show up on our subpoena of medical records. But we got a tip from an old high school friend of Francis's and we followed it."

Hurriedly, I wrote this all down. I became excited as I began to interpret the information on a more personal level. Proof of Marquesson's instability was fantastic news. For Kit. For me. For the two of us together.

I tried to read his expression. There was only a perfunctory

return of warmth. He revealed no aversion, but more a preoccupation.

"Can you tell me who gave you the tip?" I asked.

"No, of course not." His look said I had missed the point.
"You don't understand the whole of what this means," he con-
tinued, gesturing for me to write this down. "We have reason
to believe the prosecution had access to the same tip from
Marquesson's high school friend. If we can prove to the judge
that the prosecution deliberately withheld this from the Grand
Jury, it's grounds for dismissal. Estella will file for dismissal
Monday morning."

I reminded myself that attorneys filed dozens of useless
motions in any case. As little court reporting as I'd done in the
last year or more, I knew a dismissal after indictment was rare.
"But do you think that's likely?"

Kit wasn't put off by this question, but seemed to enjoy it,
allowing it to hang in the air a little longer by taking another
sip of coffee. Even with the paper cup covering his mouth, I
could make out a pleased expression. He lowered the cup to the
table.

He smiled at me, let another moment hang in the air, then
asked, "Are you aware that the judges rotate in Superior
Court?"

I nodded. At the beginning of each month Superior Court
judges in Massachusetts shift their county venue.

"Well, word is that the incoming judge on Monday is Judge
Landau. The former state rep."

There was obviously some significance I didn't immediately grasp.

"From East Cambridge. In the mideighties."

I nodded.

He reached across the table and closed the cover of my
notebook.

"We have reason to believe Landau would be sympathetic to my case."

"Why?"

He didn't answer the question, but continued. "That's why Estella is holding off till Monday to file the motion to dismiss. We both think that of all the judges in the state, Landau would be the most inclined to consider a dismissal favorably."

He smiled, and I remembered something from the database. A clip from the mideighties. It was a story about residents in Cambridge asking for legislation to curb and monitor the expanding biotech labs. Kit had been quoted as head of some business organization opposed to the bill. The story had noted that Kit had political ties in the state house. That he'd financially backed several candidates from Cambridge campaigning at the state level.

It was a measure of how far I had fallen for Kit that I was able to suppress the normal reporter revulsion at what I guessed was influence peddling. A part of me might be disgusted, but the other part knew that if the case against Kit was dismissed, there would be no more barriers. Nothing legal or ethical to keep us apart.

Now, he reached across the table for my hand, grasping it tightly and looking deep into my eyes. "Estella didn't want me to tell you any of this, but I trust you, Addy, even after today's paper."

I gazed back at him, hoping he could see in my expression that his trust was warranted.

Apparently, he did. "Being a political animal, Landau would be more inclined to dismiss the charges on Monday if the News-Tribune had just made a convincing argument to the public that I'm an honest businessman—the innocent victim in all of this." He smiled one of his patented smiles, the curve of his lip confident and sensual while his blue eyes glimmered boyishly. It was the smile that had kept me longing for him for fourteen years. "I can count on you, can't I?"

"Just get me a photocopy of the medical records," I said.

19

Just off the elevator, I grabbed the latest edition of the day's paper from the reporter stacks and scanned the headlines again. Gerard, too, had a front-page story, although his was well below the fold.

Wassermanns defy faith
in daughter's memory
By Gerard Hanley
staff reporter

I would read it later. For now, I tucked the newspaper under my arm and headed through the newsroom, a determined gait toward my word processor. I still had not heard from Dennis about the cabby, but now, with the knowledge of Marquesson's medical records, I could write an alternate lead.

Three suburban reporters were huddled in front of the bulletin board, making it impossible for me to nonchalantly search for a tearsheet of my story. "Nice piece on the widow," a voice called out as I passed. I nodded my thanks.

At my desk, I found a tacky, metallic gold pyramid, about the size of a coffee mug. It was a promotional item with the name of one of the Boston banks emblazoned along the hypotenuse. Initially a joke, the pyramid had become a tradition, an in-house trophy passed to whichever Financial reporter made Page One from the last Financial reporter to have made Page One. It had probably been left on my desk by Lorraine.

She swiveled around to watch my reaction. "Nice piece on the widow," she said with a smirk.

I thanked her and settled into my ergonomic chair for the long siege ahead of me. I had to start over with a new lead showing Kit in a different kind of action. This time, the anecdote would introduce the revelation of Marquesson's "suicidal tendencies," as opposed to the alibi of the cab ride. If Dennis and I were lucky enough to find the cabby by deadline, he could become a strong conclusion to the story instead of the lead. In fact, the whole body of the profile could build to this climax.

I began to pull out notebooks stuffed in the vertical and horizontal trays on my desk to review my notes. In my center drawer, I came across the photocopy of my brother's autopsy report pushed to a far corner. As always, I felt the chill of the document, as if the formal analysis of Rory's death somehow made it worse.

I shut the drawer firmly. It wasn't until I was on my way back to the paper in a cab that I realized I never told Kit about Karen Oblonsky. Now I knew that I had no choice but to push it from my mind, stave off the dervish of unanswered questions about Rory's death. They would no doubt resurface at 1:00 A.M., waking me with my breath stopped and heart furiously beating. But there was nothing else I could do. I had twenty-four hours to turn in a completed draft of the profile.

Mark leaned over the cubicle wall and tossed me a yellow envelope, which skipped over the surface of my blotter and landed on my lap. "Nice piece on the widow," he said, smiling as he walked off.

I opened it immediately:

McNeil,
Good job today. No wasted words. To the point.
Now get to work on Korbanics.
Lev

I reread it several times, terse as it was. Lev was never one to be long-winded in his praise, but the words themselves were not as important as the fact of the memo itself. I was back among the official recipients; Mark's casual delivery, the toss across the desk, emphasized his belief that I was expected to receive such commendations.

I slipped the memo into my drawer and snapped on my computer. After a bit, I decided to again open with a scene on the Esplanade, but this time, I'd focus on the moment Kit stared at the Cambridge skyline puzzling over Marquesson's state of mind, over "what could make any human being fling himself off a balcony."

I typed out the lead and a rough outline of the story with a sense of accomplishment. But five minutes later, as I reread it from the screen, my self-satisfaction disappeared.

There in my own words I could see the hole. The blip in my thought process. The crack in the foundation. Kit's argument with Marquesson was the key to the story—the reason Marquesson committed suicide. After all this time, all these interviews, I still didn't know what it was about.

No longer did I believe Mrs. Marquesson's theory that the fight was over her husband leaving The BioFund. But reviewing my notes, I realized that Kit's long-ago analysis that Marquesson had a "fear of failure" was also a gross simplification.

I was pretty sure that the specifics of the argument had to do with Fenton Biomedical. But I also knew that until the merger with Lavaliere Pharmaceutical was completed, Kit wasn't going to talk to me about it.

"Problem?" Lorraine asked.

"You could say that." I pushed my notebook away, as if to distance myself from my own spotty information.

"I don't suppose you had the chance to read Gerard's piece on the Wassermann autopsy?" Lorraine asked.

I grunted, but Lorraine was not put off.

"Page One. Not in the top corner like yours, of course," she continued.

I glanced at the newspaper thrown on my desk. I had a vague recollection of Anthony telling me about the family's religious opposition to the autopsy. So this was what they'd been defying their faith about. "I'd forgotten they were opposed to the autopsy," I said. "But isn't that old news by now?"

"You have to read it. Through to the end."

"I will, later," I said.

"Pretty good, you know, for Gerard," she added.

"Later," I repeated. This kind of deliberate praise from Lorraine meant I had to pay attention, but I was too wrapped up in the glaring hole in my story to take more of an interest right now. It'd just occurred to me that Marquesson, with his founders' stock, must have had the biggest stake in pushing the sale of Fenton. Perhaps he had gone overboard somehow.

I swiveled my chair toward Lorraine. "What happened with that Fenton Biomedical piece you were going to do for your column?"

She was now standing at her desk, gathering her things in a backpack, getting ready to go. For the first time, I realized how late it was. We were the only two left in the department. She turned, pleased with my interest. "I had a hell of a time getting an interview with the company president." She went on to complain in detail about some half-witted PR agent who never seemed to get her name straight.

"So did you get it?"

She smiled triumphantly. "I did—eight-thirty tomorrow morning with Raymond Beane. I'm going to make him answer some questions about first-quarter revenues."

When I asked her to explain, she told me she'd learned that Fenton Biomedical had lost its largest account, Quebec Pharmaceutical, five months ago. And that a source believed Fenton may have inflated first-quarter revenues from its contract-screening business so it could command a better stock price in a merger.

My instincts told me the pieces were falling together. "You mind if I tag along?" I asked.

She considered this a moment. "To ask about Korbanics?"

I nodded.

"I don't know, Addy. Beane was a hard man to get ahold of. I don't want him backing out on me because you piss him off."

"What if I promise to hold all my questions until after you're done?"

She thought about this another moment. "I don't know. How will I explain why you're there?"

"Say I'm a new reporter you're breaking in."

She scrutinized me a minute. "You don't look like a new reporter."

"But I am a new reporter. Back from the grave," I said, appealing shamelessly to her sympathy.

She lifted her backpack off the desk as if it were unduly weighted with rocks. "All right," she said, swinging the bag slowly over her shoulder. "But you better follow my lead."

She ordered me to meet her in the newsroom an hour before the interview so we could go over our act before taking a cab over to the Fenton office, which was in some sort of warehouse outside Kendall Square in Cambridge.

I agreed. With the specifics of the argument that set Francis Marquesson spinning and the medical records in hand, I was feeling more secure. Lev could not make any objections to the angle I was taking, my treatment of the profile—no matter what his friendships.

And if Dennis found the cabby, the alibi witness, I wouldn't just get the murder charges dismissed against Kit, I might just get a Pulitzer.

#

I changed to the Green line at the Park Street station, heading outbound toward Kenmore Square, where I'd catch the bus to Brighton. I planned a quick stop at home before meeting Dennis at the substance abuse meeting. I had to see him, not just to get an update on the cabby, but to confide in him about Karen Oblonsky. I needed his wisdom, his wider vision of the world. It was my only shot at getting any sleep tonight.

On this line, through upscale Back Bay toward Boston University and Boston College, the passengers, if tattered in bum attire, have affected the look. And with the colleges in summer session, the train was uncrowded enough after Arlington Station that I got not one, but two seats to myself.

Although I had brought a copy of the Fenton's marketing report with me, I decided to put off the heavy study for later. Instead, I spread the newspaper on my knees. Curious about what had so impressed Lorraine, I scanned Gerard's lead.

Hal and Bettie Wassermann's decision was a difficult one: Defy their faith and allow the state to perform an autopsy on their daughter Serina, or spend the rest of their lives uncertain about what really killed her.

I read through the first ten inches of the story with moderate interest. The Wassermanns' first twenty-four hours after their child's death were filled with undue pressure from both their families to uphold the Orthodox Jewish tenet not to violate the body of the deceased, and from the police to conduct the autopsy.

I turned to the jump page and despite Gerard's stilted prose, I found myself identifying with this poor family. The controversy seemed such an unfair burden to their grief. Even as the subway lights began blinking and we stalled outside Copley for no explicable reason, I continued to read, ignoring the mutterings of the passengers as I hoped for some smidgen of relief, some form of consolation for the Wassermann family.

By the time the train was moving again, the focus of the piece had shifted to the autopsy. The family, the police, and the DEA were awaiting the results. Before we hit Kenmore, I got my moment of meaning; the Wassermanns were right not to go to court to stop the autopsy. It gave investigators new insight into the toxic effects of synthetic cocaine.

> *Police now think that the synthetic drug might have caused more deaths than previously believed. Depending on the particular batch of the narcotic, it can kill two ways, according to Middlesex County Medical Examiner William Powers.*
>
> *Most often, the synthetic cocaine, which has been labeled the "serial killer," can be ten to twenty times stronger than the natural drug.*
>
> *But authorities now know that there have been some milder batches of the synthetic drug on the streets. This relatively weaker version, only two to three times as strong as the natural variety, can kill in a completely different way.*

My heart began to throb, a drumbeat of mounting panic, as I realized why Lorraine had been so insistent that I read this article through to the end.

According to Powers, the autopsy of Serina Wassermann revealed that technically, she did not die of an overdose. The charge of the drug overstimulated her central nervous system. It was an hour and a half after snorting the synthetic cocaine that the young Brandeis student died.

According to the medical examiner, the official cause of death was cardiac arrhythmia.

20

Waiting for Dennis, I stood outside the church in the parking lot, nodding distractedly to all the familiar faces who passed me on their way to the basement. Christy, the young girl with boyfriend problems, had come early to set up the coffee. She said Dennis wasn't coming, that yesterday he'd mentioned something about driving cab tonight. I refused to believe her and stayed hovering around the door, my eyes darting to each new car that crossed the curb cut.

The last hour had been a blank. I didn't remember getting off the train or catching the bus to Brighton. In fact, I remembered nothing at all except the cannonade of questions I kept asking and answering, one voice hysterical, the other urging calm.

I went round with new charges, new denials. I tried to imagine Rory in his living room chopping powder onto a plate but could not come up with the picture. My brother may have tried cocaine at parties once or twice in college, but as an adult? As a lawyer with a career at stake?

I thought of all the high-powered career people at my noontime substance abuse meeting at the hospital downtown—of Lawrence the architect and Anita the telecommunications executive. I tried to imagine my brother in their stories of "tooting" cocaine in the bathroom during business meetings, of carrying a pocket-size mirror and straw in a Brooks Brothers suit jacket. The picture would not come together, the data would not compute.

A cab pulled into the lot and parked. Dennis jumped out of the driver's door with a book in his hand. He stopped on the cement walkway when he saw me. "What's the matter? What's going on?" he asked.

I told him I needed to talk. My voice was calm but my shoulders must have been quivering because Dennis placed his hands on them to steady me. "This isn't about Warren Reid, is it?"

I could not attempt speech. I shook my head.

He read my expression intently. Clearly, I had not been in his night's plans, but quickly he reconciled himself to a change. "Look it, I was going to work tonight and check out a few more bars for Warren Reid. I just came by to drop off this step book to one of the new members. You want to drive around with me for a while?"

I waited for him in the back of cab, sitting on the wide seat, nervously fingering the leather where it was ripped and taped. Outside, it was still light, but the air was humid. The evening had gotten thick with a heavy-hanging front. Years of cigarette smoke emanated from the upholstery of the cab. I rolled down my window.

Dennis jumped into the driver's seat and turned to me. He was patient, slowly turning the silver bracelet on his arm as he gave me time to begin my outpour. After an initial hesitation, I let it out in a torrent of fears and suspicions. I began with Karen Oblonsky's coke habit and ended with the day's newspaper and my brother's cardiac arrhythmia.

He stared out the windshield, listening hard.

"But the thing is—on Rory's autopsy, they did a check for drugs. It came back negative."

He did not respond to this. Instead, he asked me how I was so sure this Karen Oblonsky had a coke problem.

I explained her mysterious disappearance after my brother's death, Quinn's lies, and finally finding out that she was in rehab at a clinic in Westwood.

"Oh yeah? That's where I dried out," Dennis said, somewhat fondly. He checked the clock of the cab. "You know they've got evening visiting hours there."

It took me a minute to understand what he was suggesting. "You mean, go out there, and ask her? Like this woman, a lawyer, would actually confess to me that she might have killed my brother?"

"She's a lawyer?" Dennis asked.

"Yeah, I told you she worked with my brother."

"You mean your brother Rory was a lawyer?" His brain had begun clicking. "A criminal defense lawyer?"

"Yeah, you knew him?"

"I didn't know your brother, but I knew of him. McNeil your last name?"

In substance abuse, which is supposed to be anonymous, this kind of information was allegedly concealed forever. I nodded.

"Oh Jesus. Your brother represented one of the guys I worked for. Not a drug bust, but a tax thing I think. He saved Henry a shit load of money. Henry raved about him."

Henry, the guy who had been with Quinn that day. The guy whose escrow fund had been pilfered. "This guy Henry, did he own an antique store?"

"You met him?"

"At the law firm. He's a drug dealer?" Obviously, being a criminal defense lawyer meant my brother defended a lot of criminals. I felt my stomach lurch, all the same.

Dennis didn't answer. Instead, he turned the ignition and reached across me to make sure the meter was off. "You've got to have a conversation with this woman or you'll spend the rest of your life wondering," he said, pulling out onto Washington Street before I could argue with him.

"What if she lies?" I objected.

He took a minute, staring through the windshield as he considered this. "You've got to ask her what went on that night. If she's been in rehab long enough, she won't be able to lie."

#

Westwood, although only twenty-five minutes southwest out of the city, had a distinctly small-town rural feel. The town center was only a couple of municipal buildings, a Catholic Church, and a couple of Colonial-style strip malls. Dennis took a left onto a long, windy country road. Eventually he turned into an affluent-looking entrance.

The buildings were set back, hidden in the old, swaying trees. Dennis drove forever to get to the front door. Buried under a canopy, it appeared impenetrable.

I told myself that I'd done this a hundred times, springing surprise interviews on people I didn't know, hoping to catch them at a vulnerable moment, off guard. I could not allow myself to admit the rawness of my nerves, the stretched feeling of my skin. I forced myself out of the cab to the portico, ringing the buzzer before I could change my mind.

An older woman came to the door and told me that I'd arrived too late. There were only ten minutes left to the hour and the rehab floor was no longer admitting visitors. I stood there, too stunned to object, as the door closed in my face.

Dennis, who had watched all this from the cab, was suddenly beside me, ringing the buzzer again. The woman who had answered the door the first time came back. Recognizing Dennis, she wore a whole new expression.

He introduced us. Lana, as it turned out, had been a counselor on his floor.

"Ten minutes could really help her head," he said, gesturing toward me. A meaningful look passed between them. She called an aide to take me to Floor D-4. Dennis said he'd wait for me in the lobby; he wanted to catch up with Lana.

In the elevator, I told the aide I was a cousin of Karen Oblonsky's, and that I'd wanted to get in to see her for a long time. "You know how she's been doing?" I asked.

"It's a big place, lady," he said, with an exasperated look.

Eventually, I was left to wait in a room filled with clusters of people on soft, plumped sofas. The windows were covered with cream-colored draperies that had not yet been drawn for the night. A mother on the sofa beside mine sat with a rail-like daughter who looked exhausted by the visit. Not far away, an elderly man was at a card table with a boy who appeared to be his grandson. Both the boy's arms were tattooed from the wrists to his elbows, a roughly sketched black-and-white snake disappearing into his sleeves.

I was prepared for Karen Oblonsky to have no cousins and to send the aide back with that message, but instead I saw him at the door, pointing me out to a broad-shouldered woman with a fluff of frosted hair.

She was wearing a baggy sweatsuit, but she walked across the room with such confidence, I could immediately visualize her in a power suit approaching the bench. As she got closer, I recalled telling Rory to shut up when he had raved on and on about her body.

"You came to see me?" she asked. Startled, I recognized the twang of my dream. The lie about Texas must have come from her origins. She was smiling at me with the kind of open smile no native offers to a stranger in New England.

"Yes, I did." I rose from the couch. Meeting her eye, I was surprised again by her warmth, and although I never expected myself to extend my hand, I found myself offering it. "Addy McNeil," I said.

She did not pull back warily or flee from the room. She took my hand and pressed it tightly. And then in the next moment, the woman I suspected of killing my brother was embracing me, and we were both in tears.

A buzzer sounded as we wept. The young girl and her mother rose from the sofa in relief. Others began to shift in their seats, saying their good-byes.

"Oh, and there's so much I want to say to you," said Karen Oblonsky, releasing me. She sat at the edge of the sofa beside me, glancing backward at an antique Big Ben clock. "I wrote that note to your parents, but I always wanted to meet you. You know, Rory talked a lot about you. He thought you were such a hot shit."

Hot shit. I could hear Rory saying it. *Brenda Starr's a hot shit.* I filled up with this long-lost praise from my brother. At the same time I missed him with such a sharp excruciating pain that I could not speak.

"Susan told me that you'd be coming, but I didn't know when," Karen spoke in a soothing voice. "You probably have a lot of questions."

I gained control of myself. "I need to know about his last night."

The aide who had led me here was now in front of us. "Visiting hour is over, ladies."

"Five minutes," Karen asked.

He shook his head, gestured at the now empty sofas around us. "You already got five minutes. It's time to go."

Karen ignored him. Her eyes, a warm brown, were intent on me. "I don't know if you understand this, but I need to make amends. I've done some crummy things for coke. Hurt a lot of people. I've got to try to make it right. I know I can never make it completely right. Not for you. But I've got to try, somehow."

The aide, unmoved by this, put his hand on her arm. "Yeah,

you can make your amends tomorrow, Karen." And then to me: "Visiting hours at 2:00 P.M." He pulled her, none too gently, and she rose from the sofa.

I stood. The aide began leading her to the door. I followed. "Can you come tomorrow?" she asked, grasping onto the door frame for support. The aide halted, annoyed.

"Just, please tell me this. I've got to know one thing, please."

"Oh, but there's so much I want to tell you. So much I think Rory would want you to know," Karen said.

The aide jerked her arm again. "I don't need this shit."

He had freed Karen from the doorway and was pulling her into the corridor. I followed, grabbing her other arm. "Please, just tell me. Were you guys doing coke that night?" I asked.

Her eyes were intense with pain, sadness. Her lids fluttered over them. "I had no idea he'd react that way."

The world stopped around me. I let go of her arm, but I was locked inside her pained expression. My heart beat with a frighteningly erratic force. "Was it the synthetic shit?"

There was an eternity of several seconds. "No one had heard of synthetic coke then, but now, it's the only thing I can figure," she said. "We did one lousy line and made love. An hour later he was dead."

21

Lying in bed, I tossed from side to side, from fury to sadness. I blamed Rory for what he had brought upon us: my poor father having to find his solace in a law school scholarship; my mother planting French thyme; and me numbing myself with Serax.

I conjured up my brother's image, first to curse his stupidity and call him a no-good loser. At length, I began to see his face that last day, when he had come to see me in the newsroom. I recalled that brooding expression, the look of conflict I'd ignored. Was he so desperate to escape? Was that why?

The picture dissolved. No longer did I see the serious thirty-five-year-old lawyer, but the geeky seventeen-year-old Rory was in high school, too tall, too earnest, too effusive for girls to go out with him.

I threw off my sheet and groped my way to my bureau, picking up the photograph of Rory at my cousin's wedding. I stared at the mystical haze the camera had caught in the foreground, remembering the bridesmaid on the barstool and my own brother blowing smoke rings. "What were you thinking?" I shouted. "Anything to get laid?"

Rory's dark, intelligent eyes gazed steadily into mine. "You stupid shit," I said, but the anger was already flowing out of me. Nothing he had done could change the way I loved him. The way I missed him. Sinking into the chair, I turned the photograph face down on the desk. After a minute, my head collapsed onto my arms and I spilled tears onto the Lucite frame.

#

Fenton Biomedical was in an unimpressive warehouse on a small, industrial street just outside Kendall Square in Cambridge. Following Lorraine's instructions, the cab let us off in front of a fenced lot, which appeared to be the company's shipping area. We walked three-quarters of the way around the two-story brick building before we found the entrance.

Lorraine, wearing the Filene's Basement business suit that she reserved for important interviews, was in the lead. I followed her along the cement walkway, up the stairs where I caught sight of myself in the plate glass of the double doors. The cuffs of my blouse were rolled to the elbow haphazardly and my trouser pleats were twisted as if I'd dressed in the cab. As I stopped before the glass to realign myself, I could see that my eyes, still swollen, had a wild look.

Lorraine stopped at the door, seeing my reflection. She turned and scrutinized my face. "You all right?"

"Fine," I said, meeting her eye so she could see that mine dilated. No use of Serax. Amazingly, in the wakeful hell of night, I hadn't made a move to the knee sock in my drawer. I'd kept thinking of what Dennis had said, about the Serax merely postponing the grief. I allowed the pain to flow in the hope that it might one day run out. That there might be an end to my losses.

By dawn, I'd forgiven my brother and no longer even blamed Karen Oblonsky. In the morning, I was filled with new anger, new fury. There was only one enemy: the makers of the synthetic cocaine.

Lorraine was still studying me. "I'm not sure if you look like you haven't had your coffee or you've had too much."

"I'll be fine," I said.

She appeared doubtful.

Inside, we were met by a gray-haired man who carried himself with more hauteur than the typical marketing director. He introduced himself as Len Oulette as he led us through a long, tiled corridor, banked on either side by laboratories.

On the left, the labs were small and L-shaped, only partially visible through large windows designed for observation. In one, a man in a white lab coat was at work under a sterile hood, injecting blue fluid into a beaker. At the bench, two women worked over microscopes. One rose to get something out of a freezer on the other wall. She did not appear to see us.

It occurred to me that this was where Joan Warner had worked. Where she had drawn blood from Kit's arm. I made a note of the layout of the lab in my notebook.

On the other side of the hall, instead of the series of three small, isolated labs, there was one large lab with several observation windows. Unlike the other labs, which had been populated, this one was dark and still. And it was configured more like an assembly line. Silver arms fingered with pipettes were paralyzed over stations along a U-shaped table.

"Is this where they do the contract screening?" Lorraine asked.

Oulette was pleased to confirm that it was, not knowing that Lorraine's primary interest in the lab was that it was dark and idle, giving her a visual scene she could use to illustrate her thesis that Fenton had lost key contracts.

He went on to explain that the silver arms were actually robots that conducted the various assays, cooking natural compounds, like bark or dirt, in fermentation broths to screen them for the active molecule—the first piece of information a pharmaceutical company needed to begin the process of creating a new drug.

Lorraine knew all this already, but she pretended to pay

attention. I had little interest in drug development and was thinking more of my lead. It was seeming more likely to me that losing a key contract with a pharmaceutical company *would* be something you'd want to hide in the midst of merger negotiations. Particularly if you had founders' stock and you were planning to retire to academia.

We followed the marketing director to the end of the hallway, where we climbed the stairs to another small reception area on the second floor. Here we were handed off to a secretary standing at the copy machine. She gestured toward an open office door, and told us Raymond Beane would be with us in a minute.

The CEO's office was spare, with nothing on the wall at all—no degrees, no oil canvases, no family photographs. Three metal file cabinets covered one expanse of painted blueboard. In the corner near a large window, three cardboard packing boxes took up a good portion of the floor.

We were placed opposite the oak desk in two chairs that were dragged in from another office. Next to Beane's empty chair, a personal computer sat on the desk return. A half-eaten yellow pencil rested on the keyboard.

"He should be here any minute." The secretary apologized once more before she left.

I sat nearest the open window, an oversize double-hung window without a screen. It led to a rusty-looking fire escape. A breeze rattled a set of microblinds that had not been properly raised.

Below, I could see the fenced parking lot. The shipping bay was closed and there was only one late-model American car parked in the lot.

Last night, on that awful drive back from Westwood, Dennis had explained why Rory's autopsy had come back negative for drugs. My brother had died in March, months before the authorities had even been aware there *was* a synthetic coke. As Anthony had said about poisons, the medical examiner's office would not have known to test for a new or unusual compound.

I felt the wound of this all over again: my brother's murder ignored. But I had to turn pain into outrage, anger into energy. I'd get this Raymond Beane character to tell me what Kit and Marquesson had been fighting about if it meant dancing around the room, playing the moron, or charging at him with my notebook in his face. I'd finish the profile and then use every investigative skill I'd acquired to find out who Integration Technologies was, who killed my brother, Serina Wassermann, Dennis's girlfriend, and the dozen or more people whom I'd thought of as merely "cokeheads" until Rory was among them.

Through the window, I saw a red Saab pulling into the driveway to park. A man in chinos, about Kit's age, bounded out and hurried toward the door.

Within minutes, Raymond Beane was at the door, introducing himself and tossing a leather saddlebag on the floor. A medium-size man who was neither fat nor fit, he stood too long before sitting, and when he sat, rose again to shake hands. His complexion was an Irish red and his dusty-looking hair diverged in a multitude of ill-placed cowlicks.

As soon has he had disengaged from the last handshake, he patted down the unruly hair at the crown and seated himself again at the desk.

Lorraine began fishing through her backpack. From my vantage, I could see she had come armed with a folder I recognized as Fenton's private financials. But she left it hidden inside the backpack and pulled out a notebook and pen, which she poised in her hands.

She told Beane that she was writing a column on the new trend among biotech startups to offset their burn rates and subsidize the costs of long-term drug development by creating ancillary businesses that generate cash. Although she didn't lie, her phrasing made it sound as if her interest was in Fenton's great success.

As intended, Raymond Beane was put somewhat at ease. He stopped jerking at his cowlick and clasped his hands on his desk. Apologizing for the disorder in his office, he gestured toward the three packing boxes on the floor. "Materials transfers to Harvard," he explained.

Lorraine was not particularly interested. "I was curious about the labs." She asked, "What do they screen?"

Beane smiled indulgently. "Things like bark, garlic, tropical vegetation—roots reputed to have healing properties. The company fiddles with the molecule to enhance those properties. We can do it a lot cheaper than the labs at the large pharmaceuticals."

"I noticed the lab was dark," Lorraine said in an offhand way.

"We run a lot of night shifts," he said.

"You mean like GM?" she asked.

He didn't get the irony, but began reciting a list of other Boston-area biotechnology companies that had gone into either blood-screening or diagnostic work to finance the production of breakthrough drugs.

Lorraine listened attentively, taking diligent notes as if she had heard none of this before. I wanted her to close in on him, ask her questions so I could ask mine.

"So when did you decide to go into contract screening as an ancillary business?" Lorraine asked.

I heard myself interrupting. "Ann-Marie Marquesson said it was all her husband's idea."

Lorraine gave me a stern look indicating it wasn't my turn yet. But my interruption did not seem to perturb Raymond

Beane. In fact, there was a small smile on his lips. "Are you the reporter doing the Kit Korbanics story they've been advertising on the radio?" he asked.

I nodded slowly.

At this point I think both Lorraine and I expected to be tossed out, but Beane continued to smile. "Ann-Marie is right. Francis wanted a profit stream. He even brought on board the combinatorial chemist who led the project."

With a look at me to shut up, Lorraine moved to reassert her control of the interview. "And who are your major customers?"

"We service several large pharmaceuticals. I'd have to check with them before I released their names to the press," Beane said. "You know the MS drug has gotten the most press, but we have other drugs in the pipeline. A very promising anti-inflammatory and something new in the area of addictions. A drug that could inhibit the receptor . . ."

He had deliberately changed course, but Lorraine adapted, altering her own tack. "But the main focus of the company has always been the MS drug, hasn't it?" she asked. "That's why Lavaliere Pharmaceutical is buying you, for the five-hundred-million-dollar-a-year market out there in treating MS."

"Yes. That's right."

"And you've invested a lot of money in the development of this drug," Lorraine continued.

He nodded again.

"A lot of personal investment, too?" This was Lorraine's acknowledgment of Beane's role in the discovery of the protein receptor, when he was a protégé of Marquesson's at MIT.

A flash of ego. "Yes," Beane answered.

"So, is it safe to say that this drug development is a key priority for you, personally?"

"Yes, it represents at least fifteen years of my work."

This was the quote Lorraine wanted; she wrote it down.

"It's an important therapy," Beane continued. "Not only for those suffering from MS, but potentially for a host of autoimmune diseases, arthritis, lupus—"

"One of my sources told me that several of the scientists working here feel they owe it to the memory of Francis Marquesson to bring that product to market," Lorraine interrupted.

Beane actually lurched at the mention of this debt to Francis Marquesson's memory. His expression grew dark. I suddenly understood that whatever conflict Kit had with Marquesson, Beane shared.

"Was Francis Marquesson perhaps a little overzealous on this front?" I suddenly asked. Lorraine kicked my ankle, but I pretended not to feel it.

"Overzealous?" Beane's hand tugged the cowlick. "What front?"

"To get this product to market, as well as to benefit personally from the sale of his founders' stock, Marquesson was willing to do anything to make sure the merger with Lavaliere came off, wasn't he?" I pressed.

Beane looked stunned by my attack. "What are you referring to?" he asked.

Lorraine was glaring at me. My hostile questioning had changed the tempo of the interview: The drums were beating. She had no choice now but to reach into her backpack and pull out the Fenton financial data.

"In here are revenue projections for contract screening that don't add up," Lorraine said. All pretense of friendliness was gone. The edge of her voice made Beane tense. He sat rigid, expressionless.

"And Mrs. Marquesson told me that her husband rejected Lavaliere's first offer in 1989 as too low," I said hurriedly. We would be thrown out soon; it was time to go in for the kill. "Francis Marquesson pushed Fenton to inflate these during the first quarter to make the company's burn rate look palatable and increase the stock price, didn't he? Kit Korbanics was furious when he found out—"

"This was not on the interview agenda we agreed to," Beane said. "I already told the *Herald*, I am not answering questions about Kit Korbanics."

"But how can these revenues be real when you've lost your largest contract?" Lorraine interjected. "I have on the record that Quebec Pharmaceutical pulled out of its contract with you in January."

"Those numbers are real!" Beane retorted.

"Are you denying you lost the Quebec account?" Lorraine said.

"They're insignificant to our revenue stream!" Beane stood up, knocking his chair aside.

"What was the conflict between Korbanics and Marquesson, then?" I badgered. "Why were they at odds?"

"You people have no idea what you're talking about," Beane replied. "It had nothing to do with first-quarter revenues. The conflict was over commitment. Marquesson talked a fair game about scientific discovery, but Kit Korbanics was the one with the real commitment, the real dedication to science."

I floundered to write this down, a wild scramble of ink on paper.

But Lorraine sprang to her feet and I was compelled to do the same. I stuffed my notebook in my satchel and swung it over my shoulder, ready for the impending eviction.

Beane stepped around the desk and was now close enough to force both Lorraine and me to take a step away, toward the window. "If you jeopardize this merger in that column of yours you'll be facing a libel suit," he said to Lorraine. "The merger has survived due diligence by Lavaliere's financial team. The cash flow analysis has been approved by the auditors."

Lorraine was not pushed from her stance. "What auditors? What firm?"

"I'm not answering any more questions," Beane said, taking another step toward Lorraine, who backed up.

As I stumbled to give her room, my foot knocked the top off one of the packing boxes. Looking down into the open box, my eyes were drawn to the brightly colored packaging material.

"You kill this merger and five years from now when you see some woman in her midthirties in a wheelchair with MS, you can consider yourself responsible," Beane was saying to Lorraine in a hot voice. "You'll get your front-page story, but you'll be the one responsible for the continued destruction of her nerve fibers."

I did not hear Lorraine's response. I wanted to get the hell out of there as fast as Beane wanted us gone. He'd put a completely new spin on my story. If Kit Korbanics wasn't the mercenary venture capitalist looking to sell out quickly and maximize the return on BioFund shares, readers might see that he wasn't mercenary enough to throw Marquesson out a window to collect on an insurance policy.

Beane personally shepherded us down the staircase and through the long, tiled corridor.

"I'll be calling your publisher," he said to Lorraine.

But Lorraine paid no attention. She deliberately stopped in front of the observation window and peered into the darkened lab. "Night shifts," she said derisively.

Book IV
Final Copy, due June 28, 1991

22

I'd been in front of my computer less than three hours re-arranging blocks of type before Mark walked into the depart-ment and demanded a printout.

"It's not due until five o'clock," I objected. I'd put together forty inches, not an inconsequential amount of copy, but it was still rough, the paragraphs of information strung together bits without glue.

"Give me the rough version," Mark ordered. "Lev wants to see it now."

I'd been intensely focused on the word, the line, the para-graph on the screen. Now I jabbed at the computer and hit the printout key. Mark turned and followed the electronic copy to the laser printer in the City room.

I glanced at Lorraine guiltily, but she would not look up from her computer screen. She was still furious with me for ruining her interview. Her plan had been to get the full list of all contract screening customers from Beane *before* going on the attack. I'd blown it, barging in too soon and making Beane defensive, leaving her with only half her weaponry.

Lorraine could prove that Fenton Biomedical had lost its premier client, Quebec Pharmaceutical, but she could not prove first-quarter revenues hadn't come from another contract screening account.

I was in a strange state of mind, numbed by exhaustion and grief, riding adrenaline to the finish line. I couldn't recall if I'd had breakfast or lunch, but there was no room in my stomach for food. Caffeine and my own blood chemicals had me wired. I couldn't deal with my screw-up of Lorraine's story. My transgression spun like a distant planet out of my mental orbit.

Gerard appeared over the cubicle wall. "Nice piece on the widow," he said.

I nodded, dully. Yesterday's front page seemed long ago.

"Have you heard the radio ad?" He shifted to his real purpose.

For a moment, I thought he meant the promotion for my story, which had been running on the three major stations. But his expression told me this was not something to my advantage. "What ad?" I asked.

"The *Herald*. They're doing their own profile on Korbanics. For Sunday."

"Kit hasn't been talking to the *Herald*," I said.

"You sure?"

The cold finger poked at my spine. I recalled the look of betrayal on Kit's face after the Ann-Marie Marquesson story yesterday. Had I misread his forgiveness? Had he decided to hedge his bets, after all?

"That's what Beane must have been talking about." Lorraine, forgetting her fury, turned around from her desk.

Dimly I remembered the CEO's reference to the *Herald* reporter. I had assumed it was a general story about the upcoming murder trial.

"So much for the *News-Tribune* exclusive," Gerard said.

"They could be doing the story without Korbanics's cooperation," Lorraine offered. She had now rolled her chair right beside mine. "Relying on sources who know him—the *Herald* does that kind of thing sometimes."

"Kit wouldn't talk to the *Herald*," I persisted, trying to sound confident. Gerard's expression was dubious.

At that moment, Lev turned the corner into the department, anger and energy pinching his face. He was holding my printout in his hand.

Even Gerard backed off, disappearing into City. Lorraine rolled quietly back to her desk.

"What the hell happened to the cab driver Korbanics was going to produce?" Lev shouted.

"He hasn't found him yet, but . . ."

"And so we attack the victim? With twenty-year-old medical records? Where the hell are these records? You better have the photocopies or it won't fly with the lawyers."

I had a sudden chill deep in my intestines. I'd gotten so wound up with Karen Oblonsky, trailing her to Westwood, I'd failed to get the photocopy of the records from Kit. I forced myself to meet Lev's eye and nodded with certainty, as if all documentation were already in my desk.

"And what's this about Korbanics's 'commitment to science'? You think anyone in their right mind is going to think a venture capitalist is committed to science?"

"That's a direct quote from Raymond Beane, the guy who heads—"

"I don't care if it's a quote from God Himself," Lev interrupted. "You've got this vague reference to a fight between Marquesson and Korbanics in the lead and then you have nothing to back it up except this generic crap about commitment to science."

There was a heavy silence. Lev was right. A part of me had known all along there was still a hole in my story, but I'd hoped to get by, writing around it.

"Just get the photocopies of these medical records upstairs to the lawyers, McNeil," he said. "And find out what the hell

Korbanics and Marquesson were fighting about."

I nodded.

He was not through with me yet. "And what about the *Herald* ads? What happened to our exclusive?"

"I don't think Kit's cooperating."

"I hope not, McNeil. For your sake."

#

By three o'clock, I'd given up on my attempts to reach Kit by phone and began hunting for my satchel. "I'm going to see Korbanics," I announced to Lorraine, who was talking to me again.

"He's not with his lawyer?"

"I keep missing him. Now they say he may have gone home for a late lunch."

"And phones don't work for you?"

"Kit's town house is only fifteen minutes away. I've got to pick up some documents, anyway."

Lorraine's eyes met mine. I realized I should have kept this to myself.

"You've got what? Two more hours to turn this in?"

"I don't have any choice. Anyway, Lev said he'd give me 'til Saturday if I got late information."

"You'd better have damn good information to bring the editor in on his day off. If not . . ." she stopped, as if she could-n't bring herself to verbalize the consequences.

"I'm not going to blow it," I said.

She shook her head, unable to offer me her confidence.

#

The late afternoon sun was searing as the cab turned onto Commonwealth Avenue; the driver lowered his visor against the glare.

On the mall, rollerbladers and bicyclers sweated visibly as they evaded each other and the Soldier of the Revolution commanding the stretch of green with his broken saber. I shifted my gaze to Kit's town house and peered at the windows for movement of a drape or glint of light on the upper floors to indicate he was home.

"You gonna pay me?" the cabby asked. I handed him a five and told him to keep the change.

I rushed out of the cab, but as I neared the wrought-iron railings around the entrance, I slowed down. It occurred to me that maybe Kit wasn't home. Maybe he was off talking to the *Herald* at a lunch counter somewhere.

I halted before the mahogany door and coached myself on self-control. I'd learn a lesson from my mistake with Raymond Beane this morning. If Kit was inside, I wouldn't even mention the *Herald* until after I had the photocopy of the medical records in my hands.

I also couldn't let myself think about Rory. Kit would see it in my eyes. I didn't have time for a full explanation of synthetic coke and Integration Technologies. I had to get back to the paper with the medical records. Stay on track or I could wind up blowing both stories.

Three college-age kids walking down Commonwealth Avenue stopped to gape at me standing under the canopy. They whispered among themselves until I realized that they knew who lived here. The brownstone was marked, like a celebrity house on a Hollywood map, only here the story was murder.

It occurred to me that unless Kit was expecting someone, he might not answer his front door—particularly if he wasn't cooperating and the *Herald* had been hounding him. I went through the alley to the back entrance. His white Porsche was parked in his spot, so I began knocking with more force, shouting his name into the double pane of his security door. There was no response.

Frustrated, I'd just about given up when my eye landed on

the red brick under which the key had been hidden. I'd never given it back. The key was still at the bottom of my satchel.

I fingered the key only a moment before thrusting it into the lock and pushing open the door. I was heartened when I saw a window left wide open in the kitchen. Kit might yet be home, working in his study, and hadn't heard me.

I walked through the empty dining room to the front parlor and stood at the base of the stairway calling his name. It occurred to me he might have gone somewhere by cab, or had Estella pick him up. By the time I climbed the stairs to the second floor, I knew all my shouting was perfunctory: I was alone.

Looking through the door to the library, I could see the phone on the desk of the attached study. I walked quickly through the dim room, heavy drapes drawn against the sunlight.

The study was equally dim, microblinds shielding out the day. It was a small room, with a modern, angled desk taking up two walls. The space-efficient shelving above held the computer processor, a brass mantel clock, and a fax-copy machine.

I'd noticed before that Kit's town house was clean, but I'd attributed this to a highly paid maid service. But his study, with its neatly organized work area, was a frightening insight into his personal preference for order.

I'd been hoping to come across a photocopy of the medical records waiting for me on the desk, but it was clear of papers. There was nothing besides a phone, a stapler, and a canister of black pens, all of them new and standing upright.

An antique credenza was along the third wall, below the tall window. It had sliding doors with the left side partially open, exposing manila file folders. On top of the credenza was a three-tier horizontal file. I began rifling through the top tray looking for the medical records Kit was supposed to have photocopied.

Suddenly, I stopped. What the hell was I doing? Technically, I'd probably just conducted a B&E and was now pilfering files. Even if the files belonged to someone you were trying to exonerate, this was still some sort of crime. If nothing else, it was sure to meet the legal definition of invasion of privacy.

I forced my attention to the phone, a high-tech cordless with two-dozen speed dials on the base. Estella's name was marked on the fifth button. I hesitated only a minute before pushing it. I got her male secretary and asked if Kit had returned.

Although he wasn't sure, the secretary thought Kit was at the meeting under way in their conference room. I told him where I was and that I urgently needed to speak to Kit. The secretary agreed to check the meeting for me and call back in a few minutes. I sank into the leather chair beside the desk to wait.

I watched the long, scratchy hands passing the Roman numerals on the mantel clock for what seemed forever. Five minutes passed. I called again and was told that Mr. Korbanics was not at the meeting. Apparently, he had not returned from lunch.

It occurred to me that Kit might be on his way home. Quickly, I got up from the leather seat and drew the miniblinds, flooding the room with an almost painful amount of sunlight. Then I took a seat on an upholstered chair from which I could see out the window.

Below, Commonwealth Ave. was filled with people. Besides the rollerbladers and bicycles, a shift of businessmen and women, off early for the weekend, were now strolling home to their condos.

I stood, restless. A stream of cabs turned onto Commonwealth from Berkeley. I waited, ready to run down to the parlor to greet Kit.

But the cabs did not slow. They continued up Commonwealth toward Mass. Ave. I sat down again in the leather chair. Ten minutes passed without a sign of Kit. I decided to phone Estella. Maybe she knew where Kit was. Facing that half-open credenza door, I changed my mind again, and dialed Lorraine at the paper.

"What's going on?" she asked. "Lev's been looking all over for you."

"What did you tell him?"

"I told him you'd be back by now. Are you still with Korbanics?"

I told her the situation. To avoid acknowledging I had a key, I made it sound as if I'd found his door open and gone inside to call him.

"Jesus Christ, you're bold," she said.

I reminded her that Kit and I had been college friends, which she seemed to accept. "Anyway, here I am waiting for him in his study." I took a breath. "And there is a credenza door open and a horizontal file on top."

The line was still.

"And of course it's wrong if I look at any of them. But there they are staring at me."

"You already broke into the house, " Lorraine commented dryly. She then added, "This is for a photocopy he already promised you?"

When I verified this, she also reminded me the information I sought was beneficial to his cause. "You know you don't have a whole lot of time to agonize."

I rifled through the horizontal file with Lorraine still on the other end of the phone. There was nothing but interoffice communications, outgoing letters to insurance fund managers, and balance sheets of companies I'd never heard of.

"Check inside the credenza," Lorraine ordered. "And while you're at it, keep your eye open for anything from Fenton

Biomedical with a list of the contract screening clients in it."

"I can't look inside the credenza," I objected.

"Oh Jesus Christ, go do it," she ordered. "You owe me."

After a quick glance at the window, I fell to my knees before the credenza, sliding the door aside to hunt through the files. There was a mixture of manila and brown-speckled accordion files held into place by a metal device that served as a bookend. None of the files, labeled in what looked like a secretary's neatly angled hand, had anything to do with his legal defense. There were no signs of Marquesson's medical records anywhere.

"Nothing with Fenton marked on it?" Lorraine asked.

"No," I said, returning the door to the partially opened state I'd found it in. The orderliness of the credenza bothered me. Not a file out of alignment, not a paper slipping out the side. I thought of what Joan Warner had said about Kit being so calculating.

"Check the desk drawers," Lorraine said. "And get the hell back here. Lev just walked into the department."

"I'm on my way," I said and hung up the phone.

The desk had a middle drawer and two on each side. Drawers were more personal, more of an invasion, and yet, it did seem a likely place to store the medical records.

Kit's middle drawer was completely empty except for a box of staples and a receipt for the fax-copy machine. It was as if he never used the desk. I opened the side drawers with less reservation.

The top drawer on the right was similarly empty. But the bottom drawer, which was deeper, held something heavy. It did not slide open with ease.

On top was a brochure of pharmaceuticals. I could not tell whether these were real drugs or proposed biotech products. Below was something boxlike. I removed it from the drawer. A smaller loose-leaf notebook slid out of it. "Corporate Records" was embossed on the side.

Inside the binder was a vinyl pouch held by the two lower rings. I pulled out a metal tool, like a notary stamp, and unclenched the teeth to read the engraving: Fenton Biomedical Corp.

Corporate records were usually kept at company headquarters, not in the desk of the venture capitalist, I knew. I put the stamp back in its pouch, and began leafing through the subject tabs marking each section. The first section contained a computer printout of documents on file with the state. The second, marked "stock certificates," was empty, as if they'd been removed. The last section was labeled "Minutes and Bylaws." I began flipping through.

> *Minutes of quarterly meeting of the directors*
> *of Fenton Biomedical Corp.*
>
> > *The quarterly meeting of the directors of the*
> > *above named corporation was held at 4:00 P.M. on*
> > *the twenty-fifth day of April, 1991, pursuant to a*
> > *waiver of notice signed by all directors. A quorum,*
> > *representing a majority of the stock ownership,*
> > *was present.*
> > *Raymond Beane was chosen as chairman of the*
> > *meeting and Francis Marquesson was chosen as secretary.*
> > *Francis Marquesson proposed a motion to conduct*
> > *an in-house audit concerning first-quarter revenue*
> > *disparities as cited at the annual meeting.*

I stopped to reread the line. Francis Marquesson had asked for the in-house audit. If Fenton had been cooking the books to make themselves look less like losers during the courtship by Lavaliere Pharmaceutical, apparently Marquesson was not behind it. I read further.

W. *Christopher Korbanics and Raymond Beane
both refused to second the motion. There being no
second, the motion was removed from the table.*

*Francis Marquesson proposed a motion to elect
himself as representative of Fenton Biomedical, to
discuss the merger terms with Lavaliere Pharmaceutical, Ltd., about proposed offer by said
company to buy a majority share.*

*The motion having no second, it was removed
from the floor. Upon a motion duly made by
W. Christopher Korbanics and seconded by
Raymond Beane, Raymond Beane was, by a
2 to 1 vote, elected as representative of Fenton
Biomedical Corp. to negotiate on behalf of
Fenton Biomedical Corp. with Lavaliere Pharmaceutical, Ltd., and to pursue all actions that would be
to the benefit of shareholders.*

*Francis Marquesson said he wanted it on the
record that he was opposed to the direction
Fenton Biomedical had taken in the last year and
a half. Raymond Beane noted, for the record, that
business objectives were pursued at the behest of
Francis Marquesson.*

*Francis Marquesson then asked that his name be
withdrawn as a member of the Scientific Advisory
Board and of the board of directors. His request was
taken under advisement by the board.*

*There being no further business before the meeting,
it was, upon a motion duly made and seconded, voted
to adjourn.*

Two months before he'd died, Francis Marquesson had resigned all positions at the company he'd founded. Apparently without telling his wife. A lead in itself.

I unlatched the three-ring prongs and removed the pertinent page from the binder. I walked to the fax-copy machine and fed it into the slot, waiting in front of it with a heavy feeling in my stomach. Not only was I making a photocopy of a document I'd technically just stolen, the document could be read two ways: Marquesson's resignation could be a sign that he had withdrawn from life, or evidence that there was plenty enough conflict at Fenton for murder.

I heard a thump downstairs and froze. Had Kit returned? My heart began pounding and I ripped the copy from the tray and looked wildly around the study for my satchel.

Another thump. I moved to the window and looked down at Commonwealth Ave. No cab or other cars were in sight. I glanced at the Fenton corporate records still lying open on Kit's desk.

As I moved toward the desk, the phone rang sharply, startling me. I answered, the photocopy still warm in my hands.

It was Kit, for the first time sounding anxious. "What's going on? What are you doing at my place?" he asked.

Hearing his voice, my heart pounded even more. I had to fend off a new flood of guilt. Trying to keep my voice steady, I told him how I'd come to his town house to find him, how I was up against a deadline and needed the copy of Marquesson's medical records.

"I've got them in my briefcase," he said.

I felt guilty again for having ransacked his office. "You're at Estella's?"

"No. I'm at Fenton going over corporate records. Estella got a tip yesterday that the DA is planning to subpoena every company The BioFund has a stake in. I wanted to go over the documents."

Beneath me on the desk were the open Fenton Corporate records I hadn't had time to read. Had these been spirited away from company headquarters? Hidden?

"The print is pretty small. It won't be legible in a fax. You want to come out here and meet me? Do you know where Fenton is?" he asked.

Apparently he hadn't talked with Raymond Beane. I told him I could find it.

When I mentioned my deadline, he suggested I take his Porsche. He would drop me off at the paper later.

The keys were in the beer stein on the kitchen counter. He said there was parking in the Fenton shipping area.

The mantel clock told me I had no alternative. I heard myself agree, and afterward, as I replaced the page into the binder, I wondered if I should call Lev and tell him what was going on. I could see him pacing back and forth between City and Financial asking everyone in his path if I was back yet. Still, instinct told me to wait until I had the photocopy of the medical records in my hand.

I returned the binder to the drawer and placed the pharmaceutical brochure over the top at the same angle. Closing the drawer, I double checked the stapler and phone on the desktop to make sure neither was askew.

With the photocopy of the Fenton minutes folded in my satchel, I ran downstairs to the kitchen to grab the car keys from the beer stein. A storm front had moved in. A wild breeze from the open kitchen window was making the blind thump like mad.

23

Outside in the alley, I approached Kit's Porsche with some misgiving. A highly polished white that would gleam on the street, the car demanded a driving proficiency I did not possess. But I couldn't let myself think about it, couldn't allow the intimidation.

I disabled the alarm and sunk into the driver's seat, which was unnervingly low to the ground. I felt each hole in the asphalt as I pulled out of the alley onto Clarendon. I idled at the light at Newbury. The car stalled. I started it again. The green Camry behind me began honking.

I turned onto Newbury Street, where I came to another stop. Rush hour traffic was immobilized by a truck double-parked in the first block. Next to me, a woman in a Ford Escort looked over to see who was driving.

I was sweating, my back sticking to the leather seat. I'd failed to crack a window and now fumbled on the door panel for the button. I couldn't find it. The horns behind me started sounding again.

Inching forward, I made it to Berkeley, where I turned. I would take Storrow Drive to the Longfellow Bridge. Against all logic, I hoped the river road would be less congested. According to the clock on the dashboard, it was ten to five.

Inbound traffic on Storrow was moving, but the heat of the

car had not yet found an escape. As I turned onto the Charles Street rotary, I spotted the air conditioner dial in the central panel and jabbed my index finger at a button. A vent spit new heat into my face.

I was attempting to go three-quarters of the way around the rotary to the bridge, but heavy traffic to my left blocked my path up the ramp. I was forced right and found myself on Cambridge Street, headed in the wrong direction, toward Government Center.

I heard a siren. A police car's lights flashed behind me. I continued up a block before I realized it was following me. I pulled over beside a Sunoco station. The police car nosed up to my tail. To my left, an ambulance spun out from nowhere, nearly glancing Kit's car as it passed. For a moment, I thought the cop and the ambulance were together, but then the cop jumped out of the cruiser and approached the car with purpose. This was not some mistake.

Anxiously, I searched for the electric window button, which I found on the driver's door, forward, parallel to the outside window. Exhaust from the street wafted in.

The cop, a heavy-set man now out of breath, regarded me intensely. He had an enormous, square face, strained by the afternoon heat. "A red light mean anything to you?"

I stared at him stupidly.

"Oh Jesus." He rolled his eyes upward. His hand went to a wide, stiff-looking hip. He glanced around as if looking for someone to share this experience. "That little rotary at Charles Street. You remember that far back?"

I narrowed my eyes in confusion. "I thought the light was yellow."

"Once upon a time," he said.

I was not sure if his disdain was real, or part of his act. In my own Volkswagen Jetta, I would have apologized, played the good, young girl. He might have waved me away with a warning. But in this Porsche, there was no innocence. No forgiveness. I met the cop's eye and waited for it to come.

"License and registration," he said, with an exaggerated shake of his head.

I dug into my satchel for my wallet. The cop surveyed my license as I began fiddling with the glove compartment. I prayed silently that Kit kept his registration there. It was locked. The cop seemed to be taking in my lack of familiarity with the vehicle. From his expression, I guessed this elicited a whole new line of suspicion.

I shut off the car and extracted the key from the ignition. Luckily it worked in the glove compartment and I found a plastic registration holder. I turned it over to the cop without looking at it.

He tapped it against his hand, turning to go back to the police cruiser. I sat waiting, my eyes on the clock. Time stopped, would not resume. I would wait in this hot, leathery car forever. The cop must have taken the added precaution of radioing the Registry to make sure the Porsche wasn't reported stolen. Cars whizzed by, heads turned. More than once, I caught a glimpse of satisfaction: The city wished me misfortune.

Five-fifteen. Lev was screaming by now. Kit was wondering where I was. I had the overwhelming sense of sabotage. The hours I'd spent in front of my computer this afternoon were futile. My lead was still vague. I had key information in my satchel that was dubiously obtained. I was destined to stop myself from getting anywhere.

In this moment of desperation, it occurred to me that when Kit read my story quoting the Fenton corporate minutes as the source, he would quickly remember the call from his town house. He'd figure out how I got them and it would be over between us.

With a heavy, down-to-the-bone knowledge, I understood I couldn't stand to lose Kit. Not so soon after Rory. I couldn't be thrown back into that empty, wide-awake aloneness that permeated every moment. The forced breathing. The timed exhale.

In the rearview window, I saw the cop approaching. I struggled to compose myself. I would not gasp for air. That much I knew.

The cop smiled as he handed the ticket through the window. The deed done, he wanted to be friends. "Oh, yeah," he said, pulling the registration from his clipboard and passing it on. "Don't forget this."

I folded the ticket inside my satchel and took the registration packet without comment. The cop was leaning forward into the window, checking out the interior, the radio, and tape-player. I heard appreciative grunts. "This six or eight cylinders?" he asked.

"Eight," I muttered. I had no idea. I wanted to get rid of him, be gone. The cop had both hands on the door as he inhaled the leather. I leaned forward to open the glove compartment.

"This is some company car, all right. What do you make? Chips? Software?" he asked.

I looked back. "What?"

"Integration Technologies. They make chips or something?"

A mistake. A name that sounded the same. I flipped open the plastic case and stared at the registration. I felt first the rush, then the halt of breath.

The cop was watching me. "You do work for Integration Technologies, don't you?"

"Chips," I heard myself say. Integration Technologies. The name Dennis had given me. The makers of the synthetic cocaine.

#

I sat there with the engine idling as the cop drove away, past me, onto Cambridge Street. Images flashed in my mind. The open box in Raymond Beane's office. The bright-colored Styrofoam popcorn. I realized now that it was the same yellow color Dennis had seen in the car trunk surrounding the synthetic coke.

I thought of the empty, dark laboratory that synthesized natural substances. Beane's explanation that production was at night.

This coke, this shit, didn't come from South America—it came out of some lab at night. I heard Dennis's voice as if he were beside me.

The two biggest stories in the city of Boston had merged into one. I knew this in my gut. I felt dead inside, unable to grasp either one of them.

My head began reeling. The certainty of innocence I'd seen in Kit's eyes. Was that false? His concern for Rory contrived?

I thought of Kit that day at the Esplanade, in front of the Arthur Fiedler statue, his recollection of a first-grade field trip that I'd confirmed. And later on the bridge. The way Kit had of looking inside me. In his bedroom, the feel of his arm tossed over mine. Kit. The one person who understood what I was missing when I was missing Rory.

Integration Technologies. Instinctively, I slipped the square of paper out of the registration packet and into my satchel. I had to shut off the car and remove the keys from the ignition to lock the empty plastic cover back into the glove compartment.

I made an illegal left at North Anderson Street to point Kit's hot white Porsche in the right direction, toward Cambridge.

24

At the front door, Kit greeted me with enough warmth to fill the hollowness in my bones. But now I thought I also sensed a wariness in his expression, an assessment of my reactions.

Inside the vacant reception area, the dimming sunlight angled through the windows, giving the office the hazy illumination of a premature dusk. Empty, the building seemed bigger than I remembered—a cavern with cold, blueboard walls.

I had hoped Kit might just hand me the photocopy of the medical records and let me go, but he gestured toward the tiled corridor indicating I should follow. He was finishing something upstairs, he said. It would just be a couple of minutes.

Passing the labs, I hesitated in front of the last observation window, before the paralyzed pipettes hanging from steel. I felt a chill. This was where they made the synthetic coke that had killed my brother.

Kit, seeing me stop, turned around and came to my side. I had a momentary sense that he was trying to read my thoughts, gauge my suspicions, but his tone gave none of this away. "They knock off early on Fridays," he was saying. "But half the scientists work Saturdays."

Kit had braced his large, elegant hands on the narrow sill of the glass window beside mine. The heart on his Irish ring still faced outward, emotionally unengaged, I noticed. Then, suddenly, I saw those hands shaking Francis Marquesson's thin neck, forcing him over. I backed away from the window. "Maybe I should just wait for you down here," I said.

"I've got stacks of documents I need to bring downstairs. It'll be quicker if you come up and help," Kit said.

His manner, so familiar and offhand, made me feel foolish. And yet, none of my muscles relaxed. I followed him through the corridor, upstairs, aware of my arms—tense at my sides— and the clench of my back teeth.

He ushered me into Beane's office. The file drawer was open, and the desk was covered with documents and bound reports. The computer had been left on. The screen-saver, a black universe, hurled red asteroids at planets.

"Let me get this stuff together and we can go." Kit picked up a stack of reports from Beane's desk and threw them in his open briefcase.

"The DA is subpoenaing all these records?" I asked.

"Not all, but we don't know which ones," he replied, as he began rifling through piles of documents, casting several aside. "Estella says they're getting desperate. They know they screwed up by not introducing the medical records to the Grand Jury."

"My photocopy is in there?" I pointed to his open briefcase.

"Yeah, hang on a minute." His eyes were shifting between two reports as he read the title covers. He dropped one on the desk and tossed the other in the briefcase. Inside was a copy of the day's *Herald*, folded in half.

"Did you know the *Herald* was doing a profile on you for Sunday?" I heard myself ask.

"Yeah, Estella mentioned it," he said, not looking up from his documents.

"Are they going to have a copy of the medical records, too?"

This must have been more shrill than I intended, because

Kit's head popped up. His eyes sought mine. "I don't renege on promises."

The microblinds on the open window rattled from the wind. I could see the packing box still open on the floor. *Could he not know? Could it be possible he didn't know what was going on?*

"Besides, we wouldn't trust the *Herald* to handle this." He pulled a sheet of paper from the inner pocket of his briefcase and put it in my hand, hovering over me as I read. We were buffered from each other by only the smallest pocket of air.

The photocopy of the records from New Guilford Hospital, as promised. Kit was watching me intently, waiting for some sign of satisfaction. I'd gotten what I wanted, what I told him was crucial to the story. I thanked him profusely, making much of my gratitude. In truth, I *was* happy to be reminded that Marquesson was certifiably unstable. Maybe the synthetic coke had been his plan.

"We don't expect the new judge will be friendly to the prosecution," Kit was saying. Was this bravado on his part, or had he really contributed that much to Landau's election campaign? His tone had grown hard, bitterly pleased with his upper hand. I had to force myself not to physically retract.

"Estella's got that much faith in this judge?" I asked, innocently.

Casually, his arm went around me. "Estella's got a lot of faith in you. She says your profile is going to ratchet up the pressure."

"Right." I pretended to scratch my shoulder so I could pull away from him. "We haven't found the cabby yet, though," I said.

"Yeah, but now you've got the medical records. That'll be powerful stuff. You'll focus on that, won't you?" He sought my eyes.

Even now, I felt his power over me, like the bottle of Serax in the nightstand. "Yes." I met his gaze.

He smiled, satisfied with my loyalty, and gestured to a stack of documents he wanted me to carry downstairs.

As I moved to grab them, I noticed a black loose-leaf binder, much like the one I'd found at Kit's town house.

"Something wrong?" he asked.

"No," I said. "We gotta get going. I . . ." I hesitated. "What's that?" I asked, pointing to the binder.

"Corporate records. Minutes and stuff. Very dull."

"You mind if I take a look?"

He gave me a funny smile. "I thought you were in a rush."

"I am. But I'm curious."

"About my fight with Marquesson? It's not in there." He picked up a stack of reports. "Take a look if you want. The DA will have them next week. I'll start bringing these downstairs."

The room was empty except for me and the flashing asteroids on the computer screen. I sat on the corner of the desk and flipped open the loose-leaf cover. It was the same, high-grade quality as the one at Kit's, but there was no "Corporate Records" embossed on the outside. Inside there was no metal stamp.

My fingertips moved on their own as I flipped through sparse pages. The typeface was identical to the minutes in my satchel. There was something titled "Actions of Stockholders by Written Consent," and then I found the date I was looking for:

Minutes of quarterly meeting of the directors
of Fenton Biomedical Corp.

The quarterly meeting of the directors of the
above named corporation was held at 4:00 P.M. on the

twenty-fifth day of April 1991, pursuant to a waiver
of notice signed by all directors. A quorum, representing
a majority of the stock ownership, was present.

Raymond Beane was chosen as chairman of the
meeting and Francis Marquesson was chosen as secretary.

Upon a motion duly made by W. Christopher
Korbanics and seconded by Raymond Beane,
Raymond Beane was, by a 2 to 1 vote, elected as
representative of Fenton Biomedical Corp. to negotiate
on behalf of Fenton Biomedical Corp. with
Lavaliere Pharmaceutical, Ltd., and to pursue all
actions that would be to the benefit of shareholders.

There being no further business before the meeting,
it was, upon a motion duly made and seconded, voted
to adjourn.

It was the same entry, adeptly edited. Removed were key paragraphs that Francis Marquesson had asked for an in-house audit of revenues, that in April, he had challenged the "direction of the company," and that he'd been so upset by the resistance, he'd resigned from the scientific advisory board and from the board of directors.

I fingered the paper. It was thin, and I imagined I could smell the heat of it, directly from a printer. Kit had been concocting fake minutes, falsifying corporate records to turn over to the state.

Unlatching the rings, I pulled the page from the binder. Kit Korbanics had contrived this set of fake corporate minutes as he had contrived my assignment to his profile. As he had contrived to make me fall in love.

I thought of our embrace in his kitchen. The spontaneity. The inevitability of our lovemaking. He'd been distracting me from questions about Fenton.

The adrenaline took over. A switch flipped. A white-hot electrical current illuminated each charged-up thought: Kit's revelation of the escrow account and his suspicions about Rory's death had been a way of drawing us together. I'd been so easy for him. Rory's little sister.

Rory. My eyes burned. I ran to the reception area and threw my satchel open on the copy machine. I thrashed through the main compartment, the jumble of notebooks and pens, until my hand landed on the registration to Kit's Porsche.

I stopped for a moment to peer down the stairwell. Kit was nowhere in sight.

Standing before the copy machine, my heart pumped wild impulses as I began stuffing documents underneath the hood. The falsified minutes I'd just found as well as Kit's car registration. I adjusted the paper size to eleven-by-seventeen and reduced the percentage of the zoom so I could get them both on one copy. Risk only one chug of the machine.

I made a printout and pulled it from the tray and quickly stuffed the copy into my satchel. The machine, instead of dying, began to whir again, rolling over the evidence a second time. Another copy spit into the tray.

I heard footsteps coming up the stairwell. I poked the End button. Nothing. I pushed harder, realized it was stuck. The machine marched on, multiplying Kit's lies.

"What are you doing?" Kit was near the top of the stairs and could hear every chug.

I kicked the machine, trying to get it to stop.

"What's going on? What are you copying?" Kit stood before me, hand on the stair rail.

I continued to kick. The copy machine scraped across a piece of metal with the return. Another copy spit into the tray. I grabbed my satchel from the top of the copy machine and slung it over my shoulder.

Kit walked to the copy machine. One of the copies had fallen to the floor. He picked it up. "What's this? My registration? What's going on, Addy?" Even now, his tone was full of concern, his eyes alarmed for my well-being.

He was directly in front of me: I could feel the heat of his body, steam from his damp, linen shirt. I backed up. "I got a ticket," I heard myself say.

"And that's what this is all about?" He sounded like a lover, willing to indulge my childishness.

I nodded. He studied the photocopy a second time. "You made a copy of the minutes?"

His eyes searched mine for an answer. I gave none. "Why, Addy? Why would you make a copy of these corporate minutes?"

"There's nothing incriminating in them," I said, at last. As if this was an explanation.

He halted again, trying to understand my tone.

"Nothing in there to give the prosecution any clues," I said.

"Clues to what?" he asked.

He met my eyes unflinchingly and I realized how sure he was of his hold on me. Rory's little sister. Still with her college crush. "You think the DA will realize they're fake?" I heard myself ask. "Or were those just for my benefit?"

His eyes narrowed. "They're not fake."

"My sources tell me Francis Marquesson resigned from the scientific advisory board that day. You want to explain why that doesn't show up in those minutes?"

His face grew hard and white. In the background, the copy machine slammed from side to side. "I don't have anything to explain," he said in an icy voice.

"Oh, yeah? How about the company that owns your car, Kit?" I continued.

He didn't answer.

"Integration Technologies." It spit out of me.

"The BioFund owns a lot of companies," he said, slowly. "That one happens to be a shell. To hold assets."

"I know what a shell is," I retorted.

He searched my face, trying to read the extent of my information. "Fenton has to do sample transports between here and MIT. We set up a corporation to own the vehicles. The Porsche, too. And Beane's car. We put them under a shell company in case there's ever an accident. It averts liability."

"How nice," I said, sarcastically.

The copy machine continued to roar out copies. Kit took a step toward me. I slid to the side.

"What's going on, Addy? What are you thinking?"

I took another step backward and found myself inside Beane's office. Kit stood at the door; his voice gained force. "Addy. Tell me what the hell is going on?"

I'd backed up another couple of feet, skirting the edge of Beane's desk. I stumbled over the packing boxes, kicking yellow popcorn all over the floor. "Check the copy machine, it's there," I said.

"What? A car registration?" His face was directly in front of mine, his eyes, sharp blue search lights. "What the hell does that prove?"

I turned away from him. The window behind me was enormous, the sill only a couple of feet from the floor, and the sash at eye level. Without a screen, it was almost like a door to the fire escape. Another shot of wind rattled the microblinds, pulled overhead.

Kit was behind me. He spun me around, gripping me by the shoulders. "You're going to explain yourself."

Even now there was confidence in his expression. As if all it would take was a little force and I'd be back in his arms, a bird under his wing. "It proves a connection to the synthetic cocaine." I glared at him. "And motive to kill Francis Marquesson."

"I didn't kill Francis," he said quietly.

"How much profit is there in an overdose, Kit? You ever calculate it? Just for fun?"

"Jesus Christ, Addy, you've lost it."

"Have I? Really? Maybe I have. I found out yesterday that Rory died of a synthetic cocaine overdose."

He let go of my shoulders, stumbled back a step. His heel kicked the packing box, but he was stunned, unaware of yellow popcorn crushed under his feet. "That's bullshit," he said. "They tested for drugs in his autopsy, you told me."

"Yeah. Normal drugs. Not synthetic coke. No one had even heard about it last March—"

"Rory didn't do drugs." Kit looked wild. "Not even in college."

"Yeah, he did. Not a lot. But he tried it a couple of times. At parties. He wouldn't tell you," I scoffed. "You were so straight."

"He was a lawyer, for Christ's sake. This isn't the eighties."

"That's right. It's the nineties. Where straight-ass businessmen make cocaine in high-tech laboratories. For profit."

Kit's face had hardened again; his will concentrated on refusing to believe.

"Rory did synthetic coke, Kit. It killed him. The cardiac arrhythmia you thought was so strange. Have you read the details of the latest overdose in the paper, or do you ignore those stories?"

"Are you saying just because he had a cardiac arrhythmia . . . ?"

"Not just because . . ." I shook my head. "Karen Oblonsky, the woman he was with, she told me."

"Karen Oblonsky?"

"Yeah."

Some recognition flickered in his face. Rory must have mentioned his upcoming date. Kit's cheek muscles tensed, mouth tightened. "That bitch gave him coke?"

"Not coke, Kit. Synthetic coke. The stuff that kills you."

Kit stepped back again, as if pummeled. Disoriented, he seemed to forget me for a minute. My eye on the door, I made a move to slide past him. But he quickly regained his bearings. He stepped to the right.

He was standing in front of me, his chest a wide blockade. One hand was on my arm, the other went to the small of my back. Firmly in his hold, I felt his current, an involuntary fire up my spine.

"You've got to believe me, Addy. I'd never do anything to hurt Rory."

I tried to pull away, but he drew me closer, his eyes beseeching me. "The whole thing was Beane's idea and Francis's goddamn chemist's. They figured out they could make the shit cheap. I'm as upset about this as you are," he said.

His hands encircled my waist. "I'm so sorry about this, Addy." He leaned over, his lips were on my neck, as if burying himself in our shared grief.

My legs weakened. His leathery scent, his familiar arms, his strength overwhelming me. I would have liked to let go. Stop the fight, fold in his arms.

From the lobby, the copy machine coughed. The engine lurched and seized. Kit Korbanics was a murderer. I pulled my satchel under my arm.

"Addy, I'm not going to let you leave like this." Kit had caught the movement; he eyed my satchel.

There was no getting out the door. I tried to twist free, pushing against him. He backed off, releasing me. Suddenly, he reached toward my satchel.

I swung sideways, turned to the open window, and threw the leather bag out onto the fire escape. It slid across the grating and stopped at the rail.

Behind me, Kit laughed, amused by my efforts. I ignored him, gave the sash an upward shove. The sash was high enough now for me to fit my leg over the sill and hunch my body through the opening.

Outside on the fire escape, I reached for the metal rail to steady myself. Below, the Porsche, parked in the gated shipping area, was the only car in sight. Even Binney Street, the closest thoroughfare, was an empty avenue of closed offices and warehouses.

I tightened the cord of my satchel and dropped the leather bag over the side. It fell onto the parking lot, pens spilling out. I pictured my body hitting the asphalt with the same force. A wind kicked in an alley somewhere. The sky was a trough of dark clouds, a low front overhead.

The ladder to the fire escape lay on the grating. It was old, cast iron. I bent down, grabbed the top of the ladder, and tried to slide it toward the opening in the fire escape. It would not budge. My hands were sore and dusted with orange. I pushed again. The ladder stood firm, rusted into place.

Kit had stopped laughing. He was standing on his side of the open window. "Addy. Don't be an idiot. Get back in here."

I ignored him, pushing again at the ladder.

"It was a temporary measure," Kit was shouting. "The company was going to go down the tubes. We were going to lose the MS drug. Nobody knew the coke would kill anyone."

I stood up and faced him. "But it did kill someone, Kit. It killed fourteen people. Fifteen people. It killed Rory."

He backed away, momentarily. Then he shoved the window sash, trying to raise it higher. When it didn't budge, he rammed it again and the window flew open with such force I thought the glass would come crashing out.

He stepped onto the fire escape. I moved away, toward the rail. He grabbed my arm, angrier now. "Listen to me. Fenton hasn't made the shit for over two months. That college girl, she got the last of what was already on the street."

"When did Marquesson find out?"

"The end of March. He got crazy with it. Every time he'd read. You know. Another one in the paper."

"Overdose?"

The term made Kit flinch. He squeezed my arm tighter. "Francis was the one who refused Lavaliere's initial offer as too low. He was the one who wanted to raise cash. He hired the chemist. That's why he freaked when that story came out about Mission Hill."

The five people who had died at once. The overdose Gerard had covered only a couple of days before Marquesson died. "So you killed him?" I asked.

"He killed himself. He was nuts." Kit let go of my arm. He was pleading with me to believe him, his eyes full of blue intensity. I reached down for the ladder a second time and with two hands tried to force it toward the opening.

Kit grabbed me by the waist and raised me up again. A drop of rain hit my face. He locked me in his arms, my back squeezed against his chest.

"I didn't kill Marquesson," he said hotly in my ear.

"You're hurting me," I said, trying to twist free and face him. He tightened his grip.

"The synthetic cocaine is over. Production stopped. You don't have to be the hero and expose it. It's over."

I twisted again.

He pinned me tighter. "For your own good. Listen to me. You want to get even. Punish me for Rory. But I didn't make him snort the cocaine."

I tried to elbow his chest, but I was defenseless against his strength. Another raindrop hit my head.

"The benzoyloxy is a derivative," he said in an even voice. "A new molecule our scientists invented. None of the chemicals in the compound is on the controlled substance list. The drug is too new to be illegal."

Dimly, I remembered Dennis saying something about this.

"Fenton had no capability to transport it out of the lab," Kit continued.

"Yeah, but Integration Technologies did." I couldn't stop myself. "The company that owns your Porsche. How you going to explain that?"

There was a long hesitation. Then his tone changed. An official line, he'd rehearsed. "I know nothing about it. My lawyer set up that corporation."

I wanted to see his face. Slap it. "You expect me to believe that?" I spit the words over the rail. "That Estella set up a corporation to transport cocaine? Without your knowledge?"

"Not Estella, Addy."

I was silent, trying to understand his meaning.

"Rory."

The grating beneath me swayed. Kit released me from his grip and I turned to face him.

"I told you I threw him business from time to time." Kit had a strange smile on his face, as if viewing himself from a distance. "Your brother had the criminal client I needed to meet. Henry had the local distribution network."

Henry. The guy with the antique shop. The escrow account. He was the drug dealer Dennis had worked for. "Rory knew about this?"

Kit had a dry laugh over his own callousness, his ability to proceed without remorse. "It doesn't matter if he knew. What matters is he was eager for the business and did the legwork to set up Integration Technologies. You look up the incorporation papers. Rory let me name him as secretary. Print a word of this and your brother's name will be in the headlines with mine."

He reached down and with one push, hurled the ladder through the opening in the fire escape. The cast iron clanged violently as it fell. The grating quaked under my feet. I reached for the rail. It vibrated from my hands up my forearms.

The fire escape continued to sway as I clung to rusted metal. There was complete silence, a howl of emptiness. Moments passed in the motionless neighborhood. We stood in steady rain.

Below, the ladder hung three or four feet above the asphalt. My satchel, stuffed with all those photocopies, lay nearby.

"I would never hurt you, Addy," Kit said, moving aside to give me clearance. He wiped a drop from his forehead and then, with a gracious sweep of his arm, gestured toward the ladder and the parking lot below. "I don't push people off fire escapes or balconies."

25

Sprinting past the endless one-story brick buildings, the glass doors locked and rigged with alarms, I clutched my satchel under my arm. I was heading toward the river, where there were hotels and cab stands. I had to get back to the paper. This was the only thing I knew.

I stopped at an intersection to catch my breath. It was pelting rain, and I wiped drops from my eyes as I checked over my shoulder for the Porsche. Kit hadn't bothered to follow me. There wasn't a car in sight, not on either side of the street.

Across the median strip, the barren warehouses, yet to be converted to high-tech commerce, were a wasteland of broken glass and vibrant weeds. I stood alone in the motionless neighborhood as I peered down the empty street.

Suddenly, I remembered: I'd spent my last five dollars on the cab to Kit's town house. I had no money, except for some change.

After four more blocks, the boulevard and a corner of the Esplanade Hotel were in view. I came upon a convenience store, tucked into one of the brick buildings. A sign on the glass door said there was a pay phone inside.

I ducked into the store and shook off the rain. A woman at the counter pointed to a nook behind the door, between the newspaper racks and a wheel of greeting cards. I tried

Lorraine's number but got a busy signal. I called Lev's direct line but reached his voice mail.

I hung up, not knowing what to do. When my brother died, I had wailed from my chest, a deep, physical agony. Now, I felt stunned, as if I'd been shot and didn't yet know where I was bleeding.

Through the glass door, I could see the cabs, all arriving at once and parading before the hotel entrance.

I punched in Dennis's phone number. It rang through to his car phone. He was outside the Fleet Center having just dropped off a fare.

Waiting for him at the door, I began rummaging through the photocopies in my satchel: I fingered the car registration in the name of Integration Technologies; the copies of corporate minutes showing Marquesson's concern about first-quarter revenues; the doctored corporate minutes, proving a cover-up. It was all still there.

The satchel was damp, the papers humid in my palm. My mind was fired by steam. I knew the chemical in the chain that had been synthesized, benzyo-something. I could describe the laboratory in which it had been done; I could explain exactly how the synthetic cocaine had been packed in glassware, protected by the trademark yellow Styrofoam.

Dennis's cab turned the corner. I felt myself getting giddy as he pulled up to the curb. I had Dennis, the anonymous source, who provided detailed background on the operation. A source who had actually transported the stuff to the safe house.

Venture Capital Finances Deadly Cocaine.

I wanted to make Kit pay for Rory's death. For Serina Wassermann's. For Dennis's girlfriend and the other twelve people I didn't know.

Never had I had such a lid on a story. A front-page story that would stun the city, catapult me to the investigative team, and probably win a national award.

A story that would assure my career.

And decimate my family.

I slid into the back of the cab, dripping over the leather. Dennis turned around, arm across the seat. "Jesus Christ. You're soaking wet. You all right?"

"Let's go."

"What's the matter? What's going on? What are you doing out here, anyway?"

"Interview."

"Jesus Christ, with who?"

I didn't answer. I was shaking.

"Did somebody hurt you?" Dennis asked.

"No. I'm all right. Please, I've got to get back to the paper. Start the car."

Dennis appraised me a minute more before pulling out onto the street.

Kit had been another drug to alleviate the pain. A suspicious bottle from the start. He'd known my weaknesses and lured me in.

I was filled with fury. Revenge. I'd make Kit Korbanics suffer badly. My mind began writing a new lead. This one featured Kit, arrogant smile on his face, stopped before the observation window of the lab, explaining how the company's dedicated scientists worked Saturdays.

Dedicated weekend work: the tone became snide. Inventing new molecules, for what? A new, improved, deadly cocaine.

Benzo-something or other. I'd call a chemist at MIT and have him look up the full name. "None of the chemicals in the compound is on the controlled substance list," I heard Kit say. "The drug is too new to be illegal."

A legal loophole he could slide through? Dennis had said the same thing. And Kit had taken care to set up Rory. Brilliant thinker that he was, he probably had a plan in place so that Henry or others in the distribution ring took the fall.

I glanced at Dennis, who was staring straight ahead, into traffic. God. Dennis himself might take the fall.

Buildings flew by. The hotel. Restaurants. A shopping mall. I couldn't write the synthetic cocaine story.

But I didn't have to exonerate Kit of Marquesson's murder either. Just because Marquesson had been treated for depression twenty years ago didn't mean Kit was innocent.

The rain had let up. Dennis switched off his wipers as we stopped at the red light. A billboard guarding the way to Charlestown proclaimed congratulations for the union of Deena and Andy, married the weekend before.

Like Serax, Kit held the upper hand. Rory's little sister. Not yet graduated from all twelve steps. I felt acute loathing. A deep, mind-altering rage.

Dennis glanced back. "You never got my message, then?"

I shook my head.

He reached into the glove compartment and flipped something over the seat that fluttered to the floor. The light had changed. My eye was on the traffic, backed up in front of the Museum of Science. "You know a detour anywhere?" I asked.

"This will only be a minute. Longer if we go around."

I glanced down at my feet and saw the photo of Kit Korbanics I'd given Dennis that night at the Bagel Man. Posed for promotion, his eyes were fixed intently, determined in their charm. I wanted to grind his picture into the floorboard with my heel.

"I had a brainstorm after I left you last night," Dennis was saying, "and decided to check the shelters—"

"Dennis, the left lane is moving."

"Addy," he objected, but still veered to the left, sticking the nose of the cab in front of a minivan that immediately began honking. Our lane of cars halted to a stop.

Dennis turned. "A friend of mine works at Pine Street—"

"Will you look?" I pointed to the lane we'd just abandoned. Cars that had been behind us were whizzing by.

"Addy, listen to me. Listen!" Dennis was shouting.

I turned away from the window.

"I found Warren Reid bunked up with the schizophrenics. Drunk as hell, planning to stay for breakfast. I showed him Korbanics's picture. He remembers picking him up on the Esplanade. Says he gave him a twenty-dollar tip."

A twenty-dollar tip. I remembered Kit's insistence on this, a quote from him somewhere in my first notebook. Dennis was pulling onto the expressway.

"The Pine Street Inn isn't far. Only a couple blocks from the paper. You want me to stop there first?" he asked.

The Pine Street Inn was a twenty-minute detour at most. If I went there, I could confirm what I knew, what I had known all along in my heart. Kit had been out on his way to the Esplanade when Francis Marquesson had thrown himself from the hotel balcony.

"This is Korbanics's alibi, right? The alibi you were waiting for?"

I could see Dennis trying to get a glimpse of me in the rearview mirror. He had searched the city for Warren Reid. Combed the bars. Driven to the shelters.

He found the cabby who was supposed to be the key to my profile. Like Perry Mason's surprise witness. My lead. Twenty minutes away.

"I'm sorry, Dennis. It's too late. Editors are waiting for me. I've got to get back."

"You could lose him," Dennis said. "People like that, they

disappear."

"I know. I know." I twisted the strap of my satchel. If I didn't get him now, Warren Reid would be gone in the morning. He could find himself at an all-day party under an overpass somewhere, or hitchhike to New Hampshire, or drink himself into a permanent coma.

Kit's alibi witness. I felt a strange sensation: a deep choke in my throat before the passage of air. So what if Warren Reid wandered off somewhere? Slipped into the night? Ended up where no one would ever hear from him again?

Kit hadn't thrown Francis Marquesson from a balcony. But he was a murderer all the same.

#

In Financial, three fluorescent rods flickered above Lorraine's desk. She was alone in the department, staring into her computer terminal with an air of intense concentration. Hearing my step, she swiveled around in her chair. "Where the hell have you been?"

I began unloading photocopies and notebooks onto my blotter, a cascade of paper. More information than I'd hoped for. More information than I wished I had.

The red light on my phone was blinking; I ignored it. "Has Lev gone home?" I asked.

"You kidding? He and Mark are upstairs in an emergency meeting with the publisher. They're trying to figure out how to lead Sunday's paper without the Korbanics profile." She repeated, "Where the hell have you been?"

Fenton, I was about to say, but stopped. I couldn't even confide in Lorraine. I couldn't show her the documents that proved that her instincts about Fenton were right. Not unless I was prepared to write the synthetic cocaine story. "Looking for the cabby," I said.

"You find him?"

"Not yet," I said.

"Then Korbanics has no alibi."

I didn't respond.

"Lev thinks you've lost it. Blowing deadlines again. Gerard is lobbying to step in. I heard him tell Lev he could put together a profile on Korbanics by tomorrow night—"

"Is Gerard still here?" City had been a warehouse of empty desks when I'd arrived. Most of the skeletal crew that worked the Friday nights had been at dinner, or outside on the sidewalk for a cigarette.

"I think he's at the database," Lorraine said. "Some kind of research."

I shifted my gaze to the corner, diagonally across the room, but the lights were dim and the file cabinets hid the desk. The database was dedicated to campaign finance records. What the hell was Gerard working on?

I thought of how gleeful I'd been about beating Gerard to the synthetic coke story. How I'd fantasized about his look of devastation when he read my exposé on Integration Technologies posted on the bulletin board.

I flipped on my computer. As I waited for it to boot, I picked up the receiver to retrieve my phone messages.

There were three messages on my voice mail—two of them earlier from Dennis. The last message was from my mother, asking me how the French thyme was doing.

I thought of the paper bag on my porch where I'd left it. The dirt and buds spilled on the floor. The root system a dried, lifeless maze.

It occurred to me that there had been other families I'd decimated in the name of journalism. The wives and children of embezzlers I'd exposed. Parents who had read the details of how their son bribed a state official, or of how their daughter's Ponzi scheme bilked the investment club.

I called up the Korbanics file and stared at the first draft of the profile, each word a submission to seduction, every sentence astoundingly naive.

"Did you find those medical records?" Lorraine asked.

I wished to God I'd returned to the newspaper empty-handed.

"Does that mean yes or no?" Lorraine asked.

I'd already broken so many rules of journalism, from sleeping with my source to allowing Warren Reid to slip away. But ignore evidence, evidence of this magnitude, already in my hand?

I gave Lorraine the photocopy of Marquesson's medical records. She scanned through, her expression growing bright. "You'd better run upstairs and show these to Lev. This changes everything."

Taking the photocopy, I stuck it inside a notebook I grabbed from the desk. I headed through the department and turned up the corridor of the newsroom toward the elevator, when suddenly I stopped. To my left, in the desk between the file cabinets, the red light of the database terminal was on.

I had not allowed myself to think about Rory, about his string of inexplicable moves, the shift to seediness, as if he'd adapted to the ethics at Keenan and Quinn. But now I could see him clearly, as if he were alive again, draped over the file cabinet. I was transfixed by his image—pale, bottled up with pain. He had waited for me so long, for the time I would not spare.

I realized now there was a whole side of my brother I hadn't known. I'd been too wrapped up in my career. I had to connect the dots. Make the story. Make the page.

I glanced at the screen. Gerard had left his key words in the search. *Landau.* He'd been boning up on the new judge on the bench.

I was jarred by the sound of the elevator in the lobby opening and Lev Grabowski calling my name.

Lev was striding through the lobby, charging toward me down the center aisle of the newsroom. Behind him, I saw Gerard coming out of the men's room. He stopped when he saw me, uncertain where to go. He knew to keep the distance between himself and one of Lev's outbursts.

I froze. What the hell would I say I'd been doing all this time? Hunting down medical records I'd told him I already had? I had to steady myself, settle my throat. Keep back the real information. The alibi witness. The cabby I'd promised him all along. I had a sudden urge to run back to my phone, erase my voice mail messages from Dennis, negate any hint of a Warren Reid.

Nervously, I flipped open the notebook to extract the medical papers. As I did, I saw a notation on the back of the page. A name and a date, allotted an entire line to itself. *Landau, July 1*. An almost illegible slant. I recognized the emotional pitch to my handwriting. I wrote this down shortly after my interview with Kit that day at The BioFund office. The day he'd forgiven me for my story about Ann-Marie Marquesson. The day I was blinded with college-age love.

To my right, the screen of the database flickered and disappeared. There was a moment of blackness as I waited. A screen saver, emblazoned with the *News-Tribune*'s logo, appeared. The letters were bright against the dark background. The cool of logic washed over me. The calm extended to my fingertips.

Lev was in front of me, screaming a barrage of questions that could not be answered at once. I didn't try to. Instead, I handed him the photocopy of Francis Marquesson's medical records.

I'd connected a new set of dots.

The Boston News-Tribune
June 30,1991

Pleading Innocent

Venture capitalist confident of judge's sympathy:
$22,000 in campaign contributions

By Addy McNeil
staff reporter

Kit Korbanics sits at the varnished walnut table at his elegant BioFund office, sipping coffee as he regards that day's unfavorable news coverage. The venture capitalist, charged with murdering his business partner, puts down his cup. But he isn't worried. Not today.

Today, he has gotten word that the judge who will rotate into Suffolk Superior Court for July is Arthur Landau.

"We have reason to believe Judge Landau will be sympathetic to my cause," he says with a sly smile.

Korbanics gazes for a moment at the river view of Boston from his conference room. Then he explains that his defense lawyer, the renowned Estella Rubin, has prepared a motion to dismiss, based on twenty-year-old medical records an associate dug up on Francis Marquesson, the partner Korbanics is charged with murdering.

Rubin was planning to hold off until tomorrow, the first of July, to file the motion to dismiss: Judge Landau's first day in this venue.

A man who says he understands both risk and value, Korbanics doesn't spell out his political connections but makes himself understood with a glint in his eye and a certain emphasis when he says the word "sympathetic."

In fact, News-Tribune *records provide background to Korbanics's broad hints. In the mideighties, when Cambridge activists began clamoring for local ordinances to restrict biotechnology laboratory research, Korbanics led the Association for Biotechnology Advancement, a lobby group that backed Arthur Landau's successful campaign for state representative (D-East Cambridge).*

And database records from the state Office of Campaign and Political Finance fill in the rest. State campaign finance law limits contributions to $1,000 per individual. But records show that contributions from Korbanics personally, The BioFund corporation, each of its investment companies, and top officers as listed in The BioFund's prospectus, add up. The total in cash contributions was $22,000 in 1986.

Korbanics was eager to make public Francis Marquesson's twenty-year-old mental health records from a Connecticut hospital on the day before the new judge would arrive.

Pleading innocence with his bright blue eyes, Korbanics put the warm photocopy in this reporter's hand. "You will focus on these, won't you?"

KORBANICS, Page 21

Gerard was standing in front of the bulletin board Monday morning reading from the tearsheet of my story from Sunday's front page. "Is Korbanics an idiot or what?" he asked with great amusement.

Beside the tearsheet, someone had pinned the picture of Kit that had been on my desk. Through the sheen of high resolution photography, his image gazed at me: strong jawline, handsome face. I averted my eyes.

Stooping to grab the day's paper from the reporter stacks, I could see Nora at her desk waving congratulations across the newsroom. I folded the paper under my arm, pretending not to see.

"Why did he tell you about the judge? What the hell was he thinking?" Gerard was still amazed.

I pulled the photo of Kit from the board and tossed it in the plastic refuse bin next to the reception desk. "He was thinking that I was his old girlfriend," I said quietly.

Gerard did not know what to make of this. At last, he decided to take it as a jab. "Yeah, right."

I met his eyes. "No. I mean it. Korbanics made the mistake of forgetting I was a reporter and thinking I was his friend."

Gerard smiled. The cleverness of journalists. The foibles of rich businessmen. "And you're not anyone's friend, right?"

It took me a minute to realize that from Gerard, this was praise. "That's right," I said flippantly.

But inside, I was struck by the irony. Actually, I was the one who'd forgotten I was a reporter and thought I was the girlfriend.

#

A yellow envelope, addressed to me in Lev's handwriting, waited at my desk. I tossed the day's paper over it, leaving the memo underneath unread. Before me, my phone blinked with messages I would not retrieve.

I'd written seventy-five inches. Not one word a lie. Not one doctored quote or distortion. The reader had been left with the impression that Kit Korbanics had something to hide.

I was prepared for Estella Rubin to claim I'd used misstatements and off-the-record information. Saturday, I'd gone through my notebooks, highlighting in pink anything I'd used in the final copy. I'd also been careful to box the few things actually said off the record. Rarely had I been so thorough in note-taking.

Lorraine, whose back was toward me when I arrived, turned and rolled her chair near to mine. The Fenton financial documents were in her lap. "Lev killed my Fenton story," she told me.

I had noticed her column was missing Sunday. I began to apologize again, but she cut me off. "He would have killed it anyway. Too much money riding on that merger without documents to back it up."

I looked away.

"And my guess is that Kit Korbanics isn't letting *you* back inside his town house." She was smiling. Another round of praise for my journalistic toughness. My newspaper machismo. My willingness to screw old friends.

"If that judge gives Korbanics a dismissal this morning, they'll be calling for his impeachment from the bench by noon," Lorraine speculated.

"Landau will have to remove himself from the case," I told her.

Lorraine considered this a moment, then accepted it as fact. "I'd say any judge would be nervous about dismissing the charges against Korbanics after your piece yesterday," she added.

I shrugged.

Lorraine studied me intently, searching my face. "Until I

read the paper Sunday, I was under the impression you thought Korbanics was innocent," she said.

"My piece never says he murdered Marquesson."

Her eyes narrowed behind her glasses. "I know. But the *Herald* profile was much kinder to him. In yours, he comes off like the kind of guy who *could* commit murder—"

"That wasn't my point," I said swiftly. "My point is that he shouldn't be able to buy a dismissal, whether he's guilty or innocent."

Lorraine took this in, gave it full consideration. "Fair enough," she said and rolled her chair back to her desk.

#

For the first few days, I was able to sustain myself on success. The memo from Lev that officially invited me back onto the investigative team and the nonstop meetings and buzz of media attention allowed me to subsist on each high-energy moment. In the space between, I thought about Kit, but only fleetingly. I had time only for anger, a wince of pain, before there was a new appointment, a new demand on my time.

But when the schedule died down, when the radio interviews were over and Lev called me into his office to talk about my next assignment, I had to think about what I had done. Because of my story, Kit Korbanics would stand trial for a murder he did not commit. Unless his own detectives located Warren Reid, he could be convicted.

I put off the synthetic cocaine story by claiming my source had not been reliable after all. This was easy for Lev to believe of a former drug addict. He wanted me to focus on political intrigue rather than crime, anyway. That had always been my strength, he said. Connecting the dots. From pockets to politicians. Finding the dirty ties.

Lev's suspicious eyes got very green when I said I didn't want to cover the Korbanics trial, that I thought Gerard capable of handling it alone. Lev glanced at Mark, who asked me later if Korbanics had said anything to threaten me. I couldn't tell him that I was certain that a man charged with murder wasn't violent. Instead I said I was burnt out. Exhausted from the long hours. Tired of revisiting old relationships and turning over the rocks.

But it was my own rock that was most disturbing. I had knowingly let an alibi witness wander away.

Still, there were fifteen or more murders for which Kit Korbanics would go unpunished. I told myself I'd gone for honesty instead of truth. The heart's assessment. Still, I wasn't altogether sure the heart was supposed to be involved in newspaper reporting.

#

The Catholic cemetery in Worcester where my brother is buried is strict about grave landscape. No artificial flowers. No shrubs over a certain height. When the red-white-and-blue floral wreath for Memorial Day started to wilt, cemetery officials rode over in a golf cart and pulled it up.

If the French thyme I was planting began creeping over to the other graves, the entire thing would be uprooted. I didn't worry about this. I could count on my mother's immaculate grave tending to keep the perennial in line.

The summer was already too hot, and I'd come wearing a Red Sox cap to protect my face from its burning rays. I also brought a spade, a gallon of water, and a newly purchased seedling from the lawn-and-garden store.

Rory's grave is in the "new section," on a pretty slope near the edge of the cemetery, closest to the woods. The headstones are larger here and the family plot is big enough to accommodate the four of us. If I should realize my mother's worst fears and die unmarried, I will rest in eternity beside my brother. I used to like that idea. Now, as I knelt before the slab of granite and the inscribed dates of Rory's existence, I dug at the dirt with some hostility.

"What the hell were you thinking?" I asked the ground.

Karen Oblonsky told me that Rory's legal work for Henry had been confined to tax issues concerning the antique store. I'd gone to see her in her Brookline apartment after she'd been released from rehab. Sitting in her living room filled with spotless white furniture, she'd hesitated to say anything bad about Rory. But when pressed, she admitted that my brother had suspected Henry might be actively involved in something criminal. Rory thought it was receiving stolen rugs.

I saw Rory in my mother's house, in the newsroom, in hotel lobbies and airports, but here at the cemetery where he was buried, I failed to bring up his image. I asked him again what he was thinking. He didn't respond.

Dennis had warned me last night not to expect to get too many answers graveside, but I had to come. Now, I dug a hole three inches deep and around. The dirt, which had a reddish tint, mounded up before my knee. I tapped the plastic pot against the grass to loosen the root ball. It did not come out easily.

My mother said French thyme was hardy. Only my extreme neglect had made it die. I knocked the plastic pot harder on the ground.

Karen Oblonsky had never heard of Integration Technologies, but she recalled that Rory had felt "uncomfortable" about the work he did for Kit Korbanics—especially after Kit became so interested in Henry.

After they'd met at the Celtics game, Kit had asked Rory for Henry's phone number with the excuse that he was looking for a Tiffany chandelier for the dining room. Rory thought this odd because Kit only dealt with the upscale antique dealers on Charles Street.

But as a new associate to the firm, Rory needed billable hours, Karen explained. He wasn't about to ask too many questions of a prestigious client like Kit Korbanics.

The plant fell into my hand. It occurred to me that it would be winter before a jury reached a verdict on Kit's murder charge. For some reason, I was comforted by the idea that the ground would be frozen.

"What the hell were you thinking?" I asked again. This time I wasn't sure if I was asking my brother or myself.

I put the thyme in the hole and piled the dirt back in around it, patting it tightly around the central stem. I heard Rory's voice, mocking me. *Brenda Starr has turned into a little Frau Flower, junior.*

I smiled to myself and wished he were around to make fun of me for this gardening. I was getting uneasy about how much I seemed to like it, and how, with the dirt under my nails, my hands looked like my mother's.

I stopped asking the grave for explanations. Rory wasn't answering any questions today. And anyway, I already knew. One slightly bad call led to a somewhat bigger misstep, and in the end, the lines once so carefully drawn were slipping under your feet.

It was then that I saw Rory's face. His eyes were full of amusement.

It was just like him to find the humor in the situation: that he had died by the combined efforts of his seedy clients, by the questions he failed to ask.

Suddenly, I imagined him wincing, aware he had caused me pain.

"Forget it," I said, and drenched the soil with the full gallon of water. I felt a cleansing as I watched it seep into the ground.

EPILOGUE

By the time Gerard got back to the newsroom, everyone already knew the verdict. Channel Five had reported it live from the Suffolk Superior Courthouse steps. I stood in the middle of the newsroom with everyone else watching as the camera interviewed Estella Rubin for her reaction.

She met the camera lens head on, and in a calm, assured voice, told the television crew that the verdict was a backlash to the national stories, the high-profile murderers who'd gotten off scot-free. She said the verdict would never stand up to an appeal.

Murder, but in the second, not first, degree.

A couple of minutes later, the TV's legal expert noted that during deliberations, the jury had asked to review testimony from a defense witness who had challenged the motive. Apparently, a large portion of the five-million-dollar payout on the key-man life insurance policy would have been claimed by the limited partners of The BioFund.

The jury decided Kit had killed in passion, rather than in calculation. It was all now another step further from the truth.

I returned to my desk and sat in front of my blank computer screen for a long time. Several people came around to ask me if I thought the jury was right. If Kit really did it. I couldn't answer.

Gerard appeared over the cubicle wall. The judge had scheduled sentencing for Monday the next week. Gerard was leaving on a winter vacation to the islands tomorrow, could I cover?

I told him I couldn't. I was booked with another assignment.

When he left, I turned back to the computer and typed three different versions of a letter to Lev stating my resignation.

#

I awoke in the dark, as if I'd heard a sound. I lay on my back feeling strange. Absent. It took me a moment to realize: My heart wasn't pounding. There was no racing of blood.

I sat up in bed to double-check the clock. The regular time: 1:00 A.M. But it was different. I felt alone, but calm. Sadness rather than anxiety. I had no need of Serax or even deep, gut breathing. I closed my eyes and lay back down, turning on my side. I slept in blackness, without dreaming, until midmorning.